Readers love the Warlock Brothers
of Havenbridge
series by JACOB Z. FLORES

Spell Bound

"I loved this book It's hard to think of anything else to say. Read it. It's a wonderful mix of young love, magic, and true love. Also, I'm dying for book two."

—Joyfully Jay

"*Spell Bound* is already listed as one of my favourite books of 2015 and I know that Jacob Z. Flores is an author I will read more of very soon."
—Gay Guy Reading and Friends

"*Spell Bound* is a delicious appetiser for a new series, but it packed a punch on its own."

—The Novel Approach

Blood Tied

"The writing is supreme, the story is an intricately woven idea that intrigued me, brought me in from the beginning."
—On Top Down Under Reviews

"This was awesome! I hope you guys decide to pick this up, and if you do, enjoy the read!"

—Boys in Our Books

"There was so much action and intrigue and I was on the edge of my seat the entire time."

—Prism Book Alliance

By Jacob Z. Flores

3
Being True
The Gifted One
Please Remember Me

Published by DREAMSPINNER PRESS
www.dreamspinnerpress.com

SOUL STRUCK

JACOB Z. FLORES

Published by

DREAMSPINNER PRESS

5032 Capital Circle SW, Suite 2, PMB# 279, Tallahassee, FL 32305-7886 USA
www.dreamspinnerpress.com

Soul Struck
© 2015 Jacob Z. Flores.

Cover Art
© 2015 Paul Richmond.
http://www.paulrichmondstudio.com
Cover content is for illustrative purposes only and any person depicted on the cover is a model.

ISBN: 978-1-63476-681-4
Digital ISBN: 978-1-63476-682-1
Library of Congress Control Number: 2015950144
First Edition December 2015

Printed in the United States of America

This paper meets the requirements of
ANSI/NISO Z39.48-1992 (Permanence of Paper).

To Mike.

From the moment we met, I was soul struck.

Introduction and Dramatis Personae

MAGIC HAS existed since the dawn of mankind. Its source is the Gate, a portal to the astral plane that powers the wonders of the world. From this gate, a new species—the *homo magus*—evolved from humans and divided into three different subspecies: *homo ater magus* or warlocks, *homo albus magus* or witches, and *homo neuter magus* or wizards.

From the moment the first human witnessed the power of this new species, the homo magus were hunted with prejudice and brought to the brink of extinction.

But the homo magus survived by forming a secret society that lives among humans.

The witch hunters still exist today, continuing their pursuit of eradicating magic. As long as they are hunted, warlocks, witches, and wizards will continue to live in secret, protecting themselves from extinction while saving humans from the new enemies and ancient threats they know nothing about.

The Blackmoors (Warlocks)

Pierce Blackmoor is the oldest of his siblings. Upon his father's death, he will assume the role of high priest of his coven. He commands lightning and often charges into battle without thinking, relying solely upon the powerful magic he wields to win the day.

Thad Blackmoor is the middle child. He is coolly logical and often aloof. He uses his ice abilities to strategic advantage. His powers have recently grown to creating snowstorms and calling forth blizzards. Knowledge is far more important to Thad than defeating his enemies.

Mason Blackmoor is the youngest of his siblings, who until recently couldn't control his magic or access his active power. Mason has since learned he is a shadow weaver, which means he can bend the darkness to his will. This is a rare and powerful warlock ability that has led to the corruption of every warlock who has ever wielded it.

Drake Carpenter, a human and boyfriend of Mason, has been made an honorary member of the Blackmoor coven. His last surviving relative,

Aunt Millie, was murdered by a vampyre. Drake is under the protection of the Blackmoors due to his part in the death of the vampyre that killed his aunt and because of his uncanny immunity to magic.

Aiden Teine recently joined the Blackmoor family after being cast out of Otherworld, the land of the fairies, when he was turned into the first vampyre fae. As a fire fae and former prince of his realm, Aiden struggles with balancing his conflicting fae and vampyren tendencies. His love for Thad has kept his more dangerous instincts at bay.

Oliver Blackmoor is the head of his family and the high priest of his coven. He is the most powerful warlock in the family, especially once he turns his entire body to stone. Though he is often distant and irritable, Oliver loves his sons and still grieves for his wife.

Priscilla Blackmoor was Oliver's wife and mother to Pierce, Thad, and Mason. She died from breast cancer nine months ago.

THE PROCTORS (WITCHES)

Charles and Camille Proctor are the high priests of their coven. Charles, who works for the Havenbridge Police Department as a detective, is capable of commanding fire while Camille has dominion over plants. The Proctors pride themselves on the white magic they practice, which connects them to the spiritual forces of the universe.

Adam Proctor is the oldest of his siblings. His guiding element of magic is air, which allows him to use it as an offensive or defensive ability. Adam has a rocky past with former friend Pierce Blackmoor. He also nurses his wounds for the unrequited feelings he had for Mason Blackmoor.

Charlotte Proctor finds herself bookended by two strong-willed siblings. She is the peacemaker in the family, and this characteristic manifests itself in her powers. Charlotte taps into the element of water, which grants her astounding healing abilities.

Miranda Proctor fancies herself the rebel in her family. She is loud and opinionated, which often gets her in trouble and sets her at odds with her family. This likely explains why Miranda and Mason Blackmoor do not get along; they are two peas in a pod. Miranda's active ability derives from the spirit element, which grants her a unique ability to teleport objects and people at will.

THE STONEWALLS (WIZARDS)

Lawrence and Rachel Stonewall are the high priests of their coven. The gray magic of wizards gives them direct access to the spirit element, which allows them to tap into powerful abilities that are kept in check by their logical ways. Lawrence is able to control minds while Rachel can cast illusions.

Edith Stonewall is the eldest of her siblings. She can erect invisible force fields for protection. She is also the most like her parents. She rarely engages with others outside her coven and is closest with her twin brother, Elliot.

Elliot Stonewall is Edith's twin brother, younger by three minutes. He is mute and cannot access his magic like others in the community. He does, however, have the ability to speak to others telepathically.

Kate and Keaton Stonewall are the youngest members of the family, and they are also twins. Neither of them has tapped into their active powers because they are still too young. Once they turn sixteen, they will learn what ability they will have at their disposal.

OTHER CHARACTERS

The Conclave is the governing body of the magical community. The three most powerful warlocks, witches, and wizards serve on the Conclave. They are charged with making and enforcing magical laws as well as ensuring the Gate is protected from all threats. The word of the Conclave is absolute, and their power is feared across the magical community.

Gerald Wa, a wizard and the only identified member of the Conclave, acts as an advisor to the protector covens. He was believed to be dead, but his death was staged to hide his ascension to the Conclave. Prior to this "death," Gerald was romantically involved with Drake's aunt Minnie. The information Gerald provides to the protector covens and more specifically to the Blackmoors often places him at odds with the rest of the governing body.

Bartram Kane lived during the Salem Witch Trials. Bartram was a powerful member of the Conclave of his time. He was also the last warlock to possess the abilities of a shadow weaver. When his son Ebenezer was burned at the stake, Bartram went mad. He spoke the forbidden *immortalitas* spell to resurrect his son but turned him into a vampyre instead.

Ebenezer Kane/Ben Crane came back to life as a vampyre after his father spoke the *immortalitas* spell. Ebenezer created other vampyren and almost destroyed the magical and human communities. It took the combined might of the Conclave to stop him. During the present day, Ebenezer took on the identity of Ben Crane. Ben has managed to decimate the Otherworld and steal the Hearthstone, the fae's most precious relic. His endgame remains a mystery, and the Blackmoors have vowed to end his reign of terror.

Chapter 1

"I'm gonna fry you like a chicken."

Blue arcs of electricity leaped from my clenched fists as I studied my opponents. They stood on either side of me, sizing me up. The cold bastard on my right had his hands folded behind his back, while the dipshit to my left stuck his thumbs in the front pockets of his jeans and sighed.

They no longer saw me as a threat.

A few months ago—hell, even a few weeks ago—I was the powerhouse. One stray static discharge from my pinky finger snagged their attention. That was when the world was right. I was the oldest, the most powerful.

At least I used to be.

"Come on, Pierce," my youngest brother, Mason, said. He dug his gloved hands farther into his jean pockets to scratch his balls. "Is this necessary?"

"Yes," I growled.

"He's got something to prove," Thad shouted to Mason from where he stood on the rear lawn of Blackmoor Manor. He combed his fingers through his strawberry blond hair before readjusting the green scarf around his neck. "We might as well drop our pants and get out the measuring tape."

Mason barked in laughter and, after removing his hand from his pocket, slapped it against his thigh. I didn't find it funny. My brothers needed to be reminded that after Dad, I was the baddest warlock in the family.

"Big talk needs to be backed up," I said. I funneled more of my magic to my hands, sending snaking lines of blue energy sizzling toward the cold ground.

"This isn't wise," Thad said. "Using our powers out in the open like this is a big risk."

Thad had to be shitting me. Blackmoor Manor was on the biggest, most isolated plot of land in all of Havenbridge. "Stop making excuses and power up."

"Or what?" Thad asked. His arched eyebrow issued just as much of a challenge as his tone. "You'll attack us anyway? What the hell will that prove?"

"Just. Power. Up."

"Come on, guys. All y'all are actin' foolish." That was Drake Carpenter, Mason's boyfriend. I usually found his Southern drawl soothing. Today it only pissed me off. Mostly because I could hear the pity in his tone. He felt sorry for me, and that only ticked me off even more.

I glared over my shoulder at where he stood shivering on the redbrick porch. He had his hands shoved into his blue North Face jacket, and his sandy blond hair dangled across his forehead. "Stay out of this, Drake. This is a family matter."

His shoulders slumped, and he took a step back as if I'd punched him.

"What the fuck, man?" Mason asked. He stomped across the dead grass toward me. The shadows cast by the weakened December sun crawled across the lawn toward my brother, most likely in response to his summons. "That's *not* cool."

No, it wasn't. We were the only family Drake had now. Well, at least the only family that hadn't come back from the dead as a vampyre. I'd make it up to Drake later. Buy him a root beer or some other crap food that he and Mason loved to ruin their bodies with. All I cared about right now was that Mason was angry enough to fight.

One down. One to go.

"I'll tell you what's not cool," I said. "Having a fucking vampyre for a boyfriend."

Thad inhaled sharply, and his face flushed.

My brothers were too predictable. It had always been easy to get a rise out of them, but now that they were no longer single ladies, it was even easier to yank their chains. Thad hated that the family still didn't fully trust his newly vamped boyfriend. What the hell was a vampyre fairy anyway?

"Don't make me hurt you," Thad said in a quiet, measured tone.

I snorted. "You've got that backward, Brainiac." He had hated that nickname ever since he was a kid, and that was the straw that broke Thad's back.

Thad, who was usually the most reserved of us all, charged. The already-chilled Massachusetts temperature dropped a few more degrees as Thad clicked on his ice powers. An icicle formed in his right hand, and he hurled it at me.

I had to admit, I was pretty fucking disappointed. An icicle? From a man who'd recently summoned a fucking blizzard?

I didn't even have to move to shrug that attack off. I nudged one of the arcs of lightning from my fist in the direction of the icicle, shattering it before it could come within twenty feet of me. "You'll have to do better than that."

"I'm planning on it," Mason said before jumping on my back. His fists struck the back of my neck.

Since I had at least forty more pounds and a lot more muscle than my little brother, the blows were more irritating than anything else. I reached back, grabbed Mason by his coat, and hurled him off me. He landed with a yelp that reminded me of a scared puppy.

Now that was what I needed.

Ice formed around my hands, cutting off my power source. I turned just in time to see Thad's fist coming right at me. I stepped out of the way and stuck out my leg, letting his momentum trip him up and send him face-first into the dead grass.

Their powers might have grown, but they still didn't know how to fight worth a damn.

I pushed more power through to my arms. Lightning streaked from my fists, splintering the ice Thad had formed in his lame attempt at muzzling my magic. I glanced at my brothers, who were once again upright, their chests heaving.

"You're about to get your ass handed to you on a platter," Mason said. Black energy hummed around his fists. He was preparing to fire off a shadow blast.

Thad didn't say a word. His upper lip curled into a snarl as he took a deep breath.

He'd done that once before, back in fairyland. He exhaled a snowstorm that almost took out that dumb fuck Ben, who'd been a major pain in our asses for the past couple of months. Lucky for me, I wasn't as big of an idiot as everyone thought I was.

"*Propellit*," I whispered with a flick of my wrist, and Thad and Mason flew backward ten feet before slamming back onto the hard ground and skidding another few inches.

Now that was fucking funny. I laughed so hard I almost pissed myself.

Thad and Mason eyed each other before nodding. They rose in unison and stood their ground.

"Finally ready to get serious?" I asked.

Thad nodded once, his jaw tense. Mason shot me a thin smile before saying, "This is gonna hurt."

Shadowy tentacles gripped me from behind. They coiled around my hands and legs, anchoring me to the ground. Another set wrapped around my chest, making it difficult to breathe. This was uncomfortable, but it didn't hurt one bit.

Pain exploded in my groin as an inky limb grabbed my junk, tugging and twisting in directions my cock and balls were never meant to travel.

I let out a cry of pain before ice formed across my lips, sealing them shut and sending sharp, stinging pinpricks coursing through my mouth. The agony was worse than fifth grade, when I kissed the flagpole in the middle of winter on a dare. It had taken me a week before I could whistle again.

I yanked against my shadowy restraints. My muscles strained, and perspiration slid down my cheek from the effort. They wouldn't budge, and the fucking tentacle between my legs wouldn't let my shit go. How the hell was I going to get out of this one?

"Just surrender already," Thad said.

"Screw that," Mason replied. "He has to do more than cry uncle. He's got to admit his days as king of the magical hill are over."

Thad nodded, a triumphant smile practically cracking his face in two. "I agree. Just admit we're more powerful than you are and we'll stop."

Like that was ever going to fucking happen. I'd rather nose-dive naked into a pile of dirty syringes. I narrowed my eyes at them in reply.

"Suit yourself," Thad said before turning to Mason. "Do you want to go first?"

He nodded and cracked his knuckles.

"Mason, stop!" Drake ran out to them. He glanced at me before turning his disappointed gaze upon them. "That's enough. I think you boys have made your point."

Oh fuck this! There was no way I was going to let a human come to my rescue. I liked Drake and all, but no one was going to pull my ass from this fire except me.

"He fucking deserves it," Mason complained to his boyfriend. "When he's not mouthing off about how powerful he is, he's shoving my face into his sweaty pit or something equally disgusting. I've had enough!"

"I hate to agree with Mason," Thad said, "but he's right. Pierce needs to be taught a lesson. He's not in high school anymore. It's time he grew up and acted like an adult."

"This isn't right," Drake added. "He's obviously tryin' to overcompensate because your powers have grown."

Who the hell was I? Shelby from *Steel Magnolias*? There was no way these bitches were gonna talk about me like I wasn't here.

I shut my eyes and blocked out the pain. It was a distraction. I had to focus only on the raw magic that had coursed through my veins since I turned twelve. I was the first Blackmoor to tap into my active power at such a young age, and I'd used that gift to get me out of tighter spots than being hog-tied and sexually assaulted by Mason's shadow puppets.

I willed the lightning within me to my fingertips. The energy crackled and burned my fingers, but I had to push past that too. I had to overload Mason's restraints, pour more and more power into my fingers until either it short-circuited my bonds or blew off my hands.

Either way, I'd be free.

"Pierce, what are you doing?"

I paid no attention to Thad. He was trying to distract me from getting free. I sent even more energy surging through my limbs. Not only were my fingers on fire, so were my arms and now my chest. I clenched my jaw so tightly my teeth started to hurt. It was like I was biting down on aluminum foil.

"You need to stop," Mason said. His voice cracked. He was clearly worried I was going to get free and kick his ass so hard he wouldn't be able to sit for a week.

More energy flooded my hands. The burning spread down my chest to my legs and up to my head. The usual low buzz of my power turned into audible crackles and pops that reminded me of a transformer ready to blow. I was almost there.

"Shut it down!" Thad screamed. "Now!"

"Listen to them," Drake yelled. "You're gonna hurt yourself."

"Fuck that!" Mason added. "He's gonna hurt us."

Damn straight I was.

Sweat ran down my face, and my body shook with electrical current. It was like I'd become a live wire. It was time.

When I opened my eyes, I didn't understand what I saw. Someone had replaced the world around me with waves of blue, orange, and yellow that formed people and trees.

What the fuck did my brothers do to me?

"Pierce, are you okay?"

I turned to my right. Someone mostly made of orange stood next to me. Lines of blue and green coursed through his body. It sounded like Thad, but it sure didn't look like him.

"Whatever you're doing, stop!"

A person made of yellow stood twenty feet ahead of me. Inside him flowed threads of silver and gold. Was that Mason? And who was that behind him? That person wasn't made of any *one* color. He reflected all colors at once, making him a being of almost pure white light.

"Do somethin'," the radiant figure said. That sure sounded like Drake, but why did he look so different from everyone else?

I switched my focus from the people to the world around me. The forest along the back of our property had been turned to a solid black with spots of green twinkling within. The sky above glowed yellow before turning to orange and then red. At the highest point in the sky, a dark blue slowly gave way to a deep violet.

In the distance, I spotted birds. A strange crystalline light surrounded them and alternating colors of yellow, blue, and green radiated off the bodies of all of them except the one flying in front. It was composed of a pink aura with threading lines of dark red and royal blue.

What made that bird so different from the others, and why did I want to go chasing after it?

"Will you listen to me, dammit?"

The orange Thad shook me by the shoulders before a brilliant blue surrounded him and sent him flying across the backyard.

What the fuck happened? I surveyed the backyard, looking for whoever attacked my brother.

"What did you do?" the yellow Mason asked as he ran to where Thad landed.

"Me?" I asked, but my voice didn't sound like my voice. Instead of words, I crackled and popped.

If only I wasn't still restrained by Mason's shadows, I'd go over and check on Thad. That was when I realized I could move my arms and my balls were no longer being squeezed to death. How long had I been free?

"Pierce, you've got to calm the fuck down."

Mason crouched by Thad, who moaned in pain.

"Is he okay?" I asked, but my voice still wasn't working right. It sounded like static.

I had to find a way to make myself understood. I pointed at Thad, planning on following the gesture with a thumbs-up to get my point across. Instead a brilliant blue line of energy exited my pointing figure and crashed right into my brothers in an explosive thunderclap. Their bodies flew across the lawn.

Holy shit! What did I just do?

"Pierce, listen to me." Drake, or the white energy that seemed to be him, slowly backed away from me. "You're out of control, man. Your power's goin' everywhere. You've got to discharge it now. Before it's too late."

What the fuck was he talking about?

I held my hand in front of my face, except it wasn't my hand. At least, not really. The flesh, blood, and bone had been replaced with lines of surging energy that arced off my body and singed everything around me.

What the hell was going on?

"Do it!" Drake yelled. "Now!"

I aimed my hands at the sky and expelled whatever had gotten into me. Never-ending streaks of deep blue shot out of my body and crackled overhead, turning the once multicolored sky into an electric blue. The snaking trails of energy crisscrossed through the firmament like a lightning storm until they made their way to the innocent birds that had progressed just over the forest behind the estate.

I watched in horror as my power fried the birds that emanated varying colors. Their fluctuating spectrum stopped the moment the blue lines of energy collided with their bodies. The bird with the pink aura tried to avoid the crackling discharge. It dipped and angled, doing its best to escape, but there was too much energy released all at once.

A stray line of power shot through its body, and it fell from the sky until eventually the blackness that was now the forest swallowed it up.

"Pierce, are you okay?" Drake asked.

With each blink of my eyes, he flashed between the flesh-and-blood Drake and the glowing white aura he'd become. It made me dizzy.

I tried to shake it off, but reality continued to warp around me.

When I took a step forward, my world went black.

I WOKE up on the couch in the living room. The weird colorful auras had disappeared and the world had returned to normal. At least until I tried to sit up.

My head throbbed. The last time I felt this badly I was in Mexico working on a business deal for my father. I'd gone out to one of the local bars, had a half a bottle of tequila, and woke up naked the following morning next to a man and a woman I couldn't have picked out of a lineup.

"He's awake."

I peered through half-closed eyes to my right. Drake sat on the leather sofa with a book on his lap. He was just as bad as Thad. He always had his nose in a book, trying to find some miracle spell that would change his aunt Millie back to human instead of the vampyre she now was.

"What happened?"

He regarded me with a strange curiosity, his brows stitched together over his cornflower blue eyes. "You don't remember?"

"I remember the world went batshit crazy," I said as I struggled to get up.

"It wasn't the world," Thad said as he and Mason entered the room. "That was all you."

Mason nodded in agreement and stood next to Drake with his arms crossed. If his eyes had been guns, I'd have been riddled with bullets.

"You better stop looking at me like that or I'm gonna rip your arm off and beat you with the bloody stump."

Mason snorted, clearly daring me to try.

"Will you two stop it?" Drake asked. He slammed the book down on the side table and stood up. Though he was clearly upset, he approached me cautiously. "Look where losin' your tempers got all y'all."

Thad nodded. The fury I'd briefly ignited in the backyard had died out. He studied me with a mixture of disappointment and fear. "Drake's right. We need to understand what happened, and we need Dad for that."

"Great! You're gonna snitch on me like you always do."

Thad's hazel eyes turned into slits. Ever since we were kids, Thad had always run to our mother like the tattletale he was. Now that she was gone, he gave Dad an earful every chance he got.

"Why not?" he asked. "You're still an ignorant dickhead."

"Oh. My. God!" Drake shook his head and ran his hand through his long sandy locks. "The three of you are worse than toddlers."

"Nuh-uh," Mason replied, sticking out his tongue.

Drake eyeballed him. "Just for that, wiseass, it's just you and your hand tonight."

"What?" Mason asked with a fat bottom lip. "I was just playing around."

Drake blew out a lungful of air. "If that's what you three want to do. Play around. Fine. Kill each other instead of figurin' this out."

"What's there to figure out?" I asked. I stood up, and the world spun for a few seconds before righting itself again. That was a close one. "I kicked their asses during our little war game. End of story." That wasn't entirely true. Something had happened to me, but I wasn't going to admit I had been out of control. I'd figure it out on my own like always.

Mason and Drake gaped at me while Thad rubbed his temples with his index fingers.

"What?"

"You're not really that dense, are you?" Mason asked. "You lost control of your powers. You almost killed us."

I sniffed. "You both look fine to me."

"That's because I brewed healing potions," Thad said. "Just when I think you couldn't be any more of a dumbass, you sink to a whole new level of stupidity."

I balled my fists and blue sparks flew from my hands. I wasn't stupid. I just didn't spend all my time with my nose in books. I had a life and plenty of more interesting places to stick my nose. "Call me stupid one more time and I'm gonna shove your face so far up your ass you could use your balls as earrings."

Thad crossed his arms and gave me his blank stare. He reminded me so much of Mom right now. I lost count of how many times she had looked at me that way. "That's your answer for everything. Violence. Someone pisses you off. You threaten to kick their ass. Can't open a jar of pickles. You smash it against the wall."

I snickered. I'd almost forgotten about that. Superman couldn't have opened the fucking thing. I was so pissed off I damn near beaned Mason in the head when I chucked it across the kitchen. He had screamed like a little bitch too. It had been damn near priceless.

"And now I've lost your attention."

I knitted my eyebrows. "What?"

"Not only do you have a hair trigger temper, but you have the attention span of a coke-snorting squirrel."

Mason snorted in laughter, and Drake brought his hand up to his mouth to cover his big grin.

I glared at Thad. "Yeah, well, maybe you're just not all that interesting. Have you thought about that?"

Okay, so that was a lame comeback. I didn't need the synchronized eyeball rolling to tell me that.

Thad glared at me before glancing at Mason. "This is our future high priest?" He turned his frosty gaze back to me. "We'll be dead within a week after Dad passes on."

Mason winced. "Thad, that's not cool."

Thad didn't respond. He continued to stare at me as if he dared me to defend myself, but I couldn't speak. My brother's words cut me to shreds. My biggest fear had always been filling Dad's shoes, and he knew that.

When we were kids, I told Thad how scared I was about shouldering the responsibility for everything. I would be in charge of the family *and* run our company. The magical and financial futures of the Blackmoors would become my responsibility, and if I failed, if the task proved too much for me, everything my family had built for the past four generations would crumble around my ears.

I wanted to rip Thad's head off his shoulders or tell him to fuck off, but I was paralyzed by the fear my brother's words had allowed to resurface.

How could I lead this family? I was no longer the most powerful, and I sure as hell wasn't the smartest.

Thad was right. The Blackmoor coven wouldn't outlast my father's life.

I turned around and shot toward the front door.

"Pierce!" Mason shouted. "Come back."

I slammed the door behind me. The chilly late-afternoon air bit deep as I hopped on my motorcycle and rode away.

FUCKING THAD. He knew exactly which buttons to push. He might not know how to fight with his fists, but with words, he was the undisputed heavyweight champion of the universe. The bastard didn't even fight fair.

He always went for the gut or the groin.

I took several deep breaths, but it wasn't to control my anger. Yeah, I was cheesed off. Who wouldn't be after what Thad had said? It was my anxiety I had to get under control. It gnawed away inside me like termites hell-bent on consuming an entire house.

I couldn't let it win. Hell, I couldn't let Thad win.

That was why I had to get out of the house. Whenever I was on my Ducati with its two-hundred-horsepower engine purring between my legs and the wind whipping through my black hair, I was invincible.

I redlined the bike and the engine roared. I shot down the road that ran parallel to the back property of Blackmoor Manor. The cold air stung my face and my adrenaline kicked into overdrive. The speed did what I expected it to do. The ravenous termites that threatened to devour me whole retreated, and I let out a defiant cry that echoed all around me.

Thad could go fuck himself for all I cared.

He might think I was stupid, and maybe I was compared to him. But I knew the truth. He envied me. He always had.

It started the day I first tapped into my active power, and it only grew when he realized he would never be high priest of our coven. I was the oldest. That burden and responsibility was mine, and there was nothing Mr. Smarty Pants could ever do about that.

I eased back on the throttle, having outrun most of my anxiety. The dense forest that had previously whipped by in a blur of brown slowed to where I could make out the trees that lined the farthest reaches of my family's estate.

I would show Thad he was wrong. I'd be the one to find Ben or Ebenezer Kane, whatever the fuck he called himself now, and force him to reveal his plans. Thad's newly evolved powers and supposedly superior intellect hadn't managed that so far. He might be able to create blizzards and snowstorms, but he wasn't able to stop Ben. He'd gotten away, and he was far too deadly to be on the loose. He might be the most powerful warlock to walk the earth. He might be a shadow weaver and a vampyre with the ability to cast blood magic, but when he crossed my path, I'd take him out.

Thad once told me I always looked for the hammer when a screwdriver would do the trick, but when you're a hammer, there's no fucking need to grab a screwdriver.

I slowed down and pulled over on the side of the road. I had to go back. Running wasn't the answer. If anything, it only proved Thad was right, that I couldn't handle the pressure of being a high priest.

I had to go home, look Thad square in his pissy hazel eyes, and tell him to bite me.

"Excuse me." A hand suddenly grasped my shoulder.

Surprised by the voice and the unexpected contact, I rose off my bike and whirled around, punching the sneaky bastard in the face. He fell on his ass and tumbled into the ditch off the side of the road.

"What the fuck, man?" I asked, setting the kickstand on my bike. There was no way my baby was going to get scratched or banged up while I dealt with whatever asshole had the balls to creep up on me. If he knocked it over and ruined the paint job, I'd kill him.

I stared down the thirty-degree angle of the ditch at the guy who lay on his back, covering his nose. I couldn't get a good look at his face, with his nose currently gushing out blood, but he looked like he'd already been through the wringer.

For some weird reason, he wore what looked like a tunic made of burlap, which was singed around the edges. Was this dipshit heading to a costume party? It was yuletide, not Samhain.

"What are you doing sneaking up on a guy like that?" I asked before surveying the forest to see if he had any friends with him. "Don't you know this is private property? Trespassers will be electrocuted."

"My apologies, sir." I must've hit him hard. Every word sounded like it ended with a *th*. And who the hell was he calling sir? I was only twenty-eight. I was definitely *not* old enough to qualify as a sir, but to this little chicken who looked no older than twenty-one, I might look like a daddy.

"Don't call me sir," I said, sliding down the ditch to him. He clearly needed help getting up. He was favoring his right arm and having trouble getting leverage or balance. "Just don't sneak up on me again."

"Yes, sir," he said as I grabbed his good arm and hauled him to his feet. He peered at me from over the hands he once again held to his face. His wide eyes indicated his apology of addressing me as "sir" again.

"That's strike number two," I said, to which he nodded.

From the constant pressure he'd been applying, the blood had stopped oozing between his fingers, but he still refused to let them fall away.

"Let me see the damage."

He nodded and removed his hands. He responded well to orders, which gave me a stiff one. I enjoyed a nice twink who knew who was in charge, and I would definitely enjoy eating the creamy filling of this particular Twinkie. Well, at least once he washed all the blood away.

Despite his horrible costume, his jacked-up nose, and blood-smeared face, he was pretty damn attractive. He had a full head of dark hair and smooth sun-kissed skin, like he'd just come from a tropical paradise. He wasn't very tall. Probably only about five foot seven, which meant I practically towered over him at six four. His baggy tunic hid most of his body, but his arms were nicely shaped. That boded well for the rest of him.

But what intrigued me the most about him were his eyes. They weren't amber or hazel with flecks of yellow or copper. They were a luminous warm gold and reminded me of honey.

My heart beat faster, and I held my breath.

There was something familiar about him, but I couldn't remember seeing him before. So why did it feel like I recognized him, as if something within me responded to something within him? It sent shivers across my flesh that vibrated down into my soul.

He cleared his throat, and I realized I'd been staring for longer than I probably should have. "You'll live," I said with a dismissive wave.

He nodded, but he refused to look me straight in the eye.

"What's your name?"

"Kale Aquilo," he replied, still inspecting the dead leaves that carpeted the ground.

Who the fuck named their kid after a vegetable? "What are you doing out here, Kale?"

He swallowed hard and fidgeted with his fingers. "I was on my way to a very important meeting, si—" His gaze briefly met mine before it flitted away. He clearly wasn't sure what to call me.

"I'm Pierce," I said.

"Well, Pierce, I, uh, ran into a bit of trouble, and now I'm, well, I'm not able to get to where I was going." He winced and clutched his arm.

I inspected the area for signs of a broken-down vehicle. "Were you in an accident?"

He hesitated. "Sort of."

What the hell did that mean? "Either you were or you weren't."

"Yes, I was."

"Well, where's your car? I can take a look at it. I'm pretty good with my hands." I dropped my voice to a low growl as the last two words left my lips. If this guy was interested, he'd take the bait. Most guys I knew would still fuck even with a busted nose and a hurt arm.

He gazed at me out of the corners of his eyes. "I'm sure you are."

Either he wasn't interested or he was being skittish. Considering I had just clocked him in the nose, I had to go with the latter. "I can give you a lift if you need one."

"Thank you," he said, still not looking at me. "But you can't take me where I need to go."

Like hell I couldn't. I could ride him all the way to Jersey and back. He'd get where he needed to be at least twice. "Look, just tell me where to go and I'll drop you off."

He shook his head and scaled the ditch up to the street. "Thank you, but no."

Who was he kidding? He was lost and shivering. I couldn't leave him out here. He'd freeze to death. "Well, I can't just leave you stranded. You'll die of exposure."

He held himself tight, rubbing his arms. He sniffed the air and sighed. "I'll be fine once my olfactory glands have recovered."

His what? "Are you talking about your nose?"

"Yes," he said with a short nod. "My sight is far more reliable, but right now my nose will have to do."

I had no clue what he was talking about. This guy might be hot and strangely familiar, but he was a weirdo. Still, I couldn't just leave him here. "How about this?" I said, walking over to my bike. "I live right behind this forest. It's a nice house, and it's warm. Why don't I take you there? You can get cleaned up, and maybe we can do something about your nose and your arm."

He inhaled deeply again and shook his head. "I suppose I have no other choice."

"Sure you do," I replied as I revved up the engine. "You can stay out here and die. That's a choice."

Without another word Kale traipsed over to where I was. He studied my bike as if it were a monster. "I've never seen one of these before."

I grinned. It was a limited edition. "It's a beauty, isn't it?"

He nodded. "It's very shiny."

Yeah, that was how you described a motorcycle that cost over two hundred and fifty grand. Shiny. "Hop on," I said with a nod to the back.

He wrinkled his brow at me before carefully sliding into the seat behind me. "What now?" he asked.

I released the kickstand and gave my beauty more juice. "Now you hang on," I hollered over the engine before rocketing down the street.

CHAPTER 2

KALE HELD me in a death grip all the way back to Blackmoor Manor. I tried to get him to relax, but the poor kid wouldn't ease up. I'd be lying if I said I didn't enjoy it. Even though it was pretty damn cold out, his warm body pressed against mine made me forget all about the icy wind that buffeted us from every direction and the awful fight I had with my brothers.

It also made me feel like I definitely knew him. His body against mine felt familiar, as if we'd done this before, even though I knew we hadn't.

After we arrived back at the house and I shut off the engine, I was disappointed when he withdrew the comforting weight of his body. Had he felt it too, or was it just me?

"That was neat," he said.

Neat? Who said "neat" anymore? He inspected every inch of the bike and trailed his fingers across the cool metal.

"Really?" I asked. "You were holding on so tight I was afraid you were gonna piss yourself."

He scrunched up his nose and shook his head. "That's gross. I'd never do that."

The strong conviction in his tone told me he was speaking the truth. Maybe he held on to me like that because he felt it too and was as confused by it as I was. Or maybe it was his way of letting me know he was okay if we got naked and rutted around like a couple of pigs. I was surprisingly okay with either.

"I'm just used to being in the driver's seat," he finally said after he finished admiring my ride.

The kid was a top? I didn't see that one coming. I'd bottomed before, but it wasn't really my thing. It was like someone was shoving a red-hot poker up my ass. It was also the only time in my life I didn't get off during sex, and I enjoyed blowing my load more than just about anything else.

"What do you call it?"

"What? Topping?"

He rubbed his chin and stared down at the bike. "What a weird name for this device."

I snorted. "Oh, my bad. I thought you were talking about something else."

He drew his brows together as if he had no clue why I was laughing.

I cleared my throat and tried to wipe the smirk from my lips. "This is a Ducati."

He repeated the word over and over again like a child learning to speak. In fact, the way he looked at it was like he'd never seen a motorcycle. Where was this guy from? "Why do I get the feeling you've never seen something like this before?"

"I have." His body tensed, and he regarded me carefully as he flashed me a big dopey smile. I could see the truth in the trembling corners of his mouth.

He was lying. I crossed my arms and gave him a hard look. "Try again."

"No, seriously, uh, I've seen a Ducati before. Especially, um, one like this," he sputtered. "I mean, who hasn't, right? They're everywhere."

No, they weren't. Only two hundred of these puppies had been made. "Why are you lying to me? You've never seen a motorcycle before. Am I right?"

"A what?" he asked.

I gestured to my bike.

"You said it was a Ducati. Why are *you* lying to me?"

I shook my head and sighed. "A Ducati is a type of motorcycle."

He let out a long exhalation and stared down at his feet. "Oh," he said. He might as well be kicking a rock with his big toe. "I'm not from around here, is all."

No shit. "Where you from? Pennsylvania? Oh, what are those people called? The ones who are really religious and don't use electricity and stuff." The idea made me cringe. Who could live without the comforts of modern society? "You Amish?"

Kale studied my expression for a moment before hesitantly nodding. Just great. A hot Amish boy who probably wore a chastity belt. Whatever I thought I felt had obviously been my imagination. "You're a long way from home, kid."

He stood taller and puffed out his chest. "I'm not a kid. I'm twenty-five."

I eyeballed him.

He frowned. "Fine. I'm twenty-two."

That sounded closer to the truth. "I thought you Amish weren't supposed to lie and shit."

He looked up at me with wide eyes. "Um, well."

I shook my head and grinned. He was obviously running away from that life, maybe trying to start over. He just clearly had no clue where to even begin. Maybe that was who he was meeting, someone who was going to help him. "How about we head inside and take care of your injuries?"

Kale rubbed his right arm as if suddenly remembering it hurt. He also inhaled deeply again. What the hell was he trying to smell?

"Still nothing?"

He shook his head. "Nope. I'm all stuffed up, thanks to you."

I felt real bad about that, and though I should apologize, I wasn't going to. Warlocks didn't say they were sorry. It was a sign of weakness, and I was feeling weak enough as it was. "Let's get you inside. I'm sure we've got something that'll fix you right up."

He did a slow sweep of Blackmoor Manor, taking in the three-story colonial house that had been in my family for over a hundred years. He followed the wooden trim up to the gray-shingled roof, his mouth agape. "This is yours?"

"Yup," I replied with a proud nod.

"I've never seen such opulence."

"Like it?"

He nodded.

I put my hand on his shoulder and led him to the front door. "Well, then, wait till you see the inside."

Kale bounded up the front steps. He reminded me of a little kid on his first outing, and I supposed he was. Living on an Amish farm his entire life, he was clearly used to more modest homes and awful clothing, judging by his tunic and handmade trousers.

He paused at the front door and glanced over his shoulder, his eyebrows arching across his forehead in anticipation.

There was an innocence about him that made me smile. I'd give anything to be full of hope like Kale. For him, life was one open road filled with endless possibilities. I sped down a one-lane highway with a preset destination that either went on forever or came to a dead end.

"Wow!" Kale said once I opened the front door and let him inside. He swept his gaze over the wreaths and mistletoe that hung about the house as decoration for Yule to the fine art that hung in the hallway. My father was a real art buff. He collected old paintings the way I bought nice rides.

Kale flitted over to the family portrait that hung in the alcove underneath the stairwell. We'd sat for that painting about two years ago. We went for a long lunch on the waterfront and spent the afternoon on the beach. It was the last great day we had as a family before my mother started getting really sick. A few months later, we learned she had cancer.

"Is this your family?" he asked.

I nodded.

"Your mother is beautiful."

"Yes, she was."

He glanced over his shoulder and the bright light in his golden eyes flickered. Why did I get the feeling he wanted to dash over and give me a hug? "I'm sorry for your loss."

I gave him a halfhearted smile. It was my standard response whenever someone offered their condolences. I didn't talk about my mother. Even though she died almost nine months ago, the pain was still too raw. Just thinking about her made it feel like I was trying to choke down a big piece of steak without chewing.

Kale returned the smile with a nod. He clearly understood this was a topic of discussion I didn't want to pursue. He turned from the painting and peeked into the living room with its white overstuffed couch and sleek black piano. He crossed the hall and poked his head into the library, where his lower jaw about hit the floor.

He entered the room, inspecting every bookshelf that contained more books than I ever cared to read. Cherrywood covered the walls across both floors. A black iron spiral staircase climbed along the far right corner to the second floor, where more bookshelves stood, protecting their leather-bound charges.

It was a beautiful room, and judging from Kale's big smile of wonder, he thought so too.

He reminded me of that kid Charlie who won the golden ticket in *Willy Wonka*. When Charlie entered that factory, he practically got a boner for all that chocolate. That was how full of wonder and awe Kale was right now.

Books apparently turned Kale's crank.

He gazed up at the huge mirror that hung over the mantle of the fireplace. It was at least ten feet high, and its reflection made the room seem twice as big as it was. "Have you read all these books?" he asked, standing in the center of the room and spinning in a circle.

"Not even close," I replied. "My brother Thad more than likely has, though. Books are his only friends." That wasn't entirely true, but I wasn't done being pissed off at Thad yet.

"There aren't a lot of books where I come from," he replied.

"I bet you have the Bible," I said, sounding more like a jackass than I intended to be.

I was just about to take back the words when Kale nodded. "Funnily enough, we do have that one. It's an interesting piece of literature."

Literature? Wasn't the Bible what his people lived by? What kind of Amish was he?

"Do you mind if I open one of these books?" he asked. He was scoping the bookshelves the way I checked out someone I considered hot.

"Go crazy," I replied.

He lingered his fingers over the spines of several books before plucking one with red leather backing off the shelf. He eagerly flipped it open, and his greedy eyes quickly devoured the first page before moving on to the next. If Kale were in any more pleasure, he'd have been moaning and touching himself.

"How's your arm?"

"My what?" he asked, tearing his attention from the book to me.

"Your arm," I replied, pointing to the limb he still held close to his body.

"Oh. Still hurts," he said before returning to the book. Clearly the joy of reading overpowered whatever pain he felt. I should get him some gauze for his nose and maybe a couple of Advil. He had to have a headache after the way my fist became acquainted with his face. But what was I going to do about his arm? I had no clue what had happened to it, and I wasn't a potion master like Thad.

With my luck, anything I'd whip up would either kill him or make his arm fall off.

"Well, look who's back."

I turned around to see my brothers and Drake descending the stairs. I had no doubt they'd been upstairs talking about me. Thad's curled upper lip told me he was still angry, while the pissy had clearly blown out of Mason's sails. He bounded down the steps to me. His big blue eyes and the smile on his lips were his way of apologizing.

"I'm glad you're back," he said as he entered the room. When he saw Kale standing across the room, he arched a big bushy eyebrow at me. "And I see you picked up something to make you feel better."

I glowered at him.

"Hi," Kale said when he realized we were no longer alone. He placed the book gingerly back where it had previously rested and trekked across the room. He wore perhaps the friendliest, most genuine smile I'd ever seen that just so happened to create a pair of dimples I suddenly wanted to lick. It made him even more attractive despite the blood still caked around his nostrils. "I'm Kale. It's nice to meet you."

He held out his hand, which he had rubbed clean on his pants, to Mason, who shook it while staring long and hard at his outfit. "What the fuck are you wearing?" he asked. "And what happened to your face?"

"Mason!" Drake scolded while I snarled at my younger brother. Mason had always been carelessly blunt.

"What?" Mason asked, as if he hadn't been rude. "He looks like a *Game of Thrones* extra who's been tortured by King Joffrey."

Kale inspected his clothing and then glanced at ours. While he wore handmade clothes that were threadbare, singed, and bloody, the rest of us sported neatly pressed shirts and designer jeans. His gaze fell to the floor and his shoulders slumped. "I guess I don't look like much."

Drake smacked Mason on the back of his head before standing next to Kale. "You look just fine," he said, glaring at his boyfriend. That look told me Mason might just be spending the night on the couch. "I'm Drake."

Kale glanced at Drake out of the corners of his eyes. "Pleased to meet you."

Thad studied Kale with his cold, penetrating gaze. I hated when he did that. It always made me feel like a lab rat instead of a warlock. "Is there a reason you've brought him here when we have much to discuss?"

"Yeah, Thad," I said. My anger enflamed my pitch. "The same reason I do everything else. To piss the shit out of you."

Thad hitched up the right corner of his mouth in a smirk. Why did ticking me off make him so happy?

"Maybe I should go," Kale said.

"No," I replied. I placed my hand on his shoulder and rubbed it. He glanced up at me and gave me a sweet smile that doused my anger. "We've got to clean you up."

"And just what happened to you?" Drake asked. "Were you in an accident?"

Kale rubbed the back of his neck and wouldn't make eye contact. He clearly didn't know how to answer the question without making the situation more uncomfortable.

"It was my fault," I replied, feeling the need to own up to my actions. When was the last time I'd done that? "Kale surprised me on the road and I punched him."

"Damn, Pierce," Mason replied, giving Kale the once-over. He'd been on the receiving end of my blows before and knew firsthand how much they hurt. "You okay?" he asked Kale.

Kale inhaled deeply, trying to test his still-clogged nose. "I'll be better once I can smell again."

Mason nodded. "Yeah, it'll come back after a few hours." He gestured with his head toward me. "That big oaf has clocked me in the nose before."

"What about your arm?" Thad asked. As always, nothing got by him. "Did my brother do that too?"

Kale chewed on his lower lip instead of replying.

Why wouldn't he answer that question? Even though I had no clue how he hurt his arm or why his clothes appeared as if they'd been burned, an overwhelming need to protect Kale surged within me. "His arm was already hurt. He said he was on his way to a meeting and had lost his way."

Kale's eyes grew wide. "Oh my," he said, looking around the room as if he was a caged bird. "I need to get going. I have to find the—" He chewed on his lip again. "I shouldn't have allowed myself to become distracted from my mission."

That was an interesting choice of words. Thad obviously thought so too. He crossed his arms and studied Kale even more closely. I had to stop myself from punching him in his pointed nose. "Not just yet," Thad replied. A smile Thad meant to be comforting broke across his lips. It made him look creepy instead, as if he had just hatched a plan. "We should take care of your injuries first. Pierce can get you some bandages, and I'm sure Mason or Drake can find some clothes that would be much better at keeping you warm while you continue your travels. I'll make you some tea."

The smile lingered on Thad's lips as Kale looked back and forth from him to me. My brother definitely had something up his sleeve, and Kale could sense it. He fidgeted with the edge of his tunic.

His evident distress tugged me toward him. "Don't worry," I said. I stood by Kale and stared at my brother. "I'll make sure you're taken care of."

Kale gazed up at me, pressing his fingers to his smiling lips. Why did I get the feeling he wasn't used to having others stick up for him, and why did it make me want to do it again?

AFTER I used alcohol to clean away most of the dried blood on his face, Kale went upstairs with Mason and Drake to find warmer clothes while I headed to the kitchen to see what Thad was up to.

As he worked busily in the kitchen, Bing Crosby's voice sang "Silent Night" over the radio. Although I wasn't a fan of how humans had taken our Yule Sabbat, dedicated to the Winter Solstice and rebirth, and commercialized it into what they called Christmas, I did enjoy the music. It sure beat what the witches clucked during the ritual.

Thad pulled several jars of herbs from the cabinet and had a pot of water set to boil on the range. He portioned out some allspice, anise, and clove, and was currently cutting up an apple. To his left were two other ingredients I couldn't identify. They didn't look like any he'd previously used in past healing potions.

"What are you up to?" I asked, leaning against the counter where he continued his prep work.

"What does it look like?" he replied. "Helping to clean up another mess you've made."

I gritted my teeth. Bing Crosby's voice gave way to Jose Feliciano singing "Feliz Navidad." There wasn't much "feliz" in this particular "Navidad." "Can you just answer my question without being a smartass?"

He glanced up from his work, obviously pondering the question. "I suppose I could," he answered. He carried the cut-up apples over to the pot and placed two slices in the water. He repeated the process with the herbs I recognized.

As he was about to do the same with the mysterious spices, I asked, "Thad, what are you doing?"

He glanced at me over his shoulder before sprinkling the spices in the water and replacing the lid. "Your friend Kale is up to something. I'm just trying to figure out what that is."

"He was in an accident, and I punched him. All he's up to is wanting to get better before he continues on his way."

Thad gave me a blank stare. It was his way of telling me to stop being so stupid. I gripped the counter until my knuckles turned white. I didn't want to fight, but Thad evidently wasn't on the same page.

"Someone we don't know shows up on our property, and he doesn't answer simple questions. The only thing he does let slip is that he's 'on a mission.' He's hiding something. I know it and so do you."

I couldn't argue with him on that. Kale was keeping a secret, but so what? Whatever it was didn't mean bad news for us. I was as certain of that as I was about my dedication to this family. Besides, we all had secrets. What right did Thad have to pry? "It's none of our business."

"Wrong," Thad replied before tossing the cutting board in the sink. Ever since we'd gotten back from Otherworld, he'd been on edge. At first I chalked it up to suddenly having a vampyre boyfriend. I'd been wrong. Something else was going on here. "You brought him into our house. You've made him our business."

"You mean the way you brought Aiden into our house after Ben turned him into a vampyre?"

His nostrils flared. "I wouldn't go there if I were you."

"Why not?" I asked, taking a few steps toward him. He clearly had no trouble being suspicious of Kale. Why couldn't I return the favor? Sure, Aiden was doing his best to control his vampyren side, and so far he'd been able to rein in his violent tendencies. He'd made enough progress that Dad had taken Aiden to the Conclave. That was where they were right now, discussing Aiden's progress and alleviating most of the Conclave's concerns with allowing a vampyre to roam free. Maybe that was the source of Thad's bad mood. He'd been prevented from going with Aiden even though he begged the old wizard Gerald Wa, his friend who served as a member of our governing body, to let him go. It didn't work.

"You brought Aiden home with us from Otherworld knowing what he was, and you placed this family in danger by letting him stay here," I continued. "How is bringing Kale here any worse than what you did?"

"First, it was Dad who let Aiden stay here. If you have a problem with that, take it up with him. But you'd have to find your balls in order to do that. You've never been able to stand up to him."

I bared my teeth. Thad was going to push me one inch too far.

"And we were talking about Kale, not Aiden. Don't be throwing one of your red herrings."

What the fuck did a fish have to do with this? "I know what we're talking about. You think I'm being careless. I'm just trying to point out that I'm not doing anything more careless than you've done."

His arched eyebrows clearly disagreed with me. "You've brought a stranger into this house. Do I need to remind you of the last time that happened? You brought Ben Crane into our lives, the enemy the Conclave had been looking for, the one who turned out to be the oldest and deadliest enemy our kind has ever faced. He almost killed us, Pierce."

I didn't need to be reminded of that, but I also wasn't going to shoulder all the blame either. None of us, not even the Conclave, had been able to sense Ben's ulterior motives or his true identity.

"Kale isn't Ben."

The teakettle behind us whistled. "Perhaps not," he replied. "But that's precisely what I intend to find out."

KALE ENTERED the kitchen with Mason and Drake in tow. His dark hair was damp from the shower he'd taken to wash the remaining blood from his face, and he'd also changed into one of Mason's outfits. He had on a gray knitted cardigan zip-up with a blue button-down shirt underneath and a pair of black jeans. The big grin he also wore told me he approved of the outfit.

My fattening cock agreed.

"What do you think?" he asked, sauntering up to the counter next to me. There were three other people in the room with us, but he asked only me. It made my belly flutter.

"You look great," I replied, my voice barely above a whisper. I was just about to rub my thumb across his cheek but pulled away and ran my fingers through my hair instead.

Kale grinned broadly and his cheeks flushed. Did he know what I was about to do? "I feel so fancy," he announced. He scooted closer, and his body's warmth spread across my skin.

"You look like a thousand percent better," Mason said, sitting across from us at the bar.

Kale twisted his lips and once again scrutinized the floor.

Before I could turn my snarl into a bark, Drake picked up a dishtowel and threw it in his boyfriend's face.

"What?" Mason asked. Could he be any more clueless?

"Like my daddy used to say," Drake answered, "a closed mouth gathers no feet."

Kale burst into laughter. "I've never heard that one before," he said. "Your dad must be a real hoot."

Sadness crept into Drake's eyes before he blinked it away. "He was," he said with a slow nod. Mason was suddenly at his boyfriend's side, wrapping his arms around him. Mason might be a pain in the ass as a brother, but as a boyfriend, he brought only joy and comfort.

"I'm so sorry," Kale said. He crossed over to Drake and was about to touch him before pulling away. "I guess I should watch what I say too."

Drake smiled and patted Kale on his shoulder. "No need to apologize. I miss my folks a ton, but I don't mind talkin' about them. I should do it more often."

"You've all suffered such loss," Kale said, surveying all of us.

"I take it your parents are still alive?" Thad asked. He poured the potion into a cup and stirred it. I still had no clue what kind of brew it was, and I wasn't comfortable with Kale drinking it. Thad wouldn't serve Kale anything harmful, but the gnawing feeling in my gut told me this was wrong. I had to bite the inside of my cheek to keep from flying over the bar and slapping the cup out of his hands.

"Yes, they are. We aren't terribly close, though," Kale admitted. His voice turned flat, and he gazed out the kitchen window. "I'm not quite who they'd like me to be."

"Because you're gay?" Mason asked. Drake shot him a glare that caused Mason to throw up his hands in surrender. "Okay, fine. I'll shut up."

Yeah, like that would ever happen.

Kale switched his gaze between Drake and Mason as if he was uncertain what the fuss was about. "No, that's not it," he answered. "My people don't judge others based on who they fall in love with. It's not really something you can control."

Drake nodded. "The heart wants what it wants."

"I suppose that's true," Kale said. "But for us it's less about the heart and more about the meeting of two kindred souls." He glanced over at me before quickly looking away.

"I'm confused," I said. "I thought you were Amish."

"That explains the clothes!" Mason added. Drake, who was beyond exasperated, shook his head in defeat.

Kale flitted his gaze around the room. We were all waiting for an answer, especially Thad. He narrowed his eyes and seemed to be holding his breath.

"Yeah, so what?"

Thad strolled over to Kale, the cup of tea in his hand. "The Amish aren't exactly tolerant of homosexual behavior."

"Oh," Kale hesitated. He avoided eye contact and rubbed his right arm. "Well, my parents aren't quite as strict."

"I see." Thad locked gazes with me. It was his way of telling me "told you so." He then returned his attention to Kale and offered him a deceptively warm smile. "Here's your tea. Your arm will feel better in no time."

Kale took the offered drink, and even though he was clearly lying, the unwavering light in his eyes spoke to me on a level I'd never listened to before. Kale wasn't like Ben. He wasn't our enemy, but we still needed the truth. Once he drank the tea, we'd have it.

"Go ahead," Thad urged. "It'll do wonders. The vapors should even clear up your blocked nasal passages."

Kale brought the cup up to his nose and took a deep whiff. "It worked," he said. He took a deep breath, and his eyes grew wide. The cup of tea fell to the floor. "You're warlocks," he said, backing away from us and staring down at the spilled liquid. "What are you trying to do? Poison me?"

"I think the question is: what are you trying to do to us?" Thad nodded to Mason, who quietly circled behind Kale, blocking the kitchen exit. Drake slid over to the door to bar that avenue of escape.

Kale locked gazes with me, his panicked expression seeking my help. His lips and chin trembled, and he surveyed the room as if he expected us to throw him into the stove and cook him.

"I mean you no harm," he said, glancing over his shoulder and spotting Mason behind him. Though he was clearly afraid, his muscles tensed and his gaze turned hard. He was ready to fight even if he was outnumbered.

He inched away from Thad until he was halfway into the kitchen. It was a good move. From where Kale stood, he had all of us in his line of sight and could counter an attack. He wasn't throwing a punch. If Ben had sent him here, he'd be fighting his way out right now.

"Why have you been lying?" I asked.

"I'm sorry," Kale said. "I didn't know you were a warlock. If you hadn't punched me in the nose, I would have been able to smell it out on you."

Thad tilted his head to one side as if this situation suddenly made sense. "Smell it on him?"

Kale placed his back against the wall, still waiting to defend himself before nodding his head.

"You're a shifter."

We gaped at Thad before returning our attention to Kale.

"Yes. I'm here on official business, I swear."

"What kind of official business?" I asked.

He swallowed hard. "To find the Conclave."

"WHY DON'T you start from the beginning?" Thad asked as we sat down in the living room. As usual, Thad took his place on the piano bench off to the right. He never joined us in the sitting area whenever we had something important to discuss. He preferred to remain apart from us, where he could observe everyone like the human microscope he was.

Mason and Drake sat on the couch across from the one where Kale and I sat. Ever since Kale's revelation, Mason had scrunched up his face, his eyes practically slits. He studied Kale as if he were the main attraction at a freak show, and it was starting to piss me off. When he noticed me glowering at him, he quickly changed his expression and looked away.

I knew exactly what was on his mind because I'd been thinking the same thing. What kind of animal did Kale shift into? He didn't strike me as a wolf. I'd always imagined they'd be big, burly guys with too much testosterone. That certainly wasn't Kale. He wasn't a wimp or anything, but he certainly wasn't intimidating in size or personality.

Kale cleared his throat to finally speak, but he was either having trouble finding his words or uncertain if he should answer the question. He fidgeted on the couch next to me. He scratched itches that had popped up on his neck, his chest, and his right leg, and he swept his gaze around the room, clearly marking the exits in case he needed a quick getaway.

I had to calm him down, or we'd never learn what he wanted with our governing body.

"No one's going to hurt you," I said.

He looked at me askance. His sparkling golden eyes told me he wanted to believe me, but his flat smile communicated distrust. I couldn't blame him. We'd been gawking at him. That would make anyone uncomfortable.

"Then why were you trying to poison me?" he asked.

"It wasn't poison," Thad replied from where he sat. He was having trouble sitting still, as if the control he'd prided himself on was slowly slipping away. "It was a combination healing and truth-inducing potion. I knew you were lying, and I wanted you to tell us what you were hiding."

Kale's easygoing, friendly demeanor disappeared. His gaze turned harder than solid rock. "My information is mine to share. You have no right forcing me to do something against my will." He scoffed as if he'd told a joke that wasn't so funny. "But I expect nothing less from your kind."

What the hell did that mean? "Hey, we aren't the enemies here," I said. "But you should know we've been through a lot these past couple of months. We've faced too many bad guys who've been trying to hurt us for reasons even we don't know. Thad was just being cautious, trying to protect his family."

My brother nodded and smiled at me. Whatever remnants of anger he had previously held against me vanished like a whisper in a windstorm.

"Pierce is right," Mason added. "After everything we've been through, we'd be stupid not to be careful. We've weathered a lot and suffered some losses." He wrapped his arm around Drake, who'd lost his aunt Millie to whatever plans Ben had up his sleeve.

The evident pain in Drake's downcast eyes relieved some of Kale's apprehension. He let out a long sigh and his muscles relaxed. He sat back and uncrossed his arms from his chest. "I'm sorry," he said. "This is my first time in Human's World, and I've been on edge since I got here. It didn't help that some strange lightning storm struck me out of the sky shortly after I crossed over."

All eyes turned to me. Well, shit. At least I knew what kind of animal Kale turned into. He was the only bird I hadn't fried.

"What?" Kale asked, following everyone's gazes to me.

I grimaced before swallowing hard. "That would be my fault," I said. "My brothers and I were goofing off on the rear lawn, and my powers got away from me."

"Got away from you?" Mason asked. "That's like saying the Hulk has anger issues."

I flipped Mason off. "Can it, fuck face."

"Wait a minute," Kale said. A frown tugged his lips downward. "You punched me in the face *and* knocked me out of the sky all in the same day?" Great. As if I didn't feel bad enough about it already, Kale had to go and look at me with big golden eyes that made me feel about an inch tall.

My chin sunk all the way to my chest. "Maybe."

Kale shook his head in disbelief. "What's wrong with you?"

"How much time do you have?" Mason asked.

I locked eyes with my younger brother, who flashed me a shit-eating grin. "You better watch out or I'll send a couple thousand volts of electricity up your ass."

"No, you won't!" Drake protested.

Mason wrapped his arms around his boyfriend and his smile stretched even broader.

"With the amount of gas that Mason emits, you'd just blow us all to kingdom come," Drake added with a sly grin.

Mason's smirk died quickly, and I busted out in laughter.

"Hey!" Mason playfully swatted Drake's shoulder. "You're supposed to be on my side."

"I'm on whatever side is upwind from you," Drake said before giving Mason a kiss.

"Are we done with the crude humor?" Thad asked. He had progressed from the piano bench to the middle of the sitting area. He shook his head at Mason and Drake before returning his attention to Kale, whose laughter shut off under the weight of my brother's penetrating stare. Thad was clearly on edge and ready for some answers. "You still haven't told us why you're here."

Kale's expression turned serious. "You're right."

When he said no more, Thad placed his hands on his hips and sighed. "Well?"

"Well, it's none of your business," Kale replied.

"I beg to differ."

Thad's reply was met with an arch of Kale's dark eyebrows. "You can beg all you want. I'm the personal emissary of the Beast King. I don't answer to you."

He had balls. I had to give Kale that. Most people wilted under Thad's interrogation, but Thad's obviously raised hackles didn't even make him blink.

"The Beast King?" I asked. That was the first time I'd ever heard that expression before. "You don't live in packs with an alpha male running the show?"

Kale drew his lips into a thin line. "And warlocks aren't evil?"

I flinched as if he'd slapped me. My kind had gotten a bad reputation. Thanks to literature and television shows, most people assumed we worshipped the devil or were demons. "A simple 'no' would've worked too," I replied.

"We can't really be talking about this right now," Thad said, wringing his hands. "Ben is still out there, and I don't think a shifter's sudden presence in our world is a coincidence."

Why was Thad acting as if he knew something the rest of us didn't? Did this have anything to do with his secret meeting with Gerald Wa?

They'd had a private powwow shortly after we returned from Otherworld, and Thad refused to tell us what they'd talked about.

"I don't know Ben or what you've all been through," Kale answered. "But I can see it's been tough."

"Yes, it has," Thad agreed. "So tell us why you're here."

Kale shook his head.

"We're the Blackmoors," Thad said, as if saying our name would suddenly get Kale to trust us. For most magical species, it might work, but our name clearly didn't register for Kale. He stared through Thad as if he had no clue what my brother was referring to.

"We're one of the protector covens," Mason added. That role made us a big deal in the magical community. We were charged with protecting the Gate, the source of all magic, and we worked for the Conclave.

Kale glanced at me, obviously looking for verification. When I nodded, he turned his attention back to Thad, who clearly waited for an answer. "While that's an impressive status for your family, that doesn't make you the Conclave," Kale said. "They are who I was sent to find and deliver my message to. I'll speak to no one else on the subject."

Thad lunged toward Kale, but I intercepted him. I grabbed him, spun him around, and placed him in a chokehold. "What the fuck do you think you're doing?" I asked. This wasn't like him at all. Thad was calm, reserved, and logical. I was the one with the hair-trigger temper.

"Let me go!" he yelled. He gripped my forearms and ice formed on my skin. I gritted my teeth, trying to block out the pain. "He knows something, and he needs to tell us."

Mason stood in front of Thad, eying the sheen of frost on my arm. "Shit, Thad. Calm down, will you?"

"Mason's right," Drake said in his Southern drawl. Whenever he was stressed, his twang became more pronounced. "This isn't helpin' any."

"Ben has to be behind it," Thad said. He grabbed my arms, which were growing increasingly numb. "I can feel it."

This wasn't anger at all. Thad was terrified. What the hell did he know? "Maybe he is," I said, speaking in as soothing a voice as I could muster while trying to get him to stop thrashing against me or from turning me into a warlock-sicle. "But if Kale's message is for the Conclave's ears only, we have to respect that."

Mason nodded. "Besides, if it's something we need to know, they'll tell us."

"Yeah, right." Even though Thad's strained voice told us he was still clearly agitated, his rigid body went slack. The advancing ice on my flesh beat a hasty retreat. "You don't trust the Conclave any more than I do."

"You're right," I said, slowly releasing Thad from my grip and scraping the frost from my skin. "They've been keeping a shit-ton of secrets. Probably more than we even know about." Thad snorted as if he knew exactly where the Conclave's skeletons were buried. "But we've figured out a lot of shit on our own, right?"

Thad reluctantly nodded, his shoulders slumped.

"We'll figure this out too. I know we will."

"I hope you're right, Pierce," Thad replied. He glanced over my shoulder and shook his head. "Because we'll have to do it without your friend."

I spun around to find Kale's spot on the couch empty. I surveyed the living room and didn't see him anywhere. I darted to the hallway. At the far end, the front door stood wide open.

Kale was gone.

CHAPTER 3

WE WAITED for Dad and Aiden to come home from their visit with the Conclave, but by the time midnight rolled around, we headed to bed. I had tried to talk to Thad, to get him to open up to me about what had him so worried.

The only answer he gave me was a pained expression. He turned away and walked into his bedroom, closing the door behind him.

I tried getting sleep, but my mind refused to shut off, which was a new experience for me. Usually once my head hit the pillow, all thought left my brain and I was out, but no matter how hard I searched for sleep, it was nowhere to be found.

My thoughts filled with Kale, about why he was here and what he wanted with the Conclave. But mostly I missed gazing down into that big smile of his that made my soul shudder.

What the hell was that about?

I got out of bed and went to the library, where I tried scrying for him. The location spell required a map, a crystal, and a possession belonging to the one you searched for. Since Kale had left the clothes he'd previously worn, I had high hopes it would work.

The crystal never landed on a specific spot on the map. It swung back and forth like a pendulum.

Shifters were clearly hard to find and almost impossible to sense. They registered as human to our senses unless they were in their animal form. It had something to do with their magic, which wasn't like ours. We got our gifts from the Gate when we evolved from humans. Shifters gained their abilities as a result of some spell I couldn't recall. For the first time, I was actually wishing I'd paid attention to all the crap Thad spouted. It clearly wasn't as useless as I once thought it was.

After my failed attempt to locate Kale, I grabbed the Grimoire, my family's book of spells, and did something I hadn't done in months. I researched.

I learned there wasn't a lot on record about the shifters besides what was in our history books. They'd been born when Sersie cast a spell that turned humans into animals. She and the other sorcerers were the result of my kind, the homo magus, breeding with humans. The magic they tapped into was different from ours. They hit a vein of wild magic that was not like the black magic warlocks accessed, and definitely nothing like the white magic of the witches or the gray magic of the wizards.

The untamed energy apparently made them crazy. Sersie used the shifters as her personal army, and she and other sorcerers started the Sorcerer War. After my ancestors kicked her ass and the asses of her half-breed allies, the first Conclave sent the shifters to a magical island called Aeaea, where they'd lived ever since.

So if they'd been banished from our world for this many centuries, why was Kale here now, and why did I get the feeling Thad had every right to be as worried as he was?

Those were the thoughts that troubled me as I lay down on the couch in the library and finally fell into a fitful sleep, but when my thoughts turned to Kale holding on to me as we sped down the highway on my motorcycle, I finally drifted off.

"GET UP, sleepyhead."

A firm shake on my shoulder followed the greeting. I grunted and turned over, plummeting off the couch I'd forgotten I'd fallen asleep on. My forehead slammed into the wooden floor and my knee knocked into the cast-iron coffee table that squatted in front of the couch.

"Fuuuuuck," I groaned. I rubbed my head with one hand and my knee with the other. This was not the way to start a brand new day.

"Blessed Yule to you too," the gravelly, faraway voice said.

After everything that happened yesterday, I completely forgot today was Yule. That meant we were going to spend a greater part of the day celebrating with the other protector covens. Oh joy! Just what I needed, a whole day of the infuriating Proctor witches and the uptight Stonewall wizards.

That promised to be about as much fun as sticking my tongue in an electrical socket.

I peeled open my eyes to find my father staring down at me, hiding a big bearded grin behind the back of his hand. Why did my family get such pleasure from my pain? "What are you doing in here?" he asked.

"Researching," I said as I slowly sat up. My mouth tasted like I'd been sucking on a piece of metal all night, and I had the beginnings of what would likely be a whopper of a headache. I needed coffee, and I needed it now.

"You were researching?" He didn't need to sound so fucking surprised either. I read things that weren't just skin mags.

"Yeah, what of it?" I slowly rose off the floor, massaging the massive kinks in my back a night on the couch managed to create. "And Happy Yule to you too."

His eyebrows drew together. "Something happened while Aiden and I were gone, didn't it?"

There was no way I was going to have a serious conversation without the eye-opening magic that was coffee. I nodded in reply before shuffling out of the library and down the hall to the kitchen. When I spotted the already brewed pot just waiting for me to gulp it down, I aimed for it like it was the fountain of youth and I was a dying man.

"Well, tell me, dammit," my father demanded as he followed me into the kitchen.

My father knew me better than that. I didn't hold conversations, no matter how serious they were, before my first cup of joe.

He strummed his fingers impatiently across the marble countertop. Dad typically was easily irritated, but right now he outdid himself, and that was a pretty impressive feat for Oliver Blackmoor. He rubbed his fingers through his coarse goatee and locked his blue eyes on to mine.

No matter how agitated he was, my routine couldn't be rushed. I poured myself a big mug of hazelnut, brought it to my nose, and inhaled.

The robust aroma lifted my droopy eyes, and when I took my first sip, I felt more like myself again. I peered at Dad over the brim of my cup. "Now what were you saying?"

He glared at me as if he were about to burn me at the stake. "Pierce." He spoke my name in the low growl he often used when I was younger. It was his way of telling me I was about to send him over the edge. Whenever I did that, he usually took me with him.

"You better sit down," I said, motioning to one of the bar stools. Reluctantly he did as I suggested and I told him about Kale.

When I was done, he sat quietly. I noticed the deep lines in his face for the first time. He'd been through a lot, and his slumping shoulders revealed he evidently carried more of a burden than even I realized.

Ever since he lost Mom, he hadn't been quite himself. He was never the most fun-loving guy in the world. He had a hair-trigger temper and was often more serious than even Thad could be, but around my mother, he turned into a schoolboy gazing into the dreamy eyes of his crush. She always had that effect on him, no matter what was going on in our lives. Now that she was gone, his balance was off. The counterweight that kept him in check had been removed, and he walked around as if he were lost.

When the shadow weaver first attacked during Mabon a couple of months ago, it got even worse. The troubles we'd faced slowly sucked the life out of him, turning him into a shadow of the person he used to be.

"Dad?" I asked, feeling the need to say something. "You okay?"

He rubbed the back of his head and nodded. "Just trying to take it all in," he replied. "So you think Ben is somehow connected to why this shifter has suddenly appeared in Havenbridge?"

"His name is Kale," I said. "But yeah, I do. So does Thad."

He blew out a lungful of air and motioned for me to get him a cup of coffee. I poured him a full mug and placed it before him. "So?" I asked after he took a sip. "What do you think?"

"I think you're probably right, and we need to find out what Ben wants in Aeaea. He took the Hearthstone from the fae. He's clearly after something the shifters have, but why?"

That was the million-dollar question.

For the past few weeks, Thad had been poring through every book in our library looking for an answer. His efforts turned up nothing. There was no record of the Hearthstone in any of the magical books.

The Conclave knew something, but they weren't spilling their guts. It made me trust them and their motives less and less.

But right now Dad didn't need to hear my doubts. He clearly had them too, even though he never once expressed them to us. He was our high priest. It was his duty to lead this family and follow the orders of the Conclave. His undying loyalty to our bosses pissed off my brothers. Mason thought Dad should openly challenge them, force them to reveal what they knew. Thad wasn't any better. My typically logical brother had lost perspective when it came to the Conclave, even though his buddy Gerald Wa was a member. Thad wanted our father to poke his nose around and see what secrets he could unearth since he had direct access to the mysterious place where the Conclave convened.

My brothers didn't understand why he didn't do any of those things, but I did.

He was protecting us.

"What's going on with you?" I asked. I sat across from him. It had been a long time since the two of us shot the shit. We were always pretty close, but after Samhain he'd been more closed off than I'd ever seen him before.

He flashed me the standard father smile, the one that was far too big to be real. It was the one that told me there was serious crap going on he didn't want me to worry about. "We've got a lot to figure out and not a lot of time to do it," he said. He glanced at his watch before taking another big sip of his coffee. "And I need to get everyone up and ready to head to the Proctors'."

I grimaced. I hated going to their house, but Yule was a white magic Sabbat, which meant we celebrated it at the Proctors'. I wasn't looking forward to being in the same room with Adam. He and I hadn't gotten along since—well, for a long time.

"You can talk to me, you know?" I grabbed his hand and squeezed it.

He squeezed it back before patting my hand with his free one. "I know that, son."

"Is everything okay with Aiden?" I asked.

The whole purpose of his trip to the Conclave's Mysterious Fortress of Secretude had been to assess Aiden's control. If he didn't impress them, we were worried they might detain him the way they once held Ben captive. We all knew how well that worked out. They inadvertently taught Ben blood magic and made him even stronger. No one wanted history to repeat itself with Aiden, and although I didn't trust the vampyre fairy, I didn't want Thad to be hurt. He loved Aiden, and while Thad might be my pain-in-the-ass little brother, the only one who could get away with hurting him was me.

"Everything went fine," Dad said before standing. "They were impressed with Aiden's control over his vampyren tendencies."

That was good news, but why did I have the feeling there was more to this story? "What time did you two get home?"

He shrugged. "Around one in the morning. We snuck in, so we didn't disturb anyone."

That was an awful long time to be gone if everything was as okay as he wanted me to believe. "Why were you there so long? What's going on?"

"Dad, you're home!"

Mason trotted into the kitchen and dashed toward Dad. He held out his fist for the bump they gave each other every day. I was slightly irritated by my brother's intrusion, but the relief in Dad's eyes told me he was grateful.

"Yes, I am," he replied before knocking his fist against Mason's. He inspected Mason from head to toe, his mouth falling open. He wore a red sweater over a tan collared shirt with khaki slacks. "You're dressed and ready to go?" he asked.

Mason's blue eyes gleamed with pride. "Yup," his wicked smile told us he was waiting for the compliments.

"I'm impressed," Dad said. "I'll make sure to thank Drake when he comes downstairs."

Mason sneered. "You know, I'm perfectly capable of dressing myself. I did it for eighteen whole years before I met Drake."

"You sure did," he agreed. "But it was usually after I'd yelled at you for thirty minutes."

I snickered, and Mason shot me a scowl. "Why are you laughing? You look like shit."

I felt like it too. I hadn't slept well, and I desperately needed a shower. The stench rising from my pits offended even me.

Before I had a chance to tell Mason to take a flying suck to my hairy ass, Thad and Aiden sauntered into the kitchen arm in arm, wearing matching pajama bottoms. The two of them had clearly been at it all night long, and judging from the fresh bite marks on my brother's neck, Thad was still feeding Aiden during their sexcapades. Thad claimed their "blood tie" helped Aiden rein in his violent vampyre instincts.

It seemed to be working. Aiden had gained enough control to pass muster with the Conclave, but I didn't like it. What would happen if those reins slipped? I'd already lost my mother. I didn't want to lose a brother too.

"Someone didn't get much sleep last night," I teased.

The apples of Aiden's fair cheeks turned cherry red, and his bottle-green eyes darted around the room. Thad beamed. He clearly wasn't embarrassed.

"Yeah, me," Mason complained. He threw open the refrigerator and pulled out the orange juice. "We need to soundproof your room."

"Right after we do yours," Thad said, snatching the orange juice carton from Mason's hands. He placed it on the counter and retrieved glasses from the cabinet. "You and Drake aren't exactly quiet." He started moaning and groaning as we'd all unfortunately heard Mason do.

Mason arched his eyebrow at Thad. "Really? Is that the game we're playing?"

"Mason, please don't," my father begged. He covered his face with his hands.

My brother didn't listen. A low whimper escaped from Mason's throat before it grew louder and louder. When Mason starting yipping like a dog, I lost it.

He nailed Thad's sex noises.

"I do *not* sound like that," Thad replied with his nose high in the air.

"Oh yes, you do," I said between fits of laughter.

Aiden wrapped his arms around Thad and squeezed him tight. "I think it's sexy."

Thad spun around in Aiden's muscled embrace. "I sound like that?"

Aiden grinned. "Only when you're really happy."

When they started kissing, Mason made gagging noises and I scrunched up my face. It was disgusting to watch your brother making out.

"Are you three done?" Dad asked from where he sat drinking his coffee and pretending as if he hadn't heard a word we'd said. Everyone nodded in reply. "Good. Pierce got me up to speed. Let's talk about Kale."

Aiden arched his eyebrows and glanced around the room. "Who?"

"I'll tell you later," Thad told Aiden. "Did Pierce also tell you he lost control of his powers?"

Dad settled his blue gaze upon me. "No, he didn't," he said with a heavy sigh.

I glared at Thad and mouthed the words *I'm going to kill you.*

"AND THAT'S it," I said after filling my dad in on the events of yesterday's war games.

"It was a bit more than that," Drake said from where he sat next to Mason at the kitchen bar. He'd entered the room while I was telling my story, wearing a blue wool collared pullover and tan pants. He was clearly ready to head over to the Proctors'. "You didn't even realize what was goin' on."

It was official. Drake had just joined my brothers on my shit list. The snitch.

"Is that true?" Dad asked. During my story he'd grown increasingly stiff. It started with his clenched jaw and worked its way to his neck, which he constantly rubbed. By the time I finished, he'd turned into one raw, taut nerve.

Aiden recognized it too. He studied Dad. He scanned his green eyes back and forth as if he were reading a book, but what Aiden was really doing was reading Dad's emotions. That was one of the perks of being a fire fairy. Aiden's eyes widened for a split second before he turned away, not realizing I was watching. He'd clearly found something.

That had to mean I was right. Something was definitely going on, and Dad was keeping us in the dark.

"Is it true?" Dad asked, repeating his question.

"It's true," Thad answered for me. "He almost killed Mason and me."

I shot him a grimace. "Don't be such a fucking drama queen. You're making this sound worse than it was."

"No, he's not," Mason said. "You know I don't generally agree with anything Thad says on principle—"

Thad glared at Mason, clearly ready to give him a pair of snow balls.

"—but you could've killed us. You were out of control. The only reason you didn't is Thad managed to utter a spell that protected us from a majority of the blast." He wrapped his arm around Drake and pulled him close. "I don't want to even think what would've happened if you'd attacked Drake."

Drake snorted. "I think we've proven I'm immune to magic. I bet it wouldn't have even touched me."

"That's not something we want to find out if we can help it," Dad said.

"Damn straight!" Mason agreed.

While it was true Drake seemed to have a certain immunity to spells, he'd yet to find himself on the receiving end of an active power. We had no idea if his ability to shake off spells carried over to a lightning bolt.

Dad settled his piercing blue eyes on me. "Is there anything else you're leaving out?"

I had to stop myself from turning the question on him. He was obviously keeping secrets from us, but I knew Dad better than anyone else did, certainly better than my brothers, who hadn't even picked up on the subtle changes in his personality and demeanor.

I nodded. "The world looked funny for a while there."

That got everyone's attention. They exchanged glances before Dad asked, "What do you mean?"

I told them how I saw the world in strange colors. That Thad had turned orange, Mason had been yellow, and Drake had been a shining white light.

"What the hell does that mean?" Drake asked.

Thad rubbed his chin in thought before looking over at Dad. "Could Pierce's visual perception have heightened to where he saw the world in terms of the auras we produce?"

"It's possible," Aiden answered. "Sometimes I can see emotions in people as easily as I can see the colors of their eyes."

Dad sat up straight, as if he'd forgotten about that part of Aiden's powers. He blinked several times and swallowed hard, clearly trying to get his emotions under control.

"Which would explain a lot," Thad said, oblivious to Dad's reaction. "Pierce's powers are energy based, and auras are basically the energy all living creatures produce. It would also explain what happened to Pierce's body while his powers were out of control. The lightning he produced seemed to crawl over his skin and almost completely replace it. It was like he was turning into pure energy. The way Dad can turn himself into stone."

"What do the different colors mean?" Drake asked. He chewed on his fingernails. Ever since Drake first became a part of this family, he'd fallen further and further down the magical rabbit hole. It apparently unnerved him more than he let on.

"Auras typically represent our thoughts, feelings, or dreams we have for ourselves," Thad answered. "In some instances they can also reflect internal strength and power."

"So I shouldn't be worried that mine was white?" Drake asked.

Thad smiled and shook his head. "In most cases a white aura means purity and innocence."

Mason leered. "He's not that innocent."

Drake blushed, his previous anxiety displaced by my brother's nauseating comment. If they started making out, I'd fry them both.

"So what the fuck does all this mean?" I asked.

"It means your powers are growing," Dad answered. "Just like your brothers' abilities recently have. Not only can you project lightning, but you can now turn into and see pure energy."

That was badass and about fucking time. "Really?" I asked. I suddenly felt taller, bigger, and stronger.

Dad nodded. "The problem is you don't have control over your powers in that form. That's something we're going to need to work on in the coming days."

"I can do that," I said with a nod.

"Until then," Dad replied, wagging his index finger, "you will *not* assume that form again. Your new abilities are extremely rare and just as destructive. You'll need to learn to control it before you can harness it."

Aw, man. Having a new power was like buying a brand-new bike. You were supposed to take it out for a joyride.

"Pierce, I mean it," Dad said. His voice was low and stern. He'd clearly guessed where my thoughts had gone.

I crossed my arms and huffed. I didn't care that I was acting like a kid who'd been given a Christmas gift he couldn't open. I'd finally tapped into more power that might finally bring my world back to order, where I was on top and my brothers cowered beneath me, and I wasn't going to be able to lord it over them. Some Yule this was turning out to be. "Fine."

Dad lingered his gaze, trying to determine if I meant what I said or if I was just placating him.

"I said 'fine,' didn't I?"

He nodded, apparently deciding he had no choice but to believe me, just like I had no choice but to believe him when he had said nothing happened with the Conclave. My gut told me something different, and seeing how Aiden reacted to reading his emotions, I'd clearly been right.

"Everyone who's not dressed needs to get changed," Dad said. "We're leaving for the Proctors' in less than an hour."

Mason complained loudly, cursing his life and Miranda Proctor. My brother hated the youngest Proctor witch more than he did calculus.

Although I wasn't looking forward to spending Yule with the witches and wizards any more than Mason was, I was going to get some answers, and if I had to use my new "aura" powers to get them, well, then that was just the way it was going to have to be.

CHAPTER 4

AN HOUR later we stood on the wraparound porch of the Proctors' modest cottage, and of course the house had been painted white. Witches had a hard-on for that color. They wore it in every fucking outfit, they bought white cars, and they lived in white houses. It was irritating.

"Could they have made any more Winter Solstice stars?" Mason asked as he flicked one of the many decorations that hung from the porch's ceiling. Cinnamon sticks made up the five-pointed stars, and they had been adorned with miniature pinecones, cranberries, and anise stars. There had to be over a dozen. These witches were like Martha Stewart on crack.

"I think it's wonderful," Aiden said. He was tall like me and had to duck under the stars so as not to hit his head on them. Unlike me, he brought his face right up to the stars and took a big whiff. "I love cinnamon."

"And I love ass," I added. "You don't see me hanging it all over the fucking place."

Mason barked with laughter while Thad and my father glared at me.

"Zip it," Dad said. His voice dropped to a deep whisper. He didn't yell when he got angry. He turned deadly quiet. "This is a Sabbat, and you will be respectful."

I nodded. Dad was right. I wasn't the loudmouthed jackass who got himself into trouble. That was Mason, and I sure wasn't the cold, aloof asshole Thad was in these situations. I was the easygoing one, the son who went with the flow and did as he was told. I didn't cause trouble or buck the system. I was the good little soldier who did as his father said and as the Conclave ordered.

That was who I needed to be because that was the only way I'd get the answers I came here for. No one, not even my family, would expect the airhead, muscled jock to have an ulterior motive.

The muffled voices inside grew louder as the front door swung open. Miranda Proctor, who seemed to always be the greeter at every damn Sabbat, stood at the door. She wore a tight white turtleneck, black leggings, and cranberry-red lipstick. The delicate features of her face turned hard as she inspected us.

"Always the last to arrive," she said with a flip of her shoulder-length chestnut-brown hair. "What are we going to do with you?"

"How about drop the attitude?" Dad asked.

Miranda inhaled sharply and her cheeks flushed.

I shifted my gaze from my father to my brothers, who stood in openmouthed shock. Warlocks didn't get along well with witches and wizards. Unless it was a Sabbat, our kind weren't supposed to mix, but Dad usually went out of his way to at least be cordial. Evidently tonight all bets were off.

"My apologies, Mr. Blackmoor," she said, stepping aside and quickly deferring to his position as high priest. "Please come in."

Dad zipped across the threshold, removing his coat and placing it on the coat rack. He glanced over his shoulder to find us gawking at him. "Get in here. Now," he said before turning around and walking into the crowded living room.

We quickly followed him inside.

"All except you," Miranda said.

I turned around to find her stepping in front of Aiden.

"Why?" he asked. He glanced down at his purple-and-black baseball sweater and black jeans. He was a big guy like me, and it was difficult to find clothes that fit our larger frames and muscular physiques properly. He'd been worried his limited wardrobe might not be suitable for the ritual. "Am I not dressed right? This is my first Yule."

But Miranda's bitchiness had nothing to do with Aiden's clothes, and despite being part vampyre, Aiden was too nice to see when someone was being a prejudiced little shit. Thad saw it clearly and went on the attack. "Let him in or I'll freeze your eyeballs in your sockets."

A grin hitched up the corner of her lips. "Try it and I'll warp your balls on the Yule Log." Warping was what Miranda called her teleportation power. It was a powerful and rare ability for witches, and whenever anyone crossed her, she always countered with the threat of teleporting one or more body parts away.

"Why do you always have to be a bitch, Miranda?" Mason asked.

"You think I'm going to let some blood sucker in my house? To feed off my family?"

"Oh," Aiden said, his gaze falling to the floor. "I'm sorry. I should just go."

"What's going on here?" a smooth masculine voice said behind us. I didn't need to turn around to know who was talking. For most of my childhood, that voice was the one that calmed me down whenever I fought with my brothers or upset my parents. It belonged to Adam Proctor, the greatest friend I'd ever had until, well, he wasn't my friend anymore.

"She won't let my boyfriend in," Thad said. He stood on the porch with Aiden, their hands clasped. "If he's not welcome, then neither am I."

"You're both welcome," Adam said. He flashed his sister a hard look, telling her to keep her trap shut.

She crossed her arms and snorted before stomping away.

"I'm sorry about that," Adam said to Aiden and Thad. "Won't the both of you please come in?"

"Are you sure?" Aiden said. He took a step forward but then stepped right back. "I don't want to make anyone uncomfortable."

Adam waved away his concerns and grabbed Aiden's hand. He gently urged him forward and across the threshold. "The family's discussed it already, and you're welcome here. Miranda already knew that."

"What do you mean your family's 'discussed' it?" Thad asked. His rigid upper lip curled into a snarl.

"Come on, Thad," Adam said, flashing the friendly smile that lit up his handsome face. "You're a smart guy. What would you do if you learned a vampyre was coming to celebrate a Sabbat with you? Are you telling me your family wouldn't sit down and discuss it beforehand?"

Adam had us there. The Proctors had a right to be concerned. Hell, we still weren't 100 percent fine with it. Aiden had the violent power of a monster within him. If he lost control, he could kill most of us before we had a chance to defend ourselves. If we were still coping with it, we couldn't expect anything less from the other families.

"Adam's right, Thad," I said. My words caused Adam to take a step back. It had been years since I had agreed with him about anything. "We'd be just as worried about protecting each other as they are."

Thad looked at me askance. He knew I was right, but he wasn't going to admit it.

Without saying another word, Thad tugged Aiden into the house.

"Well this is gonna be fun," Mason said, rubbing his hands together in devilish delight.

"Knock it off," I said, removing my coat and hanging it by Dad's. "Dad's not in the mood for your bullshit, and neither am I."

"When did you turn into such a Grumpy Gus?" Mason asked. He slid out of his coat before helping Drake out of his.

"After living with you for eighteen years," I answered, spinning him around. "Now go in there and be nice."

"You can't make me," he answered with a jut of his chin.

"But I can." Drake grabbed Mason by the back of his neck and brought their lips within inches of each other. "Be good today and I promise to be real bad tonight."

Mason leered at Drake and wrapped his arms around his boyfriend's waist. "You've *so* got a deal."

The two of them laced their fingers together and practically skipped into the living room. It took all my willpower to keep from blowing chunks.

"The more things change," Adam said at my side.

"You got that right," I mumbled.

A few months ago, Adam had developed a crush on Mason, but he'd obviously moved past that. I often wondered if he did that to get back at me. I slipped my hands into the pockets of my slacks and gave Adam a sidelong glance. He still looked good. He'd obviously been hitting the gym more lately. His tight white button-down clung nicely to his chest and biceps, and his caramel-brown hair had grown out some. He'd kept it buzzed short for years, but now he had a good four inches on top.

When I realized I'd been staring at him, I looked away. We hadn't been alone in the same room together in years, and when we did occupy the same space, we typically traded scowls and not words. Did this newfound friendliness mean he wasn't angry anymore?

"So how have you been?" he asked. Despite the confident jut to Adam's chin, he was just as uneasy as I was. His smile was far too big to be genuine, and he had trouble deciding where to place his hands. He crossed and uncrossed them in front of his chest. What gave him away the most was the way his eyes, which were a deep forest green, settled on me before quickly flitting away.

I had to clear the tremor I could feel building in my throat before I could answer. "I'm good." An awkward silence ate the world around us. We still had more slats to rebuild on the bridge between us.

"Yule miracles never cease."

Edith Stonewall stood in the middle of the hallway, gawking at us. Her long wavy black hair fell way past her shoulders, and an unusually mischievous glint reflected in her baby blues. That shocked me more than Adam's and my "conversation." Edith was usually aloof and cold, which was far truer of her wizard nature than the fiendish delight I could see in her eyes.

Despite her icy ways, Edith and I had always gotten along pretty well. Although she was my brother's age, she didn't act like an immature prick the way he did. Like Adam and me, she was the eldest in her family and the future high priest of her coven.

She understood the burden I carried.

"Hey, Edith." Grateful for the rescue, I jetted over to her side and pulled her into an embrace. Her body tensed slightly before she relaxed and hugged me back. Wizards didn't particularly like physical contact from people outside the family. "I haven't seen you since Samhain."

"I wish I could say the same for your brother," she said, glancing over her shoulder at Mason. He was in the middle of a conversation with Adam's younger sister, Charlotte. For some reason he was hopping around the room like a monkey. Although Charlotte and Drake were laughing, most everyone else glared at him as if he needed to be medicated. "He's in most of my classes. The Gate must hate me."

I laughed. "He can be a bit much."

She arched one dark eyebrow. "You think?" She diverted her gaze over my shoulder to Adam before looking back at me. "Did I interrupt anything?"

"Not at all," Adam said, strolling over from the front door where he'd been standing. "Just catching up."

"Right," she said, continuing to shift her attention back and forth between us.

Adam combed his fingers through his hair. "Well, I'm gonna get back to the guests. Have to socialize and all before the ritual." He smiled at Edith before turning to me. He opened his mouth to speak, but stopped the words from slipping from his lips. He turned on his heels and left.

"What was that all about?" She nodded her head toward Adam.

"What do you mean?" I asked as we entered the living room, which was packed with Yule decorations. On almost every flat surface sat glass votive candleholders filled with water. Floating at the top was a lit candle and a sprig of holly. Mistletoe and more Winter Solstice stars hung from practically every threshold. Icicle and dried-fruit ornaments clung to the fireplace mantle, which displayed five decorated trees made with pinecones. The entire room smelled like cinnamon and apples.

"Don't play dumb with me," she said as she shouldered past my brother, who scowled at her. "That only works on your family."

I grinned at her as we slipped by Edith's parents, who barely acknowledged my presence, and her twin brother Elliot, who was attempting to corral their younger twin siblings Kate and Keaton. Elliot was mute and could only communicate through his telepathy. He was a nice enough kid, but he didn't like me very much. Whenever he saw me coming, he turned tail and went the other way. It was something I'd gotten used to a long time ago. My size and the fact that I typically walked around with a snarl intimidated most people.

"So what's going on?" she asked when we finally cleared the crowd and the low roar their conversation created within the cramped room.

"Nothing," I said. "We were just catching up."

She gave me a blank stare.

"I hate when you look at me like that."

"I only look at you like that when you're lying to me. Which is most of the time."

"I'm not lying. At least not this time." I bared my full set of teeth.

"So you expect me to believe that after years of shooting daggers at each other from across the room, the two of you are miraculously friends again?"

"I wouldn't say that." I glanced over at Adam, who was talking to his sister Miranda. By the way they were gesturing, he was clearly reading her the riot act about how she'd treated Aiden. With any luck he'd use his wind abilities and blow off her eyebrows. "But it was the first time we'd spoken civilly to one another in quite a while."

"I know," she said, turning to see what I was looking at. "And now you can't take your eyes off him."

I focused my attention back to her. "It's not what you think," I said. "Adam and I used to be really good friends. I guess I miss that more than I realized."

"I remember," she said. "The two of you used to go everywhere together, and then one day, it just stopped. What happened?"

More than I cared to admit, but that wasn't the official party line. "You know how it goes. Warlocks and witches are supposed to hate each other." Although it wasn't the true reason our friendship ended, it was what Adam and I had agreed to tell everyone else. For both our sakes.

"You know I'm a wizard, right?" she asked, studying me carefully.

I pretended to be shocked. "You? Really?"

Edith rolled her eyes. "Do that again and I'll start calling you Mason."

I frowned. I definitely didn't want that.

After she realized I was done acting like a prick, she continued, "What I was trying to say is that I know there's more to the story between you and Adam than either of you is telling."

There was. A whole lot more, and I still felt bad about it to this day.

SHORTLY AFTER Elliot came over to drag his sister into a corner where they could telepathically talk in peace, I headed for the food table. There was a huge honey-mustard glazed ham and several sides, including a potato and parsnip dish that smelled like heaven. The table was also packed with various desserts. There was a coffee-bread wreath, which was my favorite, spiced mushroom cookies, cheese balls shaped like pinecones, nutmeg Yule logs, and a big glass jug of mulled wine.

Besides the ham and the assorted greens, there wasn't much here I typically ate. I worked out hard at the gym and avoided carbs as if they were vampyren who wanted to slash open my throat, but it was Yule. The only day of the year I let myself eat like Mason.

I cut off a super-sized piece of the coffee bread wreath, added a couple of mushroom cookies, and poured myself a glass of wine. I'd pay for this tomorrow, but I'd just double my workout routine for the next two weeks.

"Still eat like a pig on Yule, I see."

Adam stood next to me, eyeing my full plate. I grinned. "The more things stay the same," I said, completing the saying he'd started when we first talked. I cut into the Yule log, which was Adam's favorite, and placed it on a plate before handing it to him.

"Are you trying to get me fat?" he asked, attempting to sound disgusted when he had to practically wipe the drool from the corner of his lips.

"Okay, then," I said, returning the plate to the table.

He snatched the dessert from my hand. "Don't you dare."

I nudged his shoulder as he tore into the dessert. "I knew you couldn't pass that up."

"You don't know me so well," he said with a full mouth.

I cringed. Getting to know each other a bit too well had led to our parting of ways.

"Shit," he said, wiping the chocolate from his mouth. "That wasn't what I was talking about."

"I know," I said. I leaned against the table. Why couldn't I just say the two words that would make everything better? That was an easy enough answer. Eating crow wasn't something warlocks enjoyed. It lodged in our throats, refusing to budge, but I had to say the words, and Adam had to hear them. I opened my mouth, but my throat constricted.

Adam chuckled. "Don't hurt yourself," he said, patting me on my back. "I know you're sorry, and I know you stubborn warlocks would rather slit your wrists than say those two words."

He was right. That sounded much easier and less painful. "But how do you know I am?"

He gazed at the ceiling and tapped his finger on his chin. "I think I've always known. Probably from the very beginning. The look on your face and the way you stuttered and stammered after you told me—" He stopped and swallowed hard. "Well, you know."

I did, and if I'd been older, I might have handled everything much better than I did back then.

"I was just so angry and then got even more pissed off when you wouldn't apologize. The direction your life took certainly didn't help matters." He looked down at his shoes and sighed. "My pride is as much to blame for our distance as your stupidity."

Silence once again gobbled the air around us, but it wasn't as uncomfortable a weight as it had once been. It was as if some of the crushing burden had been cast aside.

"Do you think we can be friends again?" I asked.

He regarded me with eyes half-closed. "I don't know," he replied. "From what I hear, you're still a dick."

I nodded in appreciation. "I am who I am."

After a few more seconds of thought, he finally nodded. "I guess we can give it a go, but why now? After all these years."

I wasn't entirely sure. Who knows? Maybe I was finally doing the one thing Thad had always wanted me to do—grow up. "It's just time," I finally answered. "Isn't it?"

Adam's nod made me smile. I missed him as my friend and confidante. Taking our relationship one step too far had destroyed a pretty good thing. Our friendship had pissed off our parents to no end. They tried for years to sever our bonds, but we resisted. When we were the ones who sliced through the thread of our friendship, they were pleased. How would they react now?

"We're gonna rock our parents' worlds," I said, glancing at Mr. and Mrs. Proctor, who watched us from across the room.

He nodded and let out a long exhale. "I know. This petty rivalry crap our parents have going on is frustrating."

"Maybe it's time for that to change," I said. I couldn't believe I was actually parroting Mason's words from Mabon. He tried to get us to see that a couple of months ago, but we weren't ready. The animosity our parents stoked roared too high for any of us to think of dousing it, but things were changing. We were changing.

It was time to let go of our old rivalries. With Adam, Edith, and me as the next generation of high priests, we had the potential to change the magical community into anything we wanted.

"That would be nice," Adam said, but the faraway look in his eyes told me he doubted it would happen.

I had been about to ask him what was going on when the doorbell rang. All conversation stopped while everyone silently surveyed the room. All the guests who should be here were already here.

"Who is it?" I asked.

Adam shrugged in response as his parents disappeared into the hall to open the front door. A few seconds later, they reentered the room. Charles Proctor's wrinkled forehead told us more than the pretend smile that spread across his lips. "It appears we have more guests this evening."

A short, squat man with beady eyes, a long, hooked nose, and dark hair waddled over the threshold. My gaze immediately cut to my brothers, who gaped over at me. It was Leopold Edwell, a warlock who lived in Salem and whose family had hated mine ever since we were chosen to be a protector coven over them.

We hadn't seen him or his family since Mabon.

Leopold's wife, Agnes, stood behind him. She was at least five inches taller than her husband and as thin as he was fat. Next to them, their daughter Charity, who had long golden hair and a temper even worse than my father's, sneered at us.

"What the fuck are they doing here?" I asked.

"I have no clue," Adam answered.

Yule wasn't Mabon. It was a private holiday celebrated with those considered family. While the Proctors and the Stonewalls weren't our blood relatives, we were the protector covens and were honor bound to celebrate all Sabbats together. It was part of our roles as guardians of the Gate.

The Edwells shouldn't be here.

"I hope we won't be too much of an intrusion," Leopold said in his usual high-pitched voice that made my teeth ache. He swept his piercing gaze across the crowd until his eyes fell upon my father. A smile slid across Leopold's lips as he winked at my dad.

Dad clenched his hand so tightly around his drinking glass I feared it was going to shatter.

"DAD, WHAT'S going on?" I asked. My brothers and I had pulled our father into a quiet corner. Sensing we needed some private time, Drake escorted Aiden to the food table for a snack while the Edwells chatted with the high priests, who appeared extremely confused. Mr. and Mrs. Stonewall rubbed their chins almost simultaneously, studying the Edwells as if they were a problem to be solved. Mrs. Proctor, who didn't like Agnes Edwell, refused to meet the woman's cold gaze while Mr. Proctor kept rubbing the back of his head.

"I assume the Edwells are traveling and decided to stop in Havenbridge to celebrate the Sabbat." Although it was a reasonable explanation, I didn't buy it, and neither did my brothers. Thad pressed his lips together while Mason scoffed.

"Yeah, right," Mason said. "I don't trust them. Never have. Never will."

"What's there to trust?" Dad asked. "The Edwells are opportunistic parasites." His voice was low and his words came out strangled.

"You know something, don't you?" Thad asked. He studied my father's stone face. "You know why they're here."

His only reply was to shake his head. He drew his brows closer and his face tightened. He was lying, and though I wanted to find out what was going on, this wasn't the place.

Mason clearly didn't understand that. "Bullshit," he said loud enough to draw the glances of the Edwells. They grinned as if they couldn't be more pleased.

"Shut it," I whispered.

"But—"

I grabbed his neck and squeezed until Mason let out a yelp. "Save it for when we get home."

Mason sought help from our father and Thad, whose stern gazes told him they agreed with me. "Fine," he growled before I released him.

"How are the Blackmoors on this fine Yule?"

The Edwells crept behind us, their faces plastered with fake bright smiles that gave me a headache.

"We're doing fine, Leopold," Dad said, extending his hand in greeting. The shorter warlock eyed the offering, clearly not going to take it when his wife jammed her bony finger into his side. He shot her a cold look before quickly shaking and then letting go of my father's hand.

"What brings you to Havenbridge?" I asked.

"What?" Agnes asked. Her voice was much deeper than her husband's, most likely the result of the cigarettes she constantly smoked. "Are we not welcome?"

"Of course you are," I replied with a smile I did my best to make more convincing than theirs. I might have succeeded, too, if my head didn't throb as if it were about to explode. "More warlocks I can handle. More witches or wizards, not so much."

Agnes let out a throaty giggle while her husband's fake laugh was more like a shriek. Their daughter Charity, though, didn't laugh or smile. She observed.

"And how are you, Charity? It's been a while. We missed you at Mabon."

When she didn't immediately answer my question, her father answered for her. "She was abroad visiting relatives."

I nodded and briefly closed my eyes and rubbed my temples. The pain was almost unbearable. When I opened them, the world around me had changed once again. The flesh-and-blood world was no more. I saw only people composed of energy or the auras Thad had talked about back at home.

Mason was still yellow and Thad was still orange, but flares of muddied red streaked through their bodies. From what I remembered about auras, that meant they were angry. My father was composed of bright yellow energy. I had no clue what that meant, but when I peered over at the Edwells, I was greeted with deep reds, dark greens, and a black far darker than the shadows Mason commanded.

What did those colors mean?

"Son, are you okay?"

I shut my eyes. When I opened them, the world had reverted to normal. My family stared at me, their gazes filled with concern while the Edwells grimaced.

"Yeah, I'm fine. Just a bit of a headache," I replied. I glanced down at my body just to make sure I hadn't changed to pure energy again. When I saw flesh, I let out a sigh of relief.

"Maybe you should go home and lie down," Agnes advised, her lips pursed.

I shook my head. "I'll be fine. Besides, if I did that, I'd miss celebrating Yule with you, and we wouldn't want that, right, guys?" I asked, turning to my brothers, who stared at me as if they were looking at a stranger. They weren't used to me schooling my face or being diplomatic. I had to clear my throat to get their attention.

"Y-yes," Thad stammered. He tore his gaze from me to the Edwells. "An unprecedented honor at that."

"What he said," Mason replied, nodding at Thad. He didn't look at Mr. and Mrs. Edwell. He returned Charity's "fuck you" glare with his own.

"I have to ask," Leopold said, surveying the room. "Where are the new members of your family? The human and the vampyre."

Was that why they were here? We'd gotten shit from the other protector covens for bringing Drake and Aiden into our family. Did the Edwells and possibly other black magic covens have a problem with it too?

"Why?" Thad asked. He held his chin high.

"Why?" Charity asked, breaking her silence. Her question resounded like a pistol shot. "You've let our enemies inside the inner circle. That's why."

The world flashed back to energy, and blackness spread across Charity's aura like an oil spill. When I blinked it was gone. I had to get this new power under control. I couldn't chance losing it here with the Edwells. My gut told me that wouldn't be good, so I took several deep breaths.

"You don't know shit about real enemies," Mason spat. "If you did you'd know that the only reason we're still here is because of my boyfriend. He helped save our fucking asses."

"As did Aiden," Thad replied. His face flushed.

Charity snorted. "Since when do warlocks need a human and a vampyre to save them? My family never has."

"That's enough!" Leopold said. Although his tone was curt, the smile that lingered at the corners of his lips told me he couldn't have been prouder of his only child.

"I couldn't agree more," my father said, his voice barely a whisper. "This is Yule. A time to be reverent, not belligerent."

Charity's nostrils flared, and a fire burned in her eyes.

"Oliver is right. We must honor the day and nothing else. We can discuss unpleasantness another time." He wrapped his arm around his daughter's shoulders. "Let's head into the other room. I believe it's almost time for the ritual." Before walking away, he glanced over his shoulder and said, "I can't wait to meet the rest of your family."

This time I focused and willed this strange aura vision to return. Waves of colors once again exploded around me, and as the Edwells walked away, I watched the inky black color that had started with Charity spill over to her parents, turning the three of them into one dark blob.

WE GATHERED in the dining room where the Yule altar had been set up and where we'd perform the ritual that welcomed back the sun.

My brothers stood to my left and my father on my right. Even though they were a part of our family, Drake and Aiden weren't warlocks. They stood behind us, eager to witness their first Yule.

The Edwells stood across from us, whispering and nodding at Drake and Aiden. They were clearly here because of the new additions to our family, but why did I get a feeling they were here for so much more than to gawk and gossip?

Dad clearly knew more than he was letting on. His entire body was tense.

"Let's begin," Charles Proctor said, and all talking stopped. As the high priest of the white magic coven, it was his duty to lead the ritual.

He approached the table, where his family joined him. They formed a circle and held hands around the small square table, which had been decorated in light blue and silver, with evergreen boughs spread across the top. In between the greenery, silver bells and candy canes had been laid out, as well as a bowl of snow that had been collected during the very first snowstorm. White candles formed a circle in the center, with a taller golden pillar candle in the middle of the ring.

"The wheel of the year has turned once more," he began. "And the nights have grown longer and colder. Tonight the darkness begins to retreat and light begins its return once again. As the wheel continues to spin, the sun returns to us once more." He nodded toward the table, and one of the smaller candles flickered to life.

Mrs. Proctor focused her attention on the next candle and continued, "Even in the darkest hours, even in the longest nights, the spark of life lingered on. Lying dormant, waiting, ready to return. The darkness will leave us now as the sun begins its journey home." When she nodded, the second candle sparked to life.

"As the wheel turns, light returns," Adam said.

Adam's sister Charlotte spoke next. "The shadows will vanish, and life will continue."

As the youngest, Miranda went last. "We are blessed by the light of the sun."

The three siblings nodded in unison, and the three remaining smaller candles burst into flame. The rest of us gathered hands, focusing all our energy on the pillar candle, and said, "So shall it ever be." The wick on the tallest candle lit. "Blessed be," we said as one.

Conversation slowly filled the room at the ritual's conclusion. The Edwells cornered Lawrence and Rachel Stonewall, who'd clearly been attempting to avoid them. They scanned the room like trapped squirrels.

If they weren't always such cold bastards, I might have intervened, but they were, so I left them to their fate.

The Proctors and my father whispered in the corner, nodding toward the Edwells. When Dad caught me watching, he escorted Charles and Camille out of the room.

Something big was going down.

"Learn anything?" Adam asked. He had snagged another mushroom cookie and chomped on it as I stared into the living room, where my father continued his animated conversation with the Proctors. He shook his fist and moved his head in quick jerky movements.

"Nope," I replied. Camille placed her palm against her breast while Charles shook his head slowly several times. He was obviously telling the Proctors what the hell was going on, and he couldn't stand them. Why wasn't he filling in his own sons? "Have your parents said anything?"

Adam snorted. "Have you met my parents?"

He was right. My father was an open book compared to Charles and Camille. For reasons that confused the fuck out of me, the Proctors and the Stonewalls still trusted in the Conclave and kept most of what they knew to themselves. Why couldn't anyone else see there was fucked-up shit going on with our leaders?

"And you don't have any clue what might be going on?" Adam asked. "Not to be a dick or anything, but trouble has followed your family like a cloud of doom these past few months."

We did seem to be some kind of crap magnet lately what with the vampyren, the asshole Ben, and our trip to Otherworld. Why was all the shit hitting our fan?

"I don't," I finally responded. "Maybe it has something to do with Kale."

"Who the hell is that?" Adam asked.

I filled Adam in on the shifter whose innocence and wide-eyed awe had made me smile before we scared the shit out of him and made him run. When I was done, Adam crossed his arms and glared at me.

"What?" I asked.

"You can seriously ask me that right now?" He cocked his head to one side and shook it.

"*What*?"

"This is why your family gets in so much trouble," Adam said. "I know warlocks don't think they need anyone and that you can take on the world all by yourselves, but that's not the way this works. You keep things to yourselves when you should be sharing them with us."

"What did you want us to do? Walk in the front door and say, 'Happy Yule, and by the way, there's a shifter looking for the Conclave'?"

"That would certainly be better than not saying anything." Adam drew in his breath and slowly exhaled before speaking. "You kept the shadow weaver a secret after Mabon, and the fact that there was a banshee in our world during Samhain. Each time you did that, we were all caught unaware. People have died, Pierce. When is your family going to learn that it isn't one protector coven, but part of *three* protector covens?"

I stood up straight, stretching to my full height and glowering down at Adam. If he didn't watch it, he was going to take a wrecking ball to the newly built bridge between us. No one attacked my family.

"Oh, don't start that 'I'm bigger and taller than you' bullshit." Adam took a step forward and stood on his tiptoes. He didn't quite meet my six feet four inches, but he got close. "You've been pulling that crap since we were kids, and it doesn't work anymore. I'm not your enemy, but I was your best friend. You should have told me about the shifter."

"Is there no line the Blackmoors won't cross?" Charity Edwell stood next to us, a devious smile curling her pasty lips. "You invite a human and a vampyre into your family. You make a witch your best friend, and you keep secrets from the other protector covens." She stroked her slender throat and grimaced. "Your family's a disgrace."

The control I'd previously managed snapped like a worn-out fan belt. I towered over her, my face twisting with anger that begged to be released. "Shut your fucking mouth!"

My words caught the attention of the entire house.

"I've tried being nice, but you seem hell-bent on provoking me." If I were any angrier, I'd have been frothing at the mouth. "Well, you've poked the bear. What the hell are you gonna do about it?" Sparks of electricity sizzled around my fists.

She glanced around, surveying the shocked expressions that gazed back at us, and I followed her eyes across the room.

Everyone stared at me as if I were a rabid dog that needed to be put down. Fuck. I'd walked right into that one.

"That's enough," my father's stern voice said behind me. His eyes had grown bluer and colder than an approaching nor'easter. I tried to speak, but my father held up his hand, cutting off my words before they leaped from my lips.

Leopold rushed to his daughter's side, wrapping a protective arm around her as if she'd just been pulled from the jaws of a beast. "Is this the way the Blackmoors act on a high Sabbat? Threatening a member of their own order?"

"They keep secrets too," Charity added. The right corner of her lips hitched upward. "They haven't revealed there's a shifter in Havenbridge."

"A what?" Mr. Stonewall asked. His dark face turned even more serious than usual as he rounded the table and stood next to my father, who rubbed the bridge of his nose. "A shifter has left Aeaea, and we're just finding out about his now?"

"Calm down, Lawrence," my father said. "I just finished filling Charles and Camille in on what's been going on." The Proctors, who stood behind my father, exchanged glances before hesitantly nodding. "I planned on telling you and Rachel next."

"I don't believe you," Rachel said. She brushed her blonde hair behind her ears and regarded my father with the precision of a scalpel.

"Neither do I," Agnes replied. She broke ranks with her family to stand next to Rachel and placed a sympathetic hand on her shoulder. Rachel Stonewall winced at the contact. "From what I hear, you've been keeping far too many secrets."

"Our business is none of yours," my father said. "We're the protector covens. Not you."

Leopold's beady eyes grew even smaller. He didn't like being reminded of that fact. The growing redness on the tip of his sharp nose clearly revealed that. He raised a clenched hand, obviously ready to call forth his active power, and stormed over to my father. "One day, Oliver, you'll push me too far."

My father took a step forward, his fists turning to stone. He poked the smaller warlock in his plump chest with his heavy earthen hand. "Bring it."

My father and Leopold flew off their feet as if an unseen hand held them by the collars of their shirts.

"You will cease this behavior at once."

Nine robed figures, three in black, three in gray, and three in white, blinked into the room. Though their faces were hidden beneath their hoods, the anger in their collective voices was unmistakable.

The Conclave was here, but they weren't alone. Kale was with them, and even though his wide golden eyes regarded the spectacle of my father and Leopold suspended before him, when he saw me, he smiled and waved.

My breath caught in my throat, and tiny fluttering wings took flight deep within my soul.

CHAPTER 5

THE CONCLAVE stood before us in silence, their hoods most likely hiding their scowls of disapproval while my father and Leopold dangled between us. Without a word or a gesture, they slowly descended.

When their feet once again touched the floor, Dad dusted himself off and took several deep breaths while Leopold Edwell scurried toward his family like the pathetic cockroach he was.

Everyone else had backed up, leaving my father standing by himself in front of our leaders. They clearly feared the wrath he'd face for almost using his powers on a fellow warlock. The chickenshit bastards. I broke from the pack and joined my father. There was no way I was going to let him face whatever was next on his own.

A few seconds later, my brothers along with Drake and Aiden stood with us. We were a united front, and we'd face the Conclave the way we faced all our enemies—together.

Dad's squared shoulders and high chin told me he appreciated the support. The Conclave clearly didn't. Their robed bodies tensed.

"The continued insubordinate attitude of your coven disturbs us, Oliver," said one of the white-hooded figures on the right.

"Indeed." One of the wizards in gray nodded. "We'd foolishly believed our conversation yesterday had squelched such behavior."

Dad clenched his jaw so hard it popped. Was that what happened yesterday? Did the Conclave issue Dad a warning? But just what were they so fucking pissed off about?

Sure, we yanked their chain. We were warlocks. That was what we did, but we were the ones to face Ben and stop him, not once but twice. That was more than they did. What more did they want?

"The answer to your unspoken question, Pierce Blackmoor, is quite simple," said a different gray-robed figure. "We expect your unflagging loyalty."

"Endless obedience," spoke a warlock in black.

"And behavior befitting your station in our community," said one of the witches in white.

"So you want mindless drones," Mason mouthed off.

One of the figures in black snapped her attention to my little brother, who immediately fell to his knees. He clutched his head and let loose a cry of pain I'd never heard come from him before. "You will mind your manners," she said. Unlike the other members of the Conclave, her voice sounded weird. It reminded me of that dumbass Siri from my iPhone, who couldn't get anything I asked her to do right. Was she using magic to alter her speech? Why go through all that trouble?

With the exception of Gerald Wa, we had no clue who the rest of the Conclave was. They governed anonymously and in secret.

"Stop it!" Drake yelled. He kneeled next to Mason, gathering him in his arms. Thad took a step forward, but my father grabbed his arm and pulled him back. He then glanced over at me, his stern gaze telling me not to move a muscle, even though I could tell by the anger burning in his eyes he was one rash decision away from turning into stone and charging the Conclave.

"I think that's enough." Gerald, the only friend we had on the governing body, lowered his hood. He studied my family with his wise gray eyes before he exchanged a long, meaningful glance with Thad, who nodded. What the hell was that about?

Gerald stepped out of the line and crossed over to Mason, who still writhed in Drake's arms. When that warlock hag didn't immediately stop, he turned his gaze upon her. "I said enough."

Mason stopped thrashing, perspiration dripped down his cheeks, and a scowl curled his lips. "What the fuck?" he asked, trying to catch his breath. "You get mad at us for our behavior, then attack me? That's bullshit."

"That's discipline," Gerald said, although he didn't sound extremely convinced. He kneeled next to Mason and placed his hand on his forehead. A golden glow filled the cup of his hand. A second later my brother no longer winced in pain. "Better?"

Mason nodded, eying the warlock who'd hurt him. If he could get away with it, he'd most likely impale her with a shadow spike.

"That's not discipline," Aiden said, his tone regal and superior. "I see only bullying."

The Warlock Hag visibly bristled. "You may be under the protection of the Blackmoor coven, but you are not one of us," she said. "You have no voice here."

Aiden took a step forward. He was still the hotheaded prince my brother fell in love with. Maybe I could grow to like him after all. "I'm a member of the Royal Fae Court."

"Not anymore," she said.

Aiden winced. He'd been stripped of his royal standing after being turned into a vampyre.

Thad stepped forward, but Dad wrapped his arms around him and restrained him. He whispered in my brother's ear, attempting to calm him down, but the chains that held his anger in check had snapped. Ever since Thad kicked ass in Otherworld, he'd become a different man. Stronger. More confident in his power. He no longer reined in his emotions. He let them fly, and secretly I couldn't have been prouder.

But a quick glance over my shoulder told me we needed to get this runaway train back on track. If the Edwells' smiles got any bigger, their faces would crack. Whatever their game was, we were playing by their rules.

"Everyone needs to calm the hell down," I said, standing between my family and the Conclave. "This is getting us nowhere."

"What's getting us nowhere is your family's attitude," the Warlock Hag replied. She wasn't going to let up. She had a serious hate-on for us. But why?

A sharp pain pierced through my head, and one blink later, my world reverted to colorful energy. I had to learn how to control this new ability better and do something about the damn headaches. An ice pick to the eye would hurt less.

I breathed through the pain and studied the Conclave. Most of them were awash in a brown, earthy aura with lines of gold and flashes of red. That told me they were attempting to rein in their collective anger. The Warlock Hag, though, had no traces of red in her aura. She glowed with a combination of earthen tones and a soft, peaceful blue.

What the fuck did that mean?

"What do you think you're doing?" she asked. The swirling colors that briefly filled my vision vanished when she took a step forward. "You dare use your powers on me."

I clutched at my throat as unseen hands cut off my oxygen. The Warlock Hag wasn't going to let me explain. I had no control over my new power. I hadn't intentionally snooped where she clearly didn't want me to. Although I got off on pushing limits, I wasn't stupid. Using our abilities against the Conclave was considered treachery.

"Let him go," my father pleaded as I was lifted off the floor and spun around the room.

"You're killing him!" my brothers screamed in unison. Anger and fear caused their voices to crack. Knowing them, they were a few seconds away from fighting back.

If they did, the Conclave would either kill my family or bind our powers.

"Cease this!" Gerald's tone was forceful and curt. At least he was still on our side, but her torment didn't stop.

I struggled to remove what felt like sharp claws digging into my throat. My life and the lives of my family depended on it, but no matter how hard I struggled, I couldn't release the steel-like grip that threatened to kill me.

"Stop!" Kale cried out. The quiet, submissive quality of his voice had been replaced by a loud, booming command. "You're supposed to be helping me, not fighting with each other."

"The shifter is correct," Gerald said, his tone clipped. "We have more pressing concerns to deal with than this."

Slowly the world stopped spinning, and the invisible hands that were choking the life from my body disappeared. I gulped for air, and a few seconds later, I dropped to the floor in a crumpled heap.

Kale dashed to my side as my family formed a protective circle around us. "Are you okay?" He drew me onto his lap and ran his soft fingers through my hair. Why did his touch make this seem almost worth it?

"I've been better," I choked out.

"What's the matter with you?" Kale asked, staring into the black void that hid the Warlock Hag's face. "You could've killed him."

"As he almost killed you," she replied.

"It was an accident," Kale responded with an exaggerated sigh. "I already told you that."

"His powers are beyond his control," she said in a tinny, metallic tone. "The family is out of control."

"Are you insane?" Gerald asked. He marched over to the Warlock Hag and stood in front of her. His gray eyes burned with anger typically not seen in wizards. They were usually cold and logical. "This is not the place for such debates."

She surveyed the room. The Proctors and the Stonewalls stood in stunned silence while the Edwells could barely contain their glee. If it wouldn't make things worse, I'd zap out all their teeth one by one.

"Perhaps not," she said. "But as I have already stated, the defiance of the Blackmoors spreads like a plague. It must be severed before it reaches the rest."

Without another word, the Warlock Hag stepped back into the line of power the Conclave represented, and though I couldn't see her face, her body faded away and her aura blinked through for a second.

There were still no angry reds. Only blue, a splash of pink, and a bright emerald green.

"ARE YOU sure you're okay?" Dad asked as my brothers helped me to my feet.

I felt about as okay as anyone who'd almost been choked to death. My throat hurt like a motherfucker, but I was more confused than in pain. That Warlock Hag was up to something, and the pit in my gut told me the Edwells were involved somehow.

Why else would they be here, trying to stir up shit?

"Pierce?" my father asked. "Are you okay?"

"My throat's sore." Speaking those words was like rinsing with Listerine after gargling with a razor blade. "But I'll live."

"I can whip up a healing potion," Thad offered.

I shook my head. I needed the pain. It fueled my anger and my thirst for answers.

The Conclave had gathered in a secret circle on the far side of the room. Gerald's wild gestures revealed how upset he was by what just happened, but the others remained as emotionless as ever. They either didn't care I was almost killed, or secretly wanted me to die.

"I hope he kicks their asses," Mason said, nodding to Gerald.

"It's nothing more than they deserve," Thad added.

"Stop that," Dad whispered. He surveyed the room. Drake and Aiden had pulled Kale over to the ritual table to give us some privacy. The Proctors and the Stonewalls stood far enough away that they couldn't overhear our conversation while the Edwells quietly beamed in the corner. "We can't afford to say anything out of line again. Too much is at stake."

"Why didn't you tell us that sooner?" I asked. I understood Dad's need to protect us, but why keep us in the dark about shit we needed to know?

His gaze fell to the floor. "I didn't know how to bring it up. How was I supposed to tell my sons that the Conclave is contemplating removing us as the protector coven for the Order of the Black?"

"By saying those exact words," Thad replied.

"Maybe," he replied. He practically buried his chin in his chest. I'd never seen my father so defeated. He was always the epitome of strength and power. Now he resembled a dog that had been kicked one time too many.

"We'll get through this." I put my arm around his shoulders. "Like we always do."

He closed his eyes and sighed. "I hope so."

"It's clear who they want to replace us." Mason sneered at the Edwells, who pretended to be talking when what they were really doing was circling like a venue of vultures.

"That doesn't make any sense," Thad said. "Our family is far more powerful."

"But not easier to control," Dad added.

That was true. The Edwells had no spine. They did what they were told like good little soldiers. Not even the Proctors or the Stonewalls were that bad. Sure, they followed orders, but they weren't afraid to ask hard questions. The Edwells did what they were told to do. No questions asked.

That made them puppets, not a protector coven.

"But protecting the Gate is about power," I said. "The kind of power we have."

"Correct," Thad said. "Which means there's more going on than we know."

Why was the Conclave so damn secretive? Our world wasn't what it once was. We weren't separate tribes fighting each other and the humans for survival. We had carved out a place for ourselves. We were safe, and we were at peace. This covert shit wasn't necessary, especially when we had Ben Crane out there up to no damn good, with vampyren at his command.

What was gained by replacing my family with a less powerful coven?

"Is she the one leading the charge?" I asked, nodding to the Warlock Hag.

"I think so," he said with a nod. "She was certainly the most vocal at the meeting. She sees us as troublemakers, wild cards that can't be trusted or controlled. She's worried we might screw up and give Ben exactly what he wants."

"Are you sure she's a warlock?" Mason asked. "That sounds more like a wizard."

I was thinking the same thing. Warlocks weren't known to be rule followers. That Warlock Hag had to know that. It was because we broke the rules that we'd been able to get this far. What was her game?

"What did you see?" Thad asked. "When your aura power kicked in."

"She was different from the rest of the Conclave. I could see their anger, but her aura didn't show any."

"How is that possible?" Mason asked. "She almost killed you."

"No, really? I hadn't noticed."

"Now's not the time to be smartasses," Dad said. He locked eyes with Thad, and they stared at each other in silence as if they could read each other's minds. It always made me feel uncomfortable when they did that. It was like I was too dumb to figure it out on my own.

"What?" Mason asked. He was as irritated by it as I was.

"I'm not certain," Thad answered. He glanced over at the Conclave, where things appeared to be winding down. Gerald no longer pointed at the Warlock Hag, and his fists weren't shaking. "What about Gerald? Did he look more like her or the rest of the Conclave?"

I shrugged. "He was behind me when the power kicked in. I didn't see his aura." I shifted my gaze back and forth between my father and Thad. "Why?"

"I'm not certain," Thad said. "I'm working through every angle here." He clasped his hands together, his index fingers pointing up. He brought them to his mouth and tapped them against his lips. That was his brainiac pose.

"Excuse me." Kale stood behind us, along with Drake and Aiden. He shuffled his feet and wrinkled his forehead as he regarded the four of us. "I don't mean to intrude, but I just wanted to see how you were feeling."

Even with all the crap going on around me, his concern brought a smile to my lips and the butterflies in my soul flitted into my stomach. "I'm doing better. Thanks to you."

A flush crept across his cheeks as he absently ran his slim fingers through his dark hair. "I didn't do anything."

Was he kidding? If he hadn't spoken up, the Warlock Hag would have likely killed me. It took being reminded there was a mission for her to let me go.

"Of course you did," my father said. He drew Kale into a big hug. The gesture made Kale smile so broadly his dimples sunk deep in his cheeks. "I'll never forget that."

"I'm just glad you're okay," he said after my father released him.

"I guess that makes us even, huh?"

He shot me a blank stare and shook his head.

"What do you mean, no? I saved you in the forest. You saved me here. That's even."

"And what about shooting me out of the sky?" he asked, a goofy grin sliding across his lips. "Or punching me in the face?"

I groaned. Really? We were going back there? "Both were accidents."

"And both demand repayment," Kale replied. He hitched the corners of his lips upward.

Man, he wasn't cutting me any slack. In fact, he seemed to be damn well enjoying being difficult right now. The little shit was clearly a sadist, and it turned me on. "I don't like you anymore."

He flashed me a big toothy grin that told me he didn't believe a word I said.

"I'm glad to see things have quieted down over here as well."

Gerald and the Conclave gathered behind us, and though the rest of the Conclave stood relaxed, Gerald was not. His lips were pinched together.

"Are you well?" he asked me.

"I'm fine, thank you," I replied with a smile when what I most wanted to do was be sarcastic.

"Good," he said with a nod. "Because we need to address the matter that has brought the young Kale into our world."

"What's happening in Aeaea?" Charles Proctor asked. The other protector covens along with the conniving Edwells drew closer.

Gerald nodded for Kale to answer.

Kale took a deep breath, and all traces of mischief bled from his expression. The carefree, wide-eyed innocence gave way to misery. "The shifters... my people...," he said, his eyes filling with tears he attempted to wipe away. "...are dying."

KALE'S REVELATION caused a chorus of concerned voices to erupt in the room. Even though they lived separately from us on their own secluded island, the shifters were a part of the magical community. The magic that brought them into being was a part of the Gate and was a part of us. Losing something so powerful could have consequences even the Conclave couldn't foresee.

"How is this possible?" Mr. Stonewall asked. He clasped his hands together and stood rigid, a storm of concern raging across his dark face.

"That is what we need to learn," Gerald replied. "A strange anomaly is spreading through Aeaea. Its origins are unknown."

"Anomaly?" Thad asked. "What kind of anomaly?"

Gerald placed a reassuring hand on Kale's shoulder, urging him to share what he knew.

"It started a few weeks ago with one of the mammalians," Kale said. From the research I'd done last night, I learned the shifters didn't live in packs or prides according to the animal they shifted into. Their society was built around the four different types of shifters that existed— the avians, the aquatics, the reptilians, and the mammalians. "He got a really high fever. The healers did what they could to bring it down, but nothing worked. And then he—" He swallowed hard and fidgeted with the hem of the sweater he'd borrowed from Mason before he cast his gaze to the floor.

I couldn't just stand there, watching him suffer. Kale's heart was clearly breaking, so I dashed over to his side and placed my hands on his shoulders. I had to hook his chin with my thumb and index finger to get him to look at me. "I know it's hard. Take your time."

He glanced nervously around the room. "There's just so many people here," he said. "I'm not used to speaking in large groups. I'm mostly left to myself."

That broke my heart more than the pain in his eyes. "Well, then just tell me," I said. "What happened to your friend?"

His mouth fell open. "How'd you know?"

Since my mom died, I recognized loss when I saw it in others. "Lucky guess," I replied. "What was your friend's name?"

Kale twisted his lips, and the unease that clouded his usually radiant golden eyes retreated a few steps. "Brit," he whispered. "He shifted into this beautiful, powerful tiger. He was a member of the king's guard, and he didn't care that I was just a—"

"Just a what?" I asked.

He shook his head. "That's not important. He was my friend." A sob rose in his throat.

"So what happened to Brit after his fever?"

"Convulsions," he replied with a wince. He was obviously there while his friend was sick. "But that wasn't the worst part. He lost control of his shifting and partially shifted."

I'd read about that. The shifters had the ability not just to shift their entire body into their animal forms, but also to transform only parts of their bodies. An arm could be turned into a claw, or a mouth into a muzzle filled with sharp teeth. It required a great deal of energy to perform and could lead to death if maintained. "What happened?"

"He attacked the healers, wounding several," he replied. "They had to restrain him." His gaze grew hard. Shifters hated being restrained or imprisoned. It went against their animal's need to be free.

"And after that?"

Kale shook his head and sighed. My gaze could no longer hold his and fell to the floor. "He lost the ability to control his forms. He'd shift back and forth until the strain was just too much for his heart. I was there with him when he died."

"But how does this one event represent an anomaly?" Mrs. Stonewall asked. The detachment that usually reflected in her blue eyes disappeared. A mother's concern filled her gaze as she looked at Kale before glancing at her four children.

Kale lifted his head, tears streaming down his face. "Because Brit was just the first. Over the past few weeks, more shifters have come down with this strange virus, attacking and even killing others. Four have died within the king's den this past week. It's spreading all over Aeaea, and our healers have no answers. We're facing extinction, and we need help. That's why King Alexander sent me to Human's World to find the Conclave."

"And we will offer whatever assistance we can," Gerald said.

"We'll do whatever is necessary." Leopold and his family stepped forward with grins wider than Leopold's waist.

Gerald looked down his nose at the Edwells. "While the offer is… appreciated," he said, as if he had trouble finding the right word. "You're not one of the protector covens. It's time you said your farewells and returned home."

"But—" Leopold darted his gaze to the Warlock Hag. "We thought—"

"You have been misinformed," Gerald replied, glancing sideways at the colleague he clearly disliked.

"Are you sending us to Aeaea?" my father asked.

"We are uncertain," Gerald admitted. "We need to investigate further before sending anyone into the outbreak."

"But this shifter is here," Mr. Stonewall said, indicating Kale. "He may very well have infected us."

Mrs. Stonewall tugged her younger children, Keaton and Kate, closer to her while the Proctors placed protective arms around their family, as if a parent's touch might somehow shield their loved ones from harm.

"No, I haven't," Kale replied, his voice firm. "The virus only affects shifters."

"How can you know for sure?" Mr. Proctor asked. "You said your healers had no answers."

Kale rubbed his chin and glanced at Gerald. He was obviously looking for permission to share what he had yet to admit. Gerald didn't reply. He scanned the area in front of him, no longer listening to us. He only ever did that when the Conclave was holding a private magical discussion.

Once again we were being kept out of the loop. What was the reason this time?

"That's information for another day," Gerald replied. "But rest assured the virus does not threaten nonshifters."

"But how can you know that?" Thad asked.

Gerald shot my brother a warning glance. Thad took a deep breath and nodded.

"When we have answers, we will contact you but for now, we must depart." Gerald walked back to join the other robed figures in line and motioned for Kale to follow him.

"No," Kale said. "I'm not going back with you."

Gerald arched a silver eyebrow at him. "But you must."

Kale shook his head and stood his ground. "I thank you for your help, but no. I'm staying here."

None of the Conclave liked Kale's response. They silently regarded him beneath the shadows of their hoods.

"He can stay with us," I said. "We have lots of room. It won't be a problem, right, Dad?"

A tentative smile stretched across my father's lips. "Of course," he replied. "If that's okay with you."

Gerald scanned the air in front of him again before he rested his kind eyes on Kale. "As you wish," he said, causing the Warlock Hag to tense beneath her robes. Gerald turned his attention to me. "I will leave him in your care, Pierce."

He stepped back into the line, and a second later, the Conclave was gone.

CHAPTER 6

AFTER THE Conclave departed, we said our good-byes. I wasn't going to stay one moment longer under the same roof as the Edwells. The Stonewalls felt the same way as they followed us to the door. I felt bad for Adam. He and his family were stuck with the party crashers who refused to go home like Gerald told them to.

Even though Camille Proctor announced how tired she was and Mr. Proctor yawned loudly, the Edwells either didn't get the hints or ignored them. Leopold went to get more food while Agnes sat down and made herself comfortable. Charity trapped Adam in the hallway, and his wide eyes pleaded with me to rescue him. There was no way I was falling down on that sword. I flashed him a big grin and waved. He replied by flipping me off.

Kale and I got in the Mercedes with Thad and Aiden while Mason and Drake rode in my father's Jag. I expected Thad to start talking as soon as the engine started. That big brain of his never stopped, and we had lots of things to figure out. I was surprised by the silence that filled the car.

Obviously I was going to be the one to get this ball rolling. "So you've got to have some idea of what's going on," I said. "Care to share?"

Thad's reply was to focus even harder on the road.

"You mean to tell me you have no theories? I find that hard to believe."

Aiden moved his hand over to Thad's and squeezed. Why did I get the feeling Aiden had some idea of what my brother was keeping to himself?

"It's a lot to take in for anyone," Kale said.

"You have no idea," I replied. "We've been through a lot before you got here, and I have a feeling our past troubles are somehow linked to yours."

Kale's head flinched back slightly. "How's that possible?"

"I don't know. I have a feeling my brother does, though."

Thad glared at me through the rearview mirror. His hazel eyes turned to slits, and his hands gripped the steering wheel. "Just what are you accusing me of?"

"Of keeping secrets," I said. "Of telling your boyfriend what you should be telling your family."

Aiden turned around in his seat. "How'd I get dragged into this?"

"Don't play stupid with me, Aiden. I can tell you know something. You *both* know something."

"Do you?" Kale asked. He held his breath and leaned closer to the front seats. "If you know anything that might help me or my people, please tell me."

Thad glared at me hard before glancing over his shoulder at Kale. "I really don't know anything about your situation, Kale. If I did, I'd let you know."

"Then what do you know?" I asked.

Thad faced forward again but didn't answer. That was an admission if I ever saw one.

"What did Gerald tell you after we got back from Otherworld?" I asked. "And don't tell me it was nothing. You've been different since that conversation. Angrier. More on edge. And I want to know why."

"I already told you," Thad replied through gritted teeth. "He shared what the Conclave learned about vampyren by studying Ben."

That was only half the truth. "And what else? I saw those glances the two of you shared at the Proctors'. You know something about that Warlock Hag, don't you? Or you at least have some idea of what we might be up against."

Thad's chest heaved like a racehorse. Aiden rubbed Thad's shoulders before massaging the back of his neck. "I know nothing," my brother finally responded.

That was a bald-faced lie.

Thad pulled up to the house. Dad had gotten home first, and Mason and Drake stood on the porch as he unlocked the door. When the car came to a stop, Thad threw open his door before disappearing inside the house.

"Where are you going?" I asked as I followed Thad inside. My strained voice caused Dad, Mason, and Drake to shift their glances between Thad and me.

"I'm beat," Thad said as he led Aiden up the stairs.

"He knows something," I told everyone. "But he's not sharing it with us. Why?"

"Not now," Mason said. His eyes were bloodshot, and Drake leaned against his shoulder. "We need rest."

"Mason's right, Pierce. It's late," my father said. He pointed his feet toward the stairs. "We can do this tomorrow."

"Are you serious? We've got to talk about what Thad knows, the Edwells, and that Warlock Hag. There's a lot to figure out."

"Tomorrow," Thad replied from where he and Aiden had stopped on the stairway landing.

What the hell was going on now? We didn't always tell each other everything, but my family didn't let things simmer. When shit had to get done, we worked it out until we either had answers or a plan.

"I know it's easy to fret right now," Drake said, his drawl exaggerated by his exhaustion. He attempted a reassuring smile but only managed a halfhearted thin line. "But we've been through a lot tonight. After a good sleep, we'll be ready to tackle things at first light."

"Well, I don't know about that." Mason grimaced. "I'm planning to sleep late."

"Me too," Aiden said with a yawn and a stretch so big he almost smacked Mason on the head. "I'm gonna sleep like the dead."

"You are dead," Mason teased.

Drake groaned. "Really, Mason?"

"I'm just stating facts," he replied.

"How about I stick an icicle up your ass?" Thad asked.

Mason snickered. "Is that what it feels like when Aiden fucks you?"

My brothers' voices disappeared as they continued teasing each other up the stairs. I shook my head and glanced over at Kale, who shrugged beside me.

"Let me show you to the guest room," Dad said.

"If it's okay with you, Mr. Blackmoor," Kale said. "I'm gonna stay up a bit longer. I'm too wired to fall asleep."

At least I wasn't the only one who was wound up. "I'll take him up later," I said.

Dad nodded and went upstairs to bed.

"So what now?" Kale asked.

I wished I had an answer to that and all the questions that rattled around in my brain. I could do more research on auras and the meanings behind the colors. It would be a start, but I was too aggravated to focus on hours of reading. I needed to find answers some other way that was more me and less Thad.

"You okay?" Kale asked. He stitched his brows together.

I shook my head. "I need answers, and it's time to find them."

"Okay," he said. "Where do we start?"

It sure as hell wasn't the library. I needed something far more powerful. "We need the Pig's Eye."

Kale sucked in a sharp breath. "It sounds like a powerful talisman. What is it?"

I grabbed the keys to my bike. "You'll see," I said as he followed me out the door. "It's the strongest magic we've got."

WHEN I parked my Ducati in front of my favorite bar called the Pig's Eye, Kale slid off the ride and studied the redbrick building that stood at the corner of Derby and Daniels. Loud music poured out of the open front door, and about a dozen people stood on the sidewalk, smoking and carrying on.

It was a dive, but it had always cured what ailed me.

"Is this a shrine of some sort where powerful oracles gather?" Kale asked.

I grinned. It was easy to forget Kale had no clue about modern society since he grew up on a magical island in the middle of the ocean. "Yeah, something like that." I strode for the front door, anxiously anticipating the hard liquor that would either give me the focus I needed or the buzz I needed to not care. After a few steps, I realized Kale wasn't with me. He stood by the bike, wringing his hands and glancing around him. "Are you coming?"

"I don't think so," he said. "We don't have shrines in Aeaea. Magic such as this is outlawed."

"Outlawed?" I asked. "For people who can turn into animals that doesn't make a shitload of sense."

"We weren't born with the gift, nor did we evolve into our shifting abilities," he said. "It was forced upon us by one of *your* kind."

Technically sorcerers were only partly our kind, but I caught his drift. "So there's no magic at all on Aeaea?"

He shook his head. "It's brought us enough trouble as it is."

"Well, we're not on Aeaea, are we?" I asked. "Without shrines like this, people like me would go batshit crazy." I jerked my head toward the front door.

He didn't budge.

"Okay," I replied, walking backward toward the entrance. "But if the Oracles see you out here alone, they might think you're the human sacrifice they ordered."

One minute later Kale and I sat on our stools at the bar, waiting to be served.

"I can see where the sacrifices take place," Kale said as he grimaced at the sticky wooden floor and the chandelier made of deer antlers. "But what's that?" Before I could answer, he hopped off his stool and made a beeline for the jukebox.

Just like the bird he turned into, he was easily distracted by shiny.

"Hey, handsome. It's been a while."

I turned in my seat and was greeted with the blond-bearded face and light-brown eyes of a guy I banged a few weeks ago. How many fucking bartenders had I unknowingly fucked in this town? Well, if they were as hot as this one, it would probably be a lot more.

"Hey, how are you, man?" I couldn't remember his name, but it started with an *M*. I thought it was Mark. We met at Sparky's, and a couple of hours later, I had him facedown on his mattress. He might look like a top, but he was the biggest bottom I'd ever come across. Pun definitely intended.

"I'm good," he answered, leaning against the bar and running his rough finger over my forearm. "I thought you would call, though."

"Sorry about that. I've been really busy." Wait. His name wasn't Mark. It was Matt, or was it Mitch?

"Is this the Oracle?" Kale asked, sliding back up on his barstool. A shaky grin slid across his lips as he took everything in. "That's the shrine, isn't it?" He pointed at the wall of liquor that spread on the shelves behind the bar.

Mark-Matt-Mitch arched an eyebrow at Kale before glancing at me. "What's he talking about?"

Kale grimaced. "If you don't know, you're not a very good Oracle."

"He's not from around here," I told Mark-Matt-Mitch.

"No shit," the bartender said, giving Kale the once-over.

"We call them bartenders here," I said to Kale.

"Bartender?" he asked with a slow nod. "Interesting. Are you allowed to give us your name, Bartender, or is that a magical secret you guard?"

He took a step back from the bar, clearly feeling the need to put distance between him and what he thought was the poster child for crazy. "Um, it's Flynn," he said.

Flynn? Fuck, I hadn't even been close.

"What can I get you boys?"

"A whiskey for me and leave the bottle," I said. "He'll take a water."

Kale shook his head. "I don't want water. We have that back home. I want what you're getting."

"You'd be better off with water," I said. "Trust me."

"I do," he said with a firm nod. "But no water."

Hearing that Kale trusted me made me smile because I'd trusted him from the moment I stared into those big golden eyes. I didn't need Thad's potion to tell me Kale wasn't a threat.

I gestured for Flynn to bring us two glasses for the whiskey. "I don't know who's going to regret this more. You or me."

"Is whiskey a powerful potion?" Kale asked. He seemed almost giddy.

I nodded. "I thought you said this stuff was outlawed in Aeaea."

"It is, but as someone wise and powerful just told me, I'm not in Aeaea, am I?" He glanced at me and smiled. "Besides, I'm here for help, and if this helps, I'm in."

Flynn returned with the bottle and two glasses. I poured for the two of us and handed Kale the shot glass filled with the burnt-umber liquid. "Cheers!"

"An incantation?" he asked with a smile before raising his glass. "Cheers!" He mimicked me and threw back the liquid. When his eyes popped out of his head and he started coughing, I almost laughed myself right off the stool.

TWO DRINKS later I answered my earlier question. I regretted this more than Kale. The alcohol had made him chatty and sleepy at the same time. How the fuck did that even happen? He'd lay his head on the bar for a few minutes and then perk right back up and chatter nonstop.

"You know what I hate?" he asked, slurring his words.

"What?"

"The reptilians." He scrunched up his face as if he'd just taken a big bite of a lemon. "They're sneaky and I don't trust them. Caspian's the worst of them all."

Thankfully the blaring jukebox provided enough background noise to drown out our conversation. The last thing I needed right now was for someone to overhear us. Breaking the Conclave's cardinal rule about keeping magic a secret wouldn't help my family's standing any. Still, I placed my finger over my lips to remind him to keep his voice down. "Who's he?"

"King Alexander's chief advisor," Kale whispered. The tone of his voice practically accused me of being an idiot for not knowing that.

I took another sip of my whiskey while Kale inspected his empty glass. "What makes him so bad?" I asked.

"He's a snake."

"So he's sneaky?"

"Well, yeah," he said, reaching for the bottle of whiskey I'd just placed out of his reach. "Hey, gimme!"

"You've had enough," I replied, placing my hand on his chest and pushing him back onto the stool.

"Are you kidding?" he asked. "This stuff is pure magic. I'll let you know when I've had enough."

"Kale," I growled.

He jutted out his lower lip and sighed. "Fine, you big meanie."

A smile turned up the corner of my lips even though I tried to fight it. I was never a fan of babysitting bad drunks, but with Kale, it was somehow endearing. Plus, considering the alcohol Kale had already knocked back, he was doing pretty damn good. It must be his shifter metabolism or some shit. "So you were saying about Caspian?"

He snorted. "I hate that guy."

"So you've said," I replied. "But why? What makes him such a snake?"

Kale glanced at me sideways. "Um, the fact that he turns into one."

I took a deep breath and shook my head.

"Aw, don't get mad," Kale said. He swatted playfully at my chest, but instead of moving his hand away, he let it linger. "Wow. You're, like, all muscle." He knocked on my chest and grinned before he slid his hand to my shoulder and squeezed. My heart beat faster, and my cock came to life.

"What do you think you're doing?"

"Shh," he said, clumsily pressing his index finger to my lips and leaning into the space between us. His warm breath plumed across my face and sent tiny flutters traveling across my flesh. "I'm busy." Kale surfed the curve of my biceps down to my hands. My heart raced as if I were slowly climbing to the top of the biggest rollercoaster in the world, and though those kinds of rides scared the shit out of me, I held my breath, anticipating the moment when the cart tipped us over the edge.

Kale's feathery strokes moved from my forearms to my fingers. He traced a line across each digit before following the path back to my chest, where he had started. He glanced up at me. His pupils were shot, and he parted his lips. Why did it feel like he'd been touching more than just my skin, but someplace deeper where no one else had ever been?

"Are you done?" I asked, my voice low and husky.

He nodded, slowly withdrawing his hand from my chest. My cock throbbed in protest. It wanted Kale's hand to travel farther south. "Yeah. Sorry about that. It was nice to touch someone. Most people don't let me."

I couldn't understand that. Kale could touch me anytime and anywhere. "Why not?"

His expression turned sober. "Because I'm not an apex."

"A what?"

"Apex," he mumbled. "You know, a top predator. My parents are. So are most shifters. But not me. I'm at the bottom of the food chain, an embarrassment to my kind and to my parents." He snatched the bottle from my grip and poured himself another glass.

"Is it really that bad?"

He pressed his lips together and looked at me askance. "You wouldn't understand. You're the oldest, the next high priest of your coven. That makes you the most powerful of your brothers. How would you feel if you were the weakest link in your family?"

It was like a bat to the balls, a hammer to the thumb, a paper cut to your tongue. "I know what you mean."

He snorted and took a drink.

"It's true," I said. My cheeks grew warm, so I switched my gaze from Kale to the wall of liquor. Tonight was supposed to be about finding answers to all the fucked-up shit going on, not a whine fest. I hated talking about my problems. I preferred zapping things or other people. That was how I coped. Opening up and spilling my guts made me weak, but why did talking with Kale not feel that way at all? "I used to be stronger than my brothers, but I'm not anymore."

"But you're the oldest."

"I know."

He placed his hand over mine, and the contact was warm and comforting, like putting on my favorite sweater fresh out of the dryer. Man, what the fuck was going on with me? I must be drunker than I thought.

"Do you want to talk about it?" he asked.

I glanced at him sideways. "Do you want to talk about your shit?"

"Do you always answer a question with a question?"

"I don't know. Do you?"

Kale let out an aggravated groan. "Fine, you big baby." He withdrew his hand from where it rested on mine and turned me around to face him, scooting closer until our knees touched. "What do you want to know?"

It was difficult to concentrate. Just the brush of his knees against mine turned me on. Was I developing some weird knee fetish?

He poked me in the chest and waggled his bushy eyebrows. "If you can't think of a question to ask me, I've got one."

There was no way in hell I was going first. "What kind of bird do you shift into?"

He sighed and cast his gaze downward. "You're gonna make fun of me."

I hooked his chin with my thumb and brought his gaze back to mine. The pain within flooded the golden pools of his eyes, robbing them of their usual brilliance. "I'd never do that," I said. "I'm the guy with younger brothers who can now kick his ass."

"That doesn't make sense," Kale said. "I'd always been taught the oldest is the most powerful."

I nodded. "That's how it's supposed to be."

He leaned in closer, reducing the space between us to almost nothing. "What happened?"

"I don't know," I replied, and I really didn't. It happened so fast I barely realized I'd gone from the king of the hill to the loser who couldn't even climb to the top. "My brothers' powers have grown recently. Mason can manipulate the shadows, and Thad can summon a fucking blizzard."

I glanced down at my hands that once unleashed more power than anyone could take, but those days were over. My brothers could hogtie me before I even got off one blast.

"If it can happen to your brothers, it can happen to you too."

"It already has." The problem was I couldn't control it.

His eyes grew wide and bright. "Really?"

I filled him in on my strange aura vision as well as turning into energy.

Kale rubbed his hand on my thigh and smiled. "You'll figure it out."

I just hoped it happened before my family was in danger again. They were counting on me, and I couldn't let them down.

"What else is bothering you?"

I snorted. It was fast approaching midnight, and we definitely didn't have time to get into all that now.

"Tell me," he said pressing his knees harder into mine. "I want to know. Maybe we can find some answers."

Or maybe Kale was just trying to stall. "I know what you're doing. You're trying to avoid answering my question." He gave me a big, sheepish grin. The little sneak. It wasn't just reptilians that were crafty. I glanced around and lowered my voice. "So what bird do you shift into?"

He hesitated for a moment before sighing and slumping his shoulders. "A dove."

"Really?" I asked. I hadn't meant to sound so surprised, but most of the information I'd read in my family's Grimoire had mentioned big cats, wolves, and birds of prey.

He nodded. "I know. Pretty pathetic, huh? Especially since I was born to two golden eagle shifters."

"How is it possible you're a dove, then? Shouldn't you be a golden eagle too?"

He knitted his eyebrows together. "You really don't know anything about shifters, huh?"

I didn't and neither did most everyone else. "There's not a lot written about your people in our books."

He snorted. "That figures."

What the hell did that mean?

"Shifting is not a natural ability. It's magical. We shift into animals that represent our inner self. It has to do with our link to the morphogenic field."

"The *what?*"

He regarded me in silence for a few seconds. "Aren't you a warlock? Shouldn't you know about all this?"

If that comment came from anyone else, I'd knock him on his ass, mostly because it was true. I couldn't blame Kale or anyone for my piss-poor studying skills. I'd spent too many years relying on Thad. How was I supposed to be the next leader of my family if I didn't know half of what my younger brother did? "You're right," I said with a firm nod. "I should."

Instead of berating me like most people in my life, Kale launched into the explanation. "It's kind of hard to describe the morphogenic field to someone who's never experienced it, but I guess you could call it the soul of the planet, and all animals can tap into it. It's how animals can sense natural disasters, follow migratory patterns and their instincts, and sense their mates." Kale locked eyes with me before flitting them away.

What just happened? I waited a few moments, hoping he'd start up again. When he continued to study the far wall, I figured it was up to me to get us back on track, even though I had no clue what had derailed us in the first place. "So it's like natural magic?" I asked.

Kale chewed on his lip in thought before nodding. "I guess you could call it that."

It made sense. All living creatures were infused with the power of the Gate, so this morphogenic field must be how animals accessed that energy. "And since you're shifters, you can connect to this natural magic too?"

"That's right," Kale replied. "It's been that way since we were first transformed by Sersie. When I'm in this form, I'm regular human Kale, but when I shift, my senses and every part of me is connected to every other beast in the world. I can feel them out there, and I can sense their energy. We shift by tapping into the animal energy that calls out to us the most, the one that resounds with our souls."

"And the dove is what called out to you?"

He studied the bar and nodded.

"Well, what's so bad about that?" I asked. "Isn't a dove a symbol of innocence and peace?" Those were some pretty powerful ideals, in my book.

"Yes." He frowned and he fidgeted with his shirt. "So you can imagine how hard my parents took it when their youngest didn't shift into a bird of prey but into the very prey they sometimes hunted."

Ouch. That was a kick to the nuts. "But that's not your fault. You can't control who you are, and you can't be the only nonapex shifter."

"There are others," he said with a nod. "But we are the minority, and for a species that prides itself on being strong, fierce warriors, we aren't of much use to them."

"Your friend Brit didn't think so, and neither must the king. You're his personal emissary, aren't you?"

He smiled, and his gaze turned faraway. He was obviously reminiscing about the good old days with his tiger best friend. "Yeah, Brit didn't care. He was my buddy no matter what."

"And the king?"

"King Alexander has a soft spot for nonapex shifters," he replied. "Everyone in his family shifts into a big cat except his younger brother Edmund, who turns into a pig."

Holy shit. That had to hurt, and it probably made family hunting a chore. What big cats could turn down a juicy pork loin?

"But the king did it more out of pity than anything else," Kale continued. "Everyone else thinks I'm worthless."

Without thinking, I cupped his cheek in my hand. Seeing pain in his eyes was like a knife wound to the chest. I had to do something to take that pain away. "You can't let other people define you. You are who you are, and that's a pretty awesome thing to be."

"Really?" he asked. He glanced down at himself before looking me up and down. "You're not ashamed that I'm not big and powerful like you?"

I laughed and shook my head. Kale had more inner strength than he gave himself credit for. I could see flashes of it in the jut of his chin or the defiance in his eyes. He wasn't the submissive weakling he thought he was. "Power isn't everything, you know. Strength comes in other areas." Where had all this positivity been when I lost control of my powers?

He rolled his eyes and finished off my drink. "Like what?" he asked, grinning at the fact that he stole my alcohol. Had he been one of my brothers, he'd be flying off the stool right now.

"Well, there's courage, and you've got that in spades."

Kale grunted in disbelief and reached for the bottle again. This time, after pouring myself another drink, I got up and moved the bottle to the end of the bar, which was now almost empty. When I sat back down,

Kale was trying to get off the stool, but his legs weren't cooperating. He reminded me of a newly born fawn.

"It takes a lot of courage to fly here from your world. I bet everyone else was too chickenshit to come."

"Yeah, courage," he scoffed. "King Alexander ordered me to come, and I did."

"Well, the king didn't come himself, did he? And neither did Caspian or any other apex shifter. It was you, and since you've been here, I've seen you defend yourself against my family and me when you thought we were trying to poison you, and stand up for me against the Conclave. Someone without courage doesn't do those things." I draped my arm around his shoulders. "You may be a dove, but you have the heart of an eagle."

The wattage of Kale's smile grew ten times brighter. "Do you really think so?"

I slid the glass of whiskey I poured for myself over to him. "I do."

Instead of taking the drink, Kale wrapped his arms around me and pressed his lips to my cheek. I caught a whiff of cedar and citrus and filled my lungs with the intoxicating bouquet. "Thank you," he whispered.

He sat back in his chair and brought the glass to his lips, swallowing its contents in one gulp and grunting through the burn of the alcohol. I could only sit there and stare as the warmth of Kale's kiss spread throughout my body like a pebble thrown into a pond.

THIS WASN'T happening right now. Any moment I'd wake up in my bed and find out this was all a dream and that Kale wasn't dancing to the Backstreet Boys. What the fuck was that song even doing in the damn jukebox?

"This is wonderful!" Kale screamed as he basically had a seizure on the dance floor. He kicked his legs one way while his arms and head went the other. It was embarrassing but also pretty damn funny. The few remaining patrons in the bar giggled and pointed. *That* pissed me off. I had to bite the inside of my cheek to keep from giving them a lightning enema.

Kale might not win any dancing awards, but he gave it his all. That had to count for something.

"Your friend is pretty damn strange. Where'd you find him?" the bartender asked. Fuck. What was his name again? Lloyd?

"You wouldn't believe me if I told you," I answered with a chuckle.

"He doesn't strike me as your type," he said as he filled my glass with more whiskey.

That was for damn sure. I liked my men and women as wild and as slutty as possible. Kale was the complete opposite. He was someone you brought home to meet your family, which was the most dangerous type of all. "He's not," I finally said.

"Could've fooled me."

"What?" I asked, not really paying attention. Kale had added singing to his routine. According to him, "Backstreet's back all night." He even got the words wrong, and what the fuck was he hopping for? I had to stop this before he hurt himself.

"You can't take your eyes off him."

I turned to face Floyd or whatever the fuck his name was. "That's because he's drunk and I'm looking out for him."

"When have you ever looked out for someone?"

I bristled. "What the fuck do you know about what I do?"

He raised his hands in surrender. "Hey, man. I mean no offense, really. But you've got a reputation in town. You're a party guy. You prowl, you score, you go home. That's what life is about for you."

I snorted. "You don't know shit."

He leaned against the bar and arched one eyebrow in challenge. "Really? Then prove me wrong."

"I don't have to prove jack shit," I said, knocking back my drink.

"Why? Worried I'm right?"

I shook my head. "Just don't care enough."

"Then what's wrong with answering one question?"

I nodded for him to pour me another drink. "What is it?"

"What's my name?"

Fuck!

"That's what I thought," he said before turning on his heel and walking away.

A loud *thwack* got my attention, and a quick glance over my shoulder made me hop off the stool and rush over to Kale, who was kicking the jukebox. "What the hell are you doing?"

"This thing stopped," he said. He kicked the casing twice. "I think it's broken."

"Will you stop that?" I asked. "It's not broken, but you're gonna break it if you keep kicking the shit out of it."

"I want to hear more," he said, pressing his nose and hands against the glass window. "Our music back home is nothing like this."

Even though I was going to regret this even more than bringing Kale to a bar, I took a couple of dollars out of my pocket and handed it to him. "Here. Use these."

Kale took the money and eyed it. He then glanced sideways at the jukebox as if it were his mortal enemy and waved the bills at the machine. "Play music immediately."

"What the hell are you doing now?"

He studied the money and waved it again, this time with more flourish. "I command you to play." When nothing happened, he frowned at me. "These talismans are broken."

Oh for crying out loud. I snatched the dollar bills out of his hand. "It's called money," I said. I fed the money into the machine and chose a couple of songs. When Fall Out Boy started jamming, I flashed Kale a smile. "See?"

"What kind of magic is money?" he asked in wide-eyed awe.

"Don't you use any kind of currency on Aeaea? You know, exchange goods for payment."

He stared at me as if I suddenly sprouted a third eye. "That's absurd. If someone needs something, we just give it to them. There's no need to pay." He then crossed his arms and huffed.

I exhaled. "What's wrong now?"

"This music is awful," he said. "What's an Uma Thurman?"

I'd never wanted to shove my face through a jukebox more in my life. "Are you kidding me? This is real music, not that boy band crap you were hopping to on the dance floor."

Kale gasped as if I punched him. "Take that back."

"I will not," I said with a firm shake of my head. "The Backstreet Boys are not considered music."

"Is that the name of the group of minstrels who sang that delightful song?"

Minstrels?

"Well, is it?" he asked, arching one dark eyebrow at me.

Why did that adorable smirk make me want to do whatever he asked? I nodded, even though I knew exactly where this was going.

"Wonderful," he said, waving at the jukebox. "Play more of that."

"Kale—"

He crossed his arms and tapped his foot.

Oh hell no. No one got away with tapping their foot at me, but I made the mistake of looking into Kale's big golden eyes and noticing the cute little dimples on his cheeks.

I found another Backstreet Boys song and pressed play.

TEN DOLLARS and five Backstreet Boys songs later, I'd had enough. Only a few stragglers remained in the bar, and it was time to go home.

"Let's go," I said to Kale, who'd been about to ask me for more money. "We have a long day tomorrow."

"Just one more song," he said, batting his big eyelashes at me. That had worked three times already, but enough was enough.

"No, we've got to go."

Kale twisted his lips and sighed. "You're being a big meanie again."

I grabbed his hand and tugged him toward the exit. "Yeah, well, you'll live."

"I can't go yet," he protested, pulling backward.

"Kale, please. No more arguing. No more dancing. No more adorable faces. I'm tired."

"Wh-what did you say?"

I rolled my eyes. "I said I'm tired. Can we please go?"

"You think I have an adorable face?" He gripped my hand harder and leaned forward, his cheeks flushed.

Did I say that? No. That didn't sound like me at all. "I don't know what you're talking about."

"But that's what you said." He grinned up at me and swayed back and forth like a little kid who'd just been told he could have ice cream before dinner.

"I think you're hearing things," I said, playfully pulling him forward.

He tugged back. "Am not."

"Are too."

"Are you two almost done?" asked the bartender whose name I still couldn't remember. "I'm trying to keep down my dinner."

"We're done," I told him before glancing back to Kale. "But I didn't."

"Yes, you did," sang the bartender as he smirked at me.

I snapped my attention to him. "Why are you lying?"

"I'm not," he said with a shrug. "I was right here when you said it."

Well, he just cut his tip in half. I hesitantly turned back to Kale, who beamed up at me. "Told you," he said.

"Fine," I said with a dismissive gesture. "You're adorable. So what?"

His lips parted and he took a step closer to me, and it was like he was traveling more than the distance that separated us. He was moving further into my soul. When the weight of his body pressed lightly against mine, sparks of energy sizzled across my flesh, and the crackling power I constantly fought to control suddenly stabilized as if I'd finally been connected to the outlet that grounded me. I wrapped my arms around his waist and pulled him closer. I'd never felt more at peace than I was at this moment. "Pierce?"

"Yeah," I asked, almost completely breathless. My lips hovered mere inches from his.

"I have to pee, and you're squishing me."

I released him and stepped back. "Oh, sorry." I took a deep breath, shaking off the bizarre emotions that had welled up inside me, and pointed to the restroom sign toward the back of the bar. "It's back there."

Kale glanced over his shoulder and winked before sprinting toward the back.

"One more for the road?" the bartender asked while attempting to hold back his laughter. He just said good-bye to the other half of his tip.

I waved off the offer. "Nah, I'm good."

"But I'm buying," a sultry voice next to me said.

I turned to find a woman sitting at the bar. When the hell did she walk in? I would've definitely noticed her. She was smoking hot, and the way she combed her fingers through her long, dark hair in slow, leisurely strokes told me she was looking to get naked.

I wasn't even remotely interested, which was pretty damn unusual for me.

"No, thanks," I said. "I need to get home."

"What's the rush?" she asked. She turned so her body pointed directly at me instead of at the bar. She wore a tight black miniskirt and a button-down blouse with the top three buttons unfastened. If she undid one more, she'd be flashing the entire bar. She rubbed her long, bare legs together and ran her fingers along the top of her right breast. "You're not married, right?"

The bartender scoffed loudly. I scowled while she turned her smile on him. "Flynn, be a good boy and go away."

Why did everyone else know this guy's name but me?

Flynn rounded the bar and disappeared into the back room.

"Now where were we?" she asked.

"Well, you're there," I said, pointing to where she sat. "And I'm here, waiting for my friend, so we can leave." I glanced over my shoulder, but still no sign of Kale. Just how much did he have to drink? I surveyed the empty bar. Where the hell did everyone else go?

"You're not really going to let me imbibe by myself?" she asked. She grabbed a bright green drink from the bar and strutted over to me. She leaned in close, and a mixture of black velvet and musk filled my lungs. She reeked of sex.

"I really can't," I said. Even though I didn't take the drink from her hand, her violet eyes captivated me. I'd never seen that color before. When she grinned, I had to shake my head and take a step back before I knocked the drink out of her hands and took her in my arms.

"Don't fight it," she said. She advanced toward me, and I stepped back until I ran into the bar. She pressed her body against me, the glass held out to her side, as she stood on her tiptoes and drew ever closer to my mouth.

At any other point in my life, I'd be all over her, but after holding Kale in my arms and having his body against mine, my flesh practically crawled away from her.

"I'm not fighting anything, Miss—"

"You can call me Chloe," she whispered. She draped her left hand around me and strummed her fingers across the back of my muscled neck. "And I can tell you want me."

She couldn't have been more wrong if she tried.

"Pierce?"

Kale stood ten feet away. He looked from me to Chloe and back to me again, shifting his weight from one foot to the next. "Is everything okay?"

"Yeah," I said, stepping away from the hypersexed barfly and toward Kale. "It's time to go."

Chloe sighed and placed the glass down on the bar. "Fine," she said. "I guess we'll do this the hard way."

I arched an eyebrow at her. "What are you talking about?"

"The avian is coming with me."

I clenched my fists and stepped in front of Kale. "What did you say?"

A sly grin cut across her lips. "Even though I know you're not exactly the brightest in your family, don't play stupid," she said. "It's very unattractive."

"Pierce, let's go," Kale said from behind me. He placed his hands on my back, and the rising current of power leveled off, preventing me from doing what I'd normally do—force my lightning down her throat. Right now that wasn't the wisest move. I knew nothing about Chloe, and getting into a magical showdown might cause more problems than it might solve. Plus Kale could get caught in the crossfire. I had to protect him at all costs. Once he was safe, though, I'd kick her ass.

"Who are you?" Arcs of electricity sizzled from my hands to show her I wasn't a warlock to be messed with.

She clicked her tongue and waved a long red fingernail at me. "A lady never reveals her secrets."

"And you expect me to believe you're a lady?"

She cackled. "You really suck at verbal sparring, you know that? I'm sure your brother Thad will prove far more entertaining on that front."

Who was this crazy bitch, and how did she know so much about my family?

"All you have to do is hand over the avian, and you won't be hurt," she said, taking one step closer.

With Kale behind me, we both took one step back. I scanned my surroundings, looking for a way to get him out of here. "Um, that would be a no."

"Have it your way."

She lunged forward, and I fired a lightning bolt at her that sizzled the air around us. Chloe stopped and held up her hand, dissipating my magic.

What the fuck? No one had ever been able to do that before.

"Is that the best you can do?" she asked.

Not even close. "*Propellit*," I uttered and Chloe flew off her feet and slammed into the wall of alcohol behind the bar. "Kale, get out of here. Now!" I yelled as I leaped over the bar and landed on the other side.

Chloe wasn't there.

"Looking for me?" she asked.

I spun around to find Chloe behind Kale with a tiny dagger held at his tanned neck. Fuck! Knocking her behind the bar didn't work the way I planned. All I managed to do was separate myself from Kale.

Thad was right. How would I protect my family as a high priest if I couldn't protect Kale from one threat?

She hitched up the corners of her mouth in a grin. "I'd love to stay and chat, but I have what I need."

"Think again," Kale said. He shrunk in size, and the clothes he borrowed from Mason fell to the ground. A white dove flew away from Chloe, heading for the back door. I'd never seen anything more spectacular or magical in my life.

"Get your feathered ass back here," she screamed. A stream of purple energy leaped from her hands and headed straight for Kale.

I uttered the Latin word for "protect" and an invisible barrier erected itself between Chloe's magic and Kale. A loud explosion filled the bar, shattering most of the bottles behind me as her energy bounced off my spell. It gave Kale enough time to fly into one of the back rooms and hopefully out a window.

Now it was just us.

"You lose," I said, calling back my lightning.

She sighed and blew her hair out of her eyes. "Again with the lightning? You saw how well that worked the last time, right?"

"I'm a slow learner."

She nodded. "Yes, I've heard that about you. I've also heard your brothers have far surpassed you in power. That must suck balls."

I sneered at her, trying my best not to let my emotions get the best of me. She had a lot of information on my family, and I didn't have to be a brainiac like Thad to figure out where she'd gotten it.

"So how's Ben?" I asked. He was obviously lurking in the shadows and spying on us. "Still licking his wounds from the little ass kicking we gave him in Otherworld?"

She'd been trying to use the information Ben fed her to piss me off, to get me to attack first and think later, but Thad had bitched enough times about needing to think things through. That was what I was doing now, distracting her until the right opportunity presented itself.

"Don't worry about Ebenezer," she said, glancing at her red nail polish as if she'd grown bored. "I've been taking excellent care of him. What you should be concerned with is yourself."

I raised my eyebrows. "Why's that?"

She cackled. "You don't really expect me to answer that, do you?"

"Not really, but it was worth a shot." I shut my eyes, concentrating on my new power. When I opened them, the physical world had been replaced by the colorful energy all living creatures produced. A muddied red aura glowed around Chloe. It was strong and vibrant, but there was something else. A second aura comprised of dark brown stood in the center.

"So are we going to fight or stand here clucking like hens?" she asked, nodding to the arcs of lightning that fanned from my fists.

I blinked, and my vision reverted to normal. I had no clue what that second aura meant, but it was important. Figuring it out might be what it would take to defeat her. Attacking her head-on wouldn't get me anywhere. She'd just cancel out my powers again. I had to try something different, something she wouldn't expect. Something that was part Thad and part Mason.

When I lowered my hands and turned off my powers, she studied me carefully. "What are you doing?"

"I can't win against you," I said. I was still behind the bar, so Chloe couldn't see me sending snakes of electricity outward from my feet. It was difficult to concentrate on focusing my power out of my lower limbs and talk at the same time, but I had to keep her distracted and focused on me. "You're too powerful."

"Clearly," she said still eying me. "But you're far too thick-headed to just give up."

"I'm not," I said. "My family will be here soon. Kale will bring them, and they'll knock you on your ass."

"Is that what you're waiting for?" she asked. "For your brothers and your daddy to save you? Pathetic."

"You won't be saying that when you're picking your teeth off the floor."

She laughed. "You have no idea what I can do. What I'm capable of."

"So tell me. What are you, exactly?"

"You really don't know, do you?" she asked with a sad sigh. Her hands glowed with purple energy. "When Ebenezer's through with you, I hope he lets me kill you."

A flutter of wings snagged our attention as Kale flew from the back room and straight into Chloe's face. Dammit! I told him to get out of here, but he'd given me the distraction I needed.

"Move!" I yelled.

Kale fluttered away, and I forced the snaking tendrils of energy I'd sent traveling around the perimeter of the room straight into Chloe from behind, not giving her a chance to snuff out my magic again.

When the lightning struck, she shrieked as thousands of volts of electricity coursed through her.

"I'm not as dumb as everyone thinks," I said, standing over her convulsing body before directing another wave of energy into her.

Kale shifted back to his human form and crossed over to me. He was completely naked, and though I wanted to take the time to enjoy all the tanned flesh and lean muscles, I was too pissed off. "What the fuck were you doing? You could've gotten yourself killed!"

"I couldn't leave you," he said, crossing his arms. He glanced at my clenched fists and straightened his shoulders. "Instead of being a dick, how about being thankful that I helped you out?"

I growled. "I didn't need your help." What I needed was for him to be safe.

He arched one eyebrow. "Really? That's not what I saw."

"I'm the one with the magic," I reminded him. "You're just—"

"What?" he asked with an arch of one eyebrow. "A dove?"

"No," I replied, blowing all the air from my lungs. Anger was getting me nowhere, not that it ever really got me anywhere before. I only landed myself in hot water or pissed off everyone around me. It never bothered me before when it was my brothers or the other protector covens, but I didn't want that with Kale.

"Then *what*?"

I opened my mouth but immediately closed it. How was I supposed to explain what I didn't even understand? All I knew was when Kale was in danger, it was like dangling over a cliff by two fingers and not giving two shits what happened to me. The only thing that mattered was making sure he was safe.

"You're just not used to defending yourself," I finally said. "But I am, and I have the power to protect you."

Mocking laughter filled the room. I'd recognize that cackling anywhere. It was Ben.

I shot over to Kale and drew a protective arm around his waist. Though he was still upset, his tense body relaxed in response to my touch. Maybe I grounded him too.

"Where are you?" I asked, studying the shadows cast across the darkened bar.

"You're protecting the dove instead of attacking?" Ben asked. "I didn't know you had it in you to care about someone other than yourself. How useful that is for me."

I clenched my jaw so hard my teeth almost shattered.

"Pierce, look!" Kale said, pointing to the shadows that rolled across the floor of the bar and gathered around Chloe's unconscious body.

"What the hell are you up to?" I asked. Without blinking my aura vision turned on. I scanned the area, looking for an energy signature that would reveal Ben's location. All I found was darkness.

"You won't find me that way," Ben teased. The advancing shadows wrapped around Chloe like a blanket. "But this new power of yours intrigues me. I must learn what it is about the Blackmoor brothers that causes such spikes in your abilities."

"Come out of hiding and find out for yourself."

Ben laughed. "You should know me better than that by now, Pierce. I don't do anything unless it advances my cause, and there's no advantage to showing myself right now."

"Sure there is," I said. "I get to kick your ass."

"Perhaps some other time," he replied. "For now enjoy this small victory. When this is all over, your family, your species, the Conclave, and even your precious dove will be no more."

When the shadows that had covered Chloe dissipated, she and Ben's voice were gone.

BEFORE KALE and I left for home, I checked to make sure Flynn hadn't been hurt by any stray spells. I found him in the stock room, staring at the wall. Whatever whammy Chloe had hit him with still hadn't worn off, but with her gone, it was only a matter of time before it dissipated.

We hopped on my bike, and I redlined it all the way back to Blackmoor Manor, where I woke everyone up and had them meet us in the library.

"What the fuck?" Mason asked. He and Drake were the last to enter the room. His dark hair stood at rakish angles, and he stifled a yawn. "I thought we agreed to wait till the morning."

"Kale and I were attacked."

My words woke everyone up. My father stood from where he was sitting on the wingback chair, and Thad, who was curled up with Aiden on the couch, sprang to his feet.

"By who?" Thad asked. "Ben?"

I nodded. "And someone named Chloe."

"Who the fuck is that?" Mason asked. He and Drake stood on either side of Dad.

"I don't know, but she was able to cancel out my powers."

"How is that possible?" Drake asked.

My father sat back down and laced his fingers in front of his mouth. "Tell us what happened."

I filled them in and also brought Kale up to speed about our recent troubles with Ben, which included the murders during Mabon that Mason and Drake had brought to an end, and his attempt to control the fae with blood magic Thad and Aiden prevented.

"So Ben has an accomplice?" Aiden asked. "Is she another vampyre?"

I shook my head. "No. She was something else entirely. Her magic wasn't like ours. I sensed no white, gray, or black energy from her whatsoever."

"That's because she's not like us," Thad said. He stood up and paced the library. Whenever he was in brainiac mode, he wore a hole in the floor. "There's only one magical species with the ability to cancel out our powers, and that's because the energy they tap into is a bastardization of all three types of magic."

Holy shit. I hadn't even thought of that. "She's a fucking sorcerer?" I asked.

Thad nodded, and Kale gasped.

"No," he said, shaking his head. "This can't be."

The last time the sorcerers were a threat, they created and enslaved the shifters, and it was sorcery shifters feared most of all. Since sorcerers created them, Kale and his people were susceptible to being controlled by their power. That was one of the reasons the Conclave sent the shifters to Aeaea.

"I won't let anything happen to you," I said. I brushed my thumb across his cheek and locked gazes with him. His trembling lips told me he wasn't used to having someone else fight his battles for him, and while he might not need me to or want me to, I was going to do it.

"I hope you can keep that promise," Thad said from where he leaned against the fireplace. "It's obvious she's behind this virus that's infecting the shifters."

"I will," I said, but I wasn't talking to him. I was speaking to Kale. When he nodded and smiled in acceptance, I turned to the others. "I used my aura vision on her."

"And?" Thad asked.

"I saw two auras."

He shrugged. "That's not uncommon. You said I gave off orange, blue, and green."

"Yes, but your body was surrounded by orange. The blue and green were specks and lines that ran through you. That's not the way she looked at all. The outer aura was a dirty red, filled with her anger. But the second one wasn't lines or specks of color. It was shaped almost like another person, and that energy was brown."

Thad stitched his eyebrows together, and he gnawed on his lower lip. I'd stumped him. I couldn't remember the last time that happened.

"What does that mean?" Aiden asked.

"I don't know," Thad said, glancing at my father, who shrugged. He had no clue either. "I'll have to research it."

"So what do we do in the meantime?" Drake asked. He buried deep into Mason's embrace. For a human, Drake was extremely resilient, but I could see the toll this was taking on him. He'd faced far more magical crap than any other human before him.

"I don't know about you," Kale said, "but I have to return to Aeaea. My people need to know the sorcerer threat has returned."

"No," my father said.

Kale studied Dad's stern face. He stood up straight and squared his shoulders. "You won't keep me from them. You *can't* keep me from them. Once I speak the king's spell, the portal that keeps Aeaea closed off will open, and I will go home."

"And I bet that's precisely what they want you to do," my father said as he stood and crossed over to Kale. Dad placed his hands on Kale's shoulders and rubbed them. "Right now they can't get into Aeaea. The spell the Conclave erected is strong and keeps them out, but if you open the portal, what's to stop Ben and Chloe from going through it?"

Kale shifted his gaze to me, clearly hoping I'd disagree, but I couldn't. "It makes sense," I said. "I bet the entire purpose of this virus had been to get one of you here on our side so that when you went back, they could follow."

"I agree," Thad said. "Aeaea is closed to them. We have to keep it that way. My guess is that Ben is looking to rebuild his army. He'd tried it with the fae."

"And failed," Aiden added with a firm nod.

"But with a sorcerer," Thad continued, "he'd be able to command an entire island of shifters."

Kale's lips curled. "I won't allow it. There's no way I'll ever let my people fall under the sway of a sorcerer again."

"And we'll do everything we can to help." My father nodded and patted Kale's back. "I need to contact the Conclave and tell them we've figured out Ben's next move."

"That should hopefully get us in the Warlock Hag's good graces," I added.

"I certainly hope so," he said. "But I want you all to promise me something."

"What's that?" Mason asked.

He swept the room, staring deeply into all of our eyes. "We can't go off half-cocked on this one. I know you want to nail Ben's ass to the wall. Hell, so do I, but we can't make any moves without the Conclave's consent. We're walking a tightrope here. One wrong move—"

"And we're out," I said.

He nodded. "So promise me now and mean it."

We all said the words Dad wanted to hear, but my gut told me Ben was going to do everything in his power to get us to break our vows. He was pulling more strings than even we were aware of, and that frightened me most of all.

CHAPTER 7

A COUPLE of days had passed since the encounter with Chloe and Ben, and the Conclave still hadn't given us our orders. We were told to stand down and wait for a decision. It pissed me off. The longer we waited, the more time the Scheming Duo had to follow through with their plans or come up with a completely different scheme, but instead of complaining like I normally would, I used the time to study up on auras.

It turned out to be a whole lot more complicated than I thought.

Each color in a person's aura wasn't straightforward because a dark, vibrant, or muddy hue meant something different for each specific shade. I'd believed red to represent anger across the board. Boy was I wrong. A cloudy or muddy red meant anger. Dark red meant the person was grounded and self-confident while a brilliant red indicated passion and competitive energy.

The brown aura that I saw within Chloe's outer, angrier aura indicated she was afraid of letting something go. All I had to do now was find out what exactly that was and use it to our advantage.

Before I could do that, though, we had to act, but we promised Dad we would wait until the Conclave's orders came in.

That promise was starting to take its toll.

"This is bullshit!" Mason complained. "We should be doing something, *anything* but sitting here jerking each other off."

That was an image I didn't need. "And what do you want us to do?" I asked. "Call Ben on his cell?"

Mason eyed me. "Do you have his number?"

"Will you stop it?" Thad asked. He sat at his desk in the library, poring over books. He still hadn't found anything that would explain the two different auras I saw in Chloe. "You're not helping."

"I'm not helping?" Mason snorted. "I think you're confusing me with the Conclave."

Drake tugged Mason into his arms and held him. He was the only person who could calm him down these days. I never understood that before. I always thought it was a sign of weakness whenever Mason or

Thad responded to their boyfriends' touches or soothing words, but since meeting Kale, it made more sense.

Just looking at him soothed the anger that constantly bubbled like hot tar inside me. Around him I was a different person, more focused and not as easily swayed by my natural warlock instincts. He brought me peace, and whenever he touched me or gave me his dimpled smile, I changed from a snarling pit bull into a Great Pyrenees, content with lying at his feet but ready to guard my flock if needed.

How did this even happen? I lived my life according to my wants and desires. I did what felt right, when it felt right, and with *whom* it felt right. I didn't give two shits about what anyone else wanted or needed, but ever since I met Kale, that wasn't me at all.

I was protecting him, believing in him, and wanting him to feel safe. It was like I'd unearthed my soul.

What was even weirder was we hadn't even kissed yet, and I'd never wanted to kiss anyone more. Every time he got close to me, static electricity surged across my skin, pulling me like a magnet to him, and over the course of the last two days, it took all my willpower not to take him in my arms and into my bed.

But I was afraid of where that might lead.

Sex usually followed every kiss I ever shared with someone else, and I didn't want to treat him the way I'd treated so many others in my past. That had happened with Adam, and look where that got us.

Kale deserved better than that. Hell, he deserved better than me.

"What's wrong?"

I looked up from where I sat on the couch to see Kale standing over me, his eyebrows drawn together. "Just thinking," I replied.

"I could tell," he said, plopping onto the couch next to me. He snuggled against my arm and sighed. He'd been doing that for the past few days, and it made my hands tingle and an unfamiliar heat radiate through my chest. "You were a million miles away."

"Not anymore." I rested my head on top of his and inhaled the air scented with orange and cedar that wafted around him. The fragrance, combined with the weight of his body on mine, made me want to cuddle. What was wrong with me?

"I know waiting is the right thing to do, but I'm having a hard time not opening the portal and going home. I need to find out if my people are okay."

I understood that. If the shoe were on the other foot and I didn't know what was happening to my family, I'd be frying everyone within a few miles of me. "We'll get you there as soon as possible," I said. "And we'll bring our own army with us."

He glanced up at me, studying my expression. "You really think the Conclave will send you and your brothers to Aeaea with me?"

"I think they'll send all the protector covens," I said.

"Do you really think so?" Aiden asked. "They certainly didn't do that for the fae."

"This is different," Thad said, giving his boyfriend a reassuring glance. The Conclave's reaction to his situation was still a sore spot for Aiden. "We didn't know what Ben's endgame was the last time. This time we do, and to stop him, we're going to need as much fire power as we can get."

While everyone else debated what the Conclave would ultimately decide, I tuned them out. Kale had tucked his legs to his body and curled into my chest. The uncertainty was obviously eating away at him.

"You okay?" I whispered.

He shook his head and worried his bottom lip. "All this talk about fighting scares me."

"Why?"

He glanced up at me before looking away. "What good will I be in a fight?" he asked. "I'm not a lion or an owl. I'm a dove."

I hooked my thumb under his chin and forced his gaze to mine. "Will you stop that already? Back at the bar, you flew right into Chloe's face and pecked the shit out of her. She would have killed me if you hadn't done what you did."

He grinned and puffed out his chest. "Yeah, I guess I did do that."

"You sure did," I said, pressing my big finger into his dimple. The gesture broadened his smile, and his cheeks flushed as his gaze lingered on my lips. All I had to do was lean down the few inches that separated us, and our lips would meet.

But I pulled back and stood up.

Kale, who'd been leaning against me, had to brace himself with his left hand on the cushion to keep from falling over. The flush on his cheeks died, and he turned away.

"Let's get out of here," I said, holding out my hand to him.

"Why? Where are we going?" he asked.

"Away from all this," I said with a gesture to my brothers, Aiden, and Drake, whose voices were growing increasingly louder. "Someplace where we don't have to think about what's going to happen. Someplace we can just enjoy right now."

A hesitant smile stretched across his lips, and he took my hand.

I GRABBED Mason's pea coat for Kale and my leather jacket, and twenty minutes later we were in my father's Jag and heading over Ocean Avenue on the way to peace and quiet. It would do the both of us good. We'd been cooped up in the house too long, and if I stayed in there any longer, someone was going to get hurt. My money was on Mason. He'd been so much more irritating than usual that he was even starting to get on Drake's nerves. The two of them were usually too busy swallowing each other's tongues to do anything else, but they'd been snipping at each other instead.

I couldn't really blame Mason, though. He was like me. He wanted to get out there and get the job done. If we went against orders, the Edwells would be named the new protector coven for the Order of Black, and there was no way I was going to let those bastards take the honor that was rightfully ours.

"You're a million miles away again," Kale said. He sat sideways in the seat so he could look at me. "I thought the purpose of this outing was to relax and not mull everything over in silence."

"You're right," I said with a smile. "No business. Just fun."

"Does fun mean more of that magical potion you called whiskey?" he asked, baring his full set of white teeth at me.

I groaned. "No, it does not." Getting Kale buzzed once was more than enough. I still hadn't recovered from his Backstreet Boys marathon.

"Too bad," he said with an absentminded shrug. "I enjoyed the way it made me feel all warm and tingly inside. Don't you like feeling that way?" He leaned against the headrest and lingered his gaze on mine.

I did, but Kale looking at me the way he did accomplished that far more easily than the alcohol. I could get drunk on that any day of the week. "Yes, but the answer is still no."

"So what are we going to do, then?"

"I'm taking you someplace I think you're going to like. Chances are we'll be the only ones there too."

Kale narrowed his eyes and looked me up and down. "Are you taking me on a date?"

I nodded. "Wait. What?" I asked, doing a double take between Kale and the road that briefly swerved before me.

"Hey!" he complained with one hand on the seat and the other on the dashboard. Passing cars blared their horns at me. "I'd like to arrive to our date in one piece."

I didn't cuddle, and I sure as hell didn't date. I occasionally shared meals and beds with people I found attractive. Those were hookups. Dating meant something else entirely, and the idea both intrigued me and almost made me shit myself. "This isn't a date," I said, shaking my head.

"That's not what you just said."

"I wasn't paying attention."

Kale wiggled his index finger at me. "Too late. You said it's a date, so it's a date." He nodded his head once to make his point.

"Just because you say it's a date doesn't make it a date."

"Just because you say it's *not* a date doesn't mean it's *not* a date."

I scowled. "You're being difficult."

"No more difficult than you," Kale said. "Besides, I'm not the one who said it was a date in the first place. That was you."

"I told you I wasn't paying attention to what you were saying."

"Fine," he said, sitting forward in his seat again. "This was going to be my first date and all, but whatever."

I couldn't believe that. Kale had the most gorgeous eyes I'd ever seen. They were big golden pools I wanted to jump naked in to. And his lips. They reminded me of the cotton candy I used to eat whenever Mom and Dad took my brothers and me to the carnival. Then there was his skin, so soft and tanned. And his muscles, and dimples, and his cute butt that would likely fit in just one of my hands. Why wouldn't anyone on Aeaea date him?

"You can't be serious?" I finally asked.

"It's true," he said with a shrug. "I'm not an apex, remember?" As if that explained everything. Maybe on Aeaea it did. To me, it was bullshit.

I grabbed his hand and squeezed it. "Okay. It's a date."

Kale shot me a blank stare and withdrew his hand. "No, thanks. There's nothing worse than a pity date."

Oh. My. God. "That's not what this is."

He crossed his arms and locked gazes with me. "I may not be from your world, but I know a pity date when I see one. This," he said, gesturing toward me with a flourish of his index finger, "is a pity date."

I swerved the car onto the shoulder of the freeway and shut off the engine. Kale had turned away from me and was suddenly very interested in the scenery outside his window. "Will you look at me, please?"

He shook his head. "I'm good."

I'd never wanted to strangle and hug someone harder in my life. "I'm sorry," I said, uttering the words far too easily for my liking. "It's just that… well… you see…." I swallowed hard. I couldn't believe I was going to say this. "I've never been on a date before either."

Kale whipped his head around. His mouth was so wide I could've driven the Jag through it. "Are you serious?"

I cast my gaze downward and nodded.

"I don't understand."

I blew out all the air in my lungs. "Dating means getting to know someone, and I've never really cared to do that before."

"Oh." He sucked in his breath as if I'd stabbed him.

"Wait. That came out wrong."

He gave me a thin smile. "Pierce, it's okay. Really. You don't have to explain."

"Yes, I do."

Kale placed his index finger over my lips and shook his head. "I understand, and I'm sorry for pressuring you. I just thought…. Well, that doesn't matter." He turned to stare out the windshield. "Let's get to where we're going and have some fun."

I growled in frustration. "Will you stop being so stubborn and listen to me? I'm not any good at this, and you're not making it easy."

He glared at me as if I needed a tranquilizer. I couldn't blame him. I wasn't making sense, and I was swinging on an emotional pendulum I had no clue how to stop.

"I'm not the sharpest knife in the drawer or even the shiniest, so it takes me a while to get to where I need to go. Just bear with me. Please."

He turned to face me and nodded.

I took a deep breath and thought long and hard about the next words to leave my mouth. "I've never been on a date before because I've never met someone I've wanted to get to know beyond a one-time thing. I know that makes me sound like some cheap manslut, but that's who I was. I can't change it, and I'm not even embarrassed by it because that was the path I needed to be on. Do you want to know why?"

"Why?" Kale asked, turning his head and entire body in the seat so I had his complete attention.

"Because that was the path that brought me to you." Kale swallowed hard. "If I'd taken the time to get to know any of the others, I might not be here right now with you. That's not what the Gate had in store for me. It wanted me to meet you, and it wanted you to be the first person I ever went on my first date with. So, Kale Aquilo, will you please go on a date with me?"

Kale cleared his throat and nodded. "Yes. I'd like that."

I let out the breath I hadn't realized I'd been holding. "Great. Then let's get this show on the road."

After I started the car and merged back into traffic, I decided to do something else I'd never done before. I slid my hand across the console to Kale's and laced my fingers with his.

He glanced down at our entwined fingers and smiled. "Never been on a date before? Not even one?" he asked.

"Nope."

"I guess I'll find out what's wrong with you on our date, huh?"

I eyeballed him, and he gave me his big dimpled grin that almost made me crash into the barrier.

"Keep your eyes on the road while I figure out what all these buttons are for."

Kale punched some of the knobs on the dashboard and turned on the air conditioner. I switched it back off. "I'd leave those alone if I were you. Dad doesn't like any of us to mess with his controls."

"Your dad likes me," Kale said, waving my concerns away. He hit the button that turned on the satellite radio. His eyes grew wide, and he stared at me. "It's a jukebox!"

"We call it a radio when it's in the car," I said.

"Will the Backstreet Boys be in there?"

Fuck. I hoped not. "They were popular in the 1990s. Not anymore."

"How is that possible?" he asked as he kept hitting the button that cycled through the stations. On his fifth attempt, he landed on '90s on Nine.

"No," I said, shaking my head. "Please no."

A second later Kale was singing at the top of his lungs along with the Backstreet Boys. They were apparently back, and it was not all right.

AFTER THE Backstreet Boys song, which lasted an eternity, we stopped briefly at Jack-Tar, a local American tavern that made the best burgers in the entire world, before we finally arrived at Chandler Hovey Park. It was a local tourist spot in Havenbridge that overlooked the mouth of the harbor. With its pavilions, benches, places to swim, and winding paths, it was a perfect place to explore during the summer. In the winter it was a good spot to go when you wanted to be alone. Not many people visited the exposed area at the northernmost tip of town because the ocean breeze chilled you to the bone.

I slid into one of the parking slots facing the Havenbridge Light Tower and the harbor beyond, and turned off the car.

"Are we getting out?" Kale asked.

"Oh hell no," I said, digging in the bag for one of the burgers. "It's too cold out there."

Kale took the burger wrapped in paper I handed to him and stared at it. "What is this?"

"You've never had a burger before?"

He sniffed the paper. "I don't think so. It smells like burned carcass."

I chuckled. "That's exactly what it is."

He frowned. "I don't eat meat," he said after I'd taken a big bite of my burger. I almost choked, and he glowered at me. "I'm a vegetarian. Not whatever nasty thought you were thinking." His blank stare told me to get my mind out of the gutter.

I swallowed down my food. "You're a shifter, not a mind reader."

"I don't have to be one to know what you were thinking."

I flashed him a big smile before handing him the fries. "Try these. They're potatoes."

"Such a weird shape for a potato," he said. He took one of the fries out of the box and sniffed it before glancing at me to see if I was pulling his leg.

"Try it," I muttered through a mouthful of food.

He plucked one fry out of the container and closed his eyes. He placed it in his mouth, and when he bit down, his eyes grew wide. "This is delicious," he said before snagging two more fries and throwing them in after the first.

"I know," I said, snatching the burger from his lap. "Not better than the burger, though. You don't know what you're missing."

"I'm not an apex, remember? We don't hunt prey."

"So what?" I asked. "You can eat whatever the hell you want. You're here, not in Aeaea."

"You keep saying that, but you don't know anything about where I come from."

"So tell me," I said. "We're on a date, right? That's what two people on a date do. They talk about themselves. So tell me what you think I don't know."

He pondered the question over a fry. "Well, did you know we don't experience our first shift till puberty?"

I did not. Suddenly finding hair on your junk was weird enough. I couldn't even imagine how strange turning into an animal was on top of everything else. "So you live through most of your childhood knowing you're going to shift into a bird or a mammal, but you don't know what kind until you actually do?"

"That's right." He stared into the wintery sky, his eyes glassy and faraway. He'd obviously travelled back to his childhood, and the smile on his face told me it had been a happy time. "Before our first shift, life is pretty normal. We live like most humans. We play, go to school—"

"You go to school?"

"Yes," he replied with an eye roll. "We may not live in your world, but we aren't stupid. We learn how to read and write. Basic math." He paused as if there was something he was going to say, but then dismissed it. "But like I was saying, before our first shift, we imagine what animal we're going to become. Well, everyone except me."

"Really? Why?"

He shrugged. "I was never really obsessed with it. Most kids pretend-fought on the playground as the animal they thought they'd become. The adults thought it was fun to watch. I just found it annoying. To me, it didn't really matter what we became if we had no control over it. I guess that was why I felt sorry for the nonapex shifters. It wasn't their fault, but those kids got teased mercilessly in school. I didn't make fun of them, though. I talked to them even when no one else did, and I used to get bullied about it all the time."

I scowled. I didn't like the thought of someone threatening Kale. It made my hackles stand up. "Did they hurt you?"

"Not really," he replied. "Sticks and stones and all that. I didn't care, but my brother and sister did."

"You've got siblings?" It was amazing what you learned about someone else when you weren't using your tongue for other things.

"Yup. Levi and Telma. They were obsessed with being apex, and they didn't want me to associate with nonapex shifters for fear that I'd turn into one of *them*." He rolled his eyes and continued. "They wanted to become golden eagles like our parents, but Levi turned into a great horned owl, and Telma shifted into an osprey. My parents were proud. Those are two pretty damn good avians to become, but I could tell they secretly wanted us to shift as they had and as their parents had. We were the first generation of non-golden eagles."

"So the pressure was on you to be everything your parents wanted you to be. I know that feeling."

"Yeah, I guess you do." He placed his food on the console between us and shifted in his seat. "How did you handle it? The pressure, I mean."

I snorted. "By turning into an asshole."

"I can see that," he said with a nod.

"Hey!" I snarled before stealing one of his fries. "Now who's being the big meanie?"

Kale laughed. "I'm not trying to be. I'm just saying I can see it, especially since the first time we met you punched me in the nose. Or have you forgotten?"

How could I since he brought it up constantly? "No, but you didn't have to agree with me so fast."

"I call it how I see it," he said with a playful shrug. "But here's the thing. I don't think you're that way at all."

I regarded him as if he was suddenly speaking a foreign language. *Everyone* thought I was an asshole. Kale was the first person to ever doubt it. "Why do you say that?" I asked, shoving the rest of our food into the bag and tossing it into the backseat.

He patted my cheek and then fluttered his fingertips across my face, sending tiny vibrations shuddering across my flesh. "It's in your eyes," he said with a smile. "They don't match the rest of you."

I leaned into his touch to keep him from pulling away. "What do you mean?"

He scrunched up his mouth and then answered, "I first saw it after you punched me."

I groaned. "Really? We're going back there again."

He pressed his finger to my lips to shush me. "Just listen. Okay?"

When I nodded, he removed his fingers from my lips and rested his hand on my chest. The contact made my heart flutter and my cock come to life. All of a sudden, it was very interested in what was going on.

"You were talking a lot of crap, telling me that 'violators would be electrocuted' and other nonsense."

I chuckled. That had been a good one, but Kale's even stare told me he didn't agree. In fact, if I didn't shut it, he'd shove his burger down my throat to keep me quiet. I pressed my lips together and nodded for him to continue.

"Even though you were scowling and clenching your fists, your eyes were soft and gentle. You were worried you'd hurt me."

He was right. The miserable look on his face when I struck him and how tentative he was around me had wrenched my gut. "I felt bad about it." I reached out to touch him, but I withdrew my hand. I was too afraid even the slightest graze might somehow make whatever was happening between us disappear like a spell gone wrong. "But I couldn't say that. I'm a warlock. We don't feel bad about shit."

He exhaled and shook his head. "That damn warlock pride."

Yeah, it was a bitch. We had reputations to uphold. "It's not easy being a warlock, you know? We're considered the muscle, the bad boys. If we're not causing trouble, we might as well be a witch or a wizard."

A grin stretched across Kale's lips as he studied me, and it was like he was looking at the real me, the one no one else, not even my family, saw. "But you know what?" he asked. "Despite that reputation, and even though I tried to leave, you wouldn't let me. You brought me to your house and bandaged me up. You've been watching out for me, taking care of me ever since then. Hell, you practically pitched a fit when I came back to help you with Chloe."

I couldn't argue with him there. I hadn't been that cheesed off since my war game with Thad and Mason.

"You were thinking of me, not about you, and I think you do that more than people realize or more than you'd like to admit. Your anger isn't because you're an asshole. You're angry because you *do* care, and caring scares the shit out of you."

Tears welled up in my eyes, and I had to blink them away. My anger had always been the mask I gave to the world, to protect me and to keep everyone else from guessing the truth Kale had seen. "I am scared," I said, swallowing a huge lump in my throat.

"Of what?" he asked, scooting closer to me so all I could see was his golden eyes and all I could smell was citrus, cedar, and a hint of sweat that made my pulse race.

When I opened my mouth, fears I'd never allowed to pass my lips before came tumbling out. "Of life after my mother's death, of my brothers or father getting hurt, of failing, of being a disappointment, of Ben, of vampyren and roller coasters, of never being good enough, of being alone, of never finding someone like my brothers have, and a whole shit-ton of insecurities that gnaw away at me every single fucking day."

Kale practically crawled over the console. He wrapped his arms around me and held me close. I clutched on to him, fighting back the emotions that welled up inside me and threatened to tear down the fortress I'd built around my heart and my soul.

Against Kale, those fortified walls didn't stand a chance. With each soothing word or caress, the bricks started to crumble.

"You remember when you said I had the heart of an eagle?" he asked.

"Yeah," I said with a sniff.

"Well, you've got the heart of a dove."

The words fluttered across my flesh and resonated deep within my sighing soul.

I sat up and rubbed the back of my palm across his face. Sliding my hand across his smooth, tanned skin, I stared deep into the golden eyes that had struck me like a lightning bolt the first time I gazed into them.

Kale leaned forward and smiled. "Why are you looking at me that way?" he asked as he tangled his fingers through my hair.

There were too many ways to answer that. I was looking at him without fear standing between us. I was looking at him because he was the most beautiful man I'd ever seen. Because he made my heart dance and my palms sweat. Because of the tiny scar above his eyebrow that I'd never noticed before. Because I wanted to know how he got that scar. Because I wanted to know everything there ever was to know about Kale Aquilo. Because my body had never longed to be this close to someone else in all my life.

But the simplest answer was the one that finally escaped my lips.

"Because I want to kiss you," I finally replied. "But since this is our first date, I'm supposed to wait until I take you back home."

Kale's cheeks dimpled with his big, bashful smile. He wound his fingers around my hair and gently tugged me closer. "Do you really want to wait till I'm headed back to Aeaea?"

That was the easiest question of all to answer. "No."

He inched closer, his hot breath spreading across my lips and my cheeks, filling my lungs with the sweetness he exhaled. "Then kiss me."

I pressed my lips against Kale's, and a current even stronger than I could generate pulsed through my quivering body. It traveled across my skin and deep into my soul, where it flipped on a circuit that had never been touched and filled my trembling, shuddering body with energy it had never experienced.

Kale wrapped his arms around my neck, shivering as if the energy that coursed through me sizzled through him. He moaned and panted into the kiss. He parted his lips, and darted his tongue into my mouth. I twisted my tongue around his, tempting him deeper inside me.

He clawed at my shirt and my shoulders, trying to rip my clothes to shreds, and I nibbled a ragged path from his chin to his neck. I gently chewed on the sensitive flesh, and Kale gasped in response. He held my face tightly to him with one hand while he surfed the other up my thigh toward my aching cock.

When he grabbed my dick, I growled and pulled his smaller body over the console and onto my lap. He ground his ass against my swollen prick, and found my mouth with his again. His tongue dove past my lips as he caressed my face, my shoulders, and my chest.

We had too many clothes on, and they had to come off. I gripped his waist, thrusting against him, trying to rip the fabric that separated us with the friction I was creating.

"I want you so bad," Kale mumbled into the kiss.

And I wanted him. I needed to feel his smooth skin against mine, my lips upon his chest, and my cock inside his ass, but this wasn't the right time. If we did it here and now, it would make this moment in time no different than any of the other sweaty grope sessions I'd had before this.

Kale deserved better than that and so did I, so with strength I didn't think I possessed, I grabbed Kale's cheeks and pulled us out of the kiss.

"What's wrong?" he asked, his eyes half-closed and his pupils shot. He strained against my grip, trying to mold his lips to mine again.

"We can't."

"Sure we can," he said, wiggling his way out of my grip. He shoved his hand beneath the waistband of my jeans and grabbed my cock before diving onto my lips. The sensation of his warm hand around my boner and his writhing tongue in my mouth made me gasp. My previous determination briefly wavered to his persuasive hand and mouth, but no matter how bad I wanted this, we had to stop.

We'd get to where we both wanted to go. Just not now, and not like this.

"Kale," I said, pulling free from his soft lips. "Stop."

He leaned his forehead against mine and panted. "Why?"

I skimmed my hand up his back and squeezed his shoulders. "I want our first time to be somewhere special, not in the front seat of my dad's car."

Kale blew out a lungful of air and nodded. "I suppose you're right," he said as he attempted to cross back over to his side of the car, but when he lifted his right leg, it wouldn't move. "Um, I think I'm stuck."

I tried to see what the problem was, but his body blocked my view. "Where?"

"My foot," he said. "It's caught on something hard."

I chuckled. "Well, I know what it's not."

"Very funny," he said with a playful smack to the back of my head. "Reach down there and let me loose."

I licked my lips and gazed up at him. "I don't know. I kinda like you helpless and trapped on top of me."

He leered down at me before pressing his lips to mine once again. "You were the one who wanted to stop. If you've changed your mind, just let me know," he said in a low, throaty whisper.

Fuck! If I didn't get him off me now, not even a lightning bolt to my nuts could stop me. "Okay, okay," I said, breaking from the kiss. "I'll get you loose."

He frowned down at me. "You *are* a big meanie."

I rolled my eyes and reached down to where his foot was jammed between the door and the driver's seat. From what I could feel, his jeans had somehow gotten caught in the seat railing. I pulled hard on the fabric, and one rip later, he was free.

Kale climbed over to his side of the car and inspected the torn jeans with a wrinkle in his brow. "I hope Mason isn't too upset."

"I think he'd be more upset to learn that you were grinding his jeans against his brother's boner."

His face flushed. "Well, I'm not going to tell him that."

I laughed. "I think those jeans are yours now, anyway."

Kale let out a long sigh. "So now what?"

I know what my erection wanted. If it had arms, it would be strangling me right now. "You tell me."

He glanced out the window and then smiled back at me.

"Oh no," I said, shaking my head. "It's too cold outside."

"I think we can both use some cooling off, don't you think?"

"No. Not gonna happen."

Kale wrapped his arms around my neck and leaned in. His lips hovered so close the heat that radiated from his body made me sweat. "Please," he said before he once again pressed his mouth against mine.

TWO MINUTES later we were walking away from the car.

It was freezing outside, but Kale's kiss managed to persuade me to leave the comfortably warm interior of the Jag for the cold Massachusetts day. My balls had crawled so far inside my body I feared they were now ovaries, and my cock wasn't pleased either. I'd gone from a hard nine inches to an inch if I was lucky.

"Oh, stop being a Grumpy Gus," Kale said at my side as we walked across the rocks on our way to the small stretch of beach that lined the harbor.

"I'm not grumpy," I growled. "I'm cold!" I shoved my hands inside my leather jacket, which did nothing to protect me from the occasional bluster, and when the wind swept across the parts of my body still covered with sweat from our makeout session in the car, I shivered.

"Have you always been a big baby?" he asked, giving me the stink eye.

"You better watch it or you're gonna find yourself going for an unexpected dip," I said, nodding toward the cold water before us.

Kale snorted. "Try it," he said with an arch of an eyebrow. "I'll just shift and fly away."

I didn't like the sound of that. Now that I'd held him in my arms and kissed his lips, I didn't want him to go anywhere. I pulled him to my side. "You better not."

His lingering gaze and big dimples told me he understood what I meant. "Don't worry," he said, leaning against me. "I'm not going anywhere right now."

"What does that mean?"

He stole his gaze from mine and looked out into the cold, gray sky. "I don't live here, remember?"

Well, fuck. I almost forgot about that. Kale eventually had to go home once all this shit was over. What was I going to do, then? I'd never met someone like him before, someone who actually saw past my bullshit and bravado.

He'd flown not only into my life but into my soul.

"I'm not leaving right now, you know?"

I nodded and tried my best to not pout, but I pressed my lips into a thin smile. The song that had begun within my soul sputtered like a scratched vinyl record before falling completely silent. I'd lost so much recently—my mother, my place of power in my family—and now I was faced with the fact that Kale would head home and turn into another memory of a happier time.

The walls inside me went back up. Brick by brick.

I shook the fear from my body like dust and focused on the world around us. Though there were a few boats bobbing on the gray, choppy waters, we were alone. The wind cut across the beach, sending icy sprays along the sand and into the air. Overhead, drab clouds scuttled across a lifeless sky.

The scenery looked as bleak as I still felt.

"I'll just come and see you," I finally said.

"I doubt the Conclave will allow it."

"They can take a flying suck to my hairy ass," I said, and I meant it. It was time for me to embrace what I wanted whether it scared me or not, and no one, not even the Conclave, was going to stop me.

"That's not exactly the best attitude to take right now, is it?"

I grumbled. He was right. Demanding to go to Aeaea would likely piss off the Conclave. At the very least, it would bunch that Warlock Hag's panties in a knot.

"You're still worrying about the Conclave and the Edwells?" Kale asked.

Yeah. That and about a trillion other things that I'd been able to escape until now, like when and how I'd ever get to see Kale again once he went back home. "It doesn't make sense. Why replace my family with a less powerful one?"

Kale shrugged. "I've never understood the Conclave, and I definitely don't trust them."

He'd said that before, and up until recently, I'd always believed the Conclave was revered and respected across the magical community, but that wasn't the case. The fae despised the Conclave, and now the shifters. "Why is that?"

Kale stood taller and gazed out at the beach before us. "The Conclave had promised to look out for us and protect us. When push came to shove, they took care of themselves instead."

"What do you mean?"

He looked at me crossways. "Are you sure you want to know?" he asked. "You've said there's not much about us in your books. I'm guessing that's been for a reason."

I stopped and tugged Kale into my arms, craning down to press my lips to his. "I want to know everything about you and your people."

He nodded and rested his head on my chest for a moment. Our chests heaved as one, and it was like all the physical barriers that separated us had fallen and turned us into an extension of the other. After he let out a content sigh, he slipped out of our embrace and grabbed my hand, tugging me farther down the beach.

"A few years after arriving on Aeaea, we had our first visitors."

That didn't make sense. Shifter Island was protected by a spell. "How is it possible? The enchantment should have kept everyone out."

"Everyone except humans."

I stopped and gaped at him. "What?"

"My people were surprised, too, when Cyrus the Great made it past the barrier. After conquering most of Persia, he'd crossed the Mediterranean and headed for Europe. He never made it. A storm destroyed his ship, and he and his people would have died if the aquatics hadn't saved them and brought them to Aeaea. My people healed their injuries, but when they tried to leave, they couldn't. The spell that had been meant to keep them out kept them prisoner instead. They blamed us and attacked."

I couldn't believe what I was hearing. Why had this been kept from the rest of the magical community?

"We asked the Conclave for help, but they denied it. They were too busy with their own problems, and since they didn't keep their promise, we were defeated," he said with a loud sigh. "We'd never fought before."

"That's not true," I said. "You fought for Sersie and the sorcerers."

He nodded. "But not of our own accord. We were told what to do. We had no real concept of how to fight except what our instincts told us. It wasn't enough against Cyrus and his skilled warriors. They beat us, and Cyrus declared himself our ruler." Kale's expression turned harder than steel. "He tortured and killed whoever didn't do what he said."

"That's awful," I said. I placed my hands on his shoulders and rubbed away the tension the history lesson had caused. "You obviously found a way to defeat him."

He nodded with a proud jut to his chin. "Only because of Jerrick, our first Beast King."

"Did he shift and kick their asses?" I asked with a wicked grin.

"Oh yeah," he said with a proud laugh. "But it's even better than you might think."

"How so?"

"Well, Cyrus's men had been whipping a bunch of shifters who'd upset them, and Jerrick shifted into his bear form and mauled them. The guards came, surrounding him with spears, but just before they could strike their fatal blow, Jerrick shifted into an owl and flew away."

"He did what?" Kale had told me avians shifted into avians, and mammals into mammals. "How is that even possible?"

He shrugged. "There are some theories, but we aren't sure. Jerrick was the first and only one of our kind to transform into an animal outside his species, and he transformed into all four types. Cyrus's men didn't know what to do, and Jerrick's sudden transformation rallied all the shifters. Instead of cowering as slaves, we attacked and defeated Cyrus and all his men. They tried to escape on a raft, but Jerrick followed them into the ocean with other aquatics and capsized their boat. According to our history, the ocean turned red that day."

I had trouble taking all this in. Not only was there so much we didn't know about Kale and his people, but one of his kind had been able to do something that shouldn't be done. He was a mammalian who'd also shifted into an avian, aquatic, and reptilian. All magic, even natural magic, had rules I'd once believed were carved in stone. I couldn't harness white magic any more than a witch could tap into black magic, but Thad proved that false when he commanded the fae's magic in Otherworld to beat the snot out of Ben. Maybe what Thad and Jerrick had done wasn't a fluke. Perhaps in times of great distress, the rules of magic could be bent if the will behind it was strong enough to make it happen.

Could that be what happened to my brothers and to me?

If that was the case, it explained Ben's fascination with and the Conclave's fear of our abilities. A grand magical game was being played, and the Blackmoors were proving to be the wild cards.

I WAS quiet for most of the walk back to the car. I'd been trying to understand everything, to find out why I felt I'd stumbled onto an important puzzle piece.

But then I remembered something Kale said that hadn't registered until now. "You said Cyrus and his men were the 'first visitors.' Have there been others?"

Kale nodded. "Over the years the aquatics have rescued many people who would have drowned in our waters. We bring them and their belongings to Aeaea. It's how we collect weapons, technology, and even books. Like the human's Bible."

"What do you do with them?" I asked. "Do they become slaves?"

Kale stopped walking and glared at me. "What the hell kind of question is that? We don't enslave others, especially since we were created to be slaves for the sorcerers."

I raised my hands and waved them in surrender. "Okay. That was a dumb question."

He crossed his arms and nodded. "I won't argue with you on that."

Despite the scowl, I pushed my luck with another question. "So the humans can't leave once they are on your island?"

The sneer faltered when Kale nodded. "The spell prevents them from leaving, so they live among us. They have their own settlement on the northernmost tip of the island."

Why were humans and shifters allowed to live together when separating humans from the magical community had been the Conclave's goal? "Are they prisoners?"

"Most think they are, but no. They aren't," he said with a firm shake of his head. "They are free to roam the island, and some even serve as teachers in our schools."

Now it made sense how Kale knew the shifter virus only affected his people. They had humans living on the island with them who most likely hadn't been affected. That was why Gerald and the Conclave hadn't shared that tidbit with us.

It was a weakness in the spell.

If this was general knowledge, someone like Ben or Chloe could figure out how to use it to their advantage, unless—

"How many humans are on Aeaea?"

Kale chewed on his lower lip as he considered his answer. "It was only a couple of hundred, but in the past few years, we've encountered many ships in trouble."

"So how many, then?"

"About a thousand."

"And how many shifters?"

"About three times that," he answered.

Fuck. What better way to take over the island than by slowly building a landing party and then letting loose a virus to reduce the number of shifters? I grabbed Kale's hand and pulled him toward the car. "We need to get home, and we need to get to Aeaea. Now."

CHAPTER 8

As I barreled down the highway, I explained my fears to Kale.

"But that doesn't make sense," he said as he mulled things over. "How would the humans even know about Aeaea?"

"Ben or Chloe," I replied. "We know they're working together, but we have no clue how long it's been going on. Everything that Ben has done since Mabon has been well-thought-out. He'd told us in Otherworld that we were always two steps behind him, and dammit, he was right."

"How could he have done all this from his prison?" Kale asked. "You told me the Conclave had him locked up until a few months ago, when he escaped. If what you're saying is true, he'd have to either have gotten out sooner than the Conclave said, or he's working with someone else, someone with so much power that they were able to keep the Conclave in the dark this whole time."

Was there some other unseen player on the board? It certainly made sense, but it was a question I didn't have an answer to. I couldn't focus on that right now. We had to deal with what we did know and hope the rest fell into place along the way. Somehow Ben had his hand in the new human arrivals on Aeaea, and whatever he was up to, he'd been planning it for a long time. Hell, he was over three hundred years old and had spent most of that time locked up and tortured by the Conclave. He had plenty of opportunities to come up with a scheme for revenge. We just had to figure out what this part of his plan was, and stop it before it was too late.

He was already a warlock, shadow weaver, and a vampyre who could cast blood magic, who had three other vampyren under his sway, and who was working with a sorcerer. We couldn't let him add an army of shifters to his arsenal as well.

I dug my phone out of my pocket and called home. A loud succession of beeps blared in my ear. Fuck. That couldn't be good. I tried Dad's cell and got the same annoying sound. The same thing happened when I tried Mason or Thad. What the hell had happened while we were out?

I dialed Adam's number. When he answered on the second ring, I exhaled the breath I'd been holding.

"Well, well," he said on the other end. "You're either drunk and need a ride, or in jail and need bail money."

"Adam, listen to me," I said, my tone short and curt. "I need you to call Edith and get both your families over to Blackmoor Manor."

"Okay," he said. I could practically hear him scratching his head in confusion. "Mind telling me why?"

"Ben's already got people on Aeaea. He knew that by attacking Kale and me at the bar he'd make us think he was trying to find a way to the island, but he wasn't. He was trying to stop us from getting there before he'd set his plan in motion."

It was the only explanation that made sense. With the power Ben and Chloe had at their disposal, they could have just taken Kale if that was what they truly wanted.

"What?" His voice trembled. "How do you know?"

"I'll explain everything later. Just get everyone to my house. Fast. No one's answering at home, and I don't know why." I hung up the phone and threw it onto the console. If my family was hurt or worse, there'd be nothing left of Ben or Chloe when I was done.

"Why don't we just go to Aeaea now?" Kale asked. "I can get us there with the king's spell."

"Because I need to make sure my family's okay. Besides, we can't do this alone," I answered. "We need all the firepower we can get. I have a feeling we're going to be walking into the middle of a war."

"DAD!" I yelled as Kale and I ran into my house. "Where are you?"

Mason emerged from the kitchen, wearing pajama bottoms and a T-shirt. "We're right here," he said. He regarded me as if I needed a straightjacket. "What's the matter with you?"

We darted into the kitchen, where everyone was eating a late-night snack. I let out a huge sigh of relief. I thought for sure Ben and Chloe had gotten here first.

"What the hell's up with your phones?" I asked. "I tried calling."

"The phone never rang," Dad said. He crossed over to the landline and picked it up. "Hm. No dial tone."

"My phone's dead too," Drake added.

After checking their phones, Thad and Mason nodded.

Ben had to be behind the dead phones, but why?

"What's going on?" Dad asked.

When I finished filling them in, my family sprang into action. They raced upstairs to get ready. By the time the Proctors and the Stonewalls arrived, everyone was dressed and ready to kick ass.

"What's the meaning of summoning us here?" Mr. Stonewall asked. A scowl marched across his dark face as I led everyone down the hall to the library.

Edith sighed. "I already told you, Dad. Pierce says Aeaea is under attack."

Mrs. Stonewall eyed me suspiciously. "And just how did you come by this piece of intelligence?"

"I figured it out."

The Stonewalls and the Proctors exchanged glances with each other before glaring at me. They obviously didn't think I could find my way out of a closet.

"Why do you have to be such dicks?" Mason asked.

Thad nodded. "Pierce's reasoning is sound. It would behoove you all to listen."

All eyes were suddenly on me, but I wasn't ready to tell this story again, not until our final guests arrived. "I'll tell you everything when the Conclave gets here."

"I haven't summoned them," my father said. He looked over at Mr. Proctor and Mr. Stonewall, who shook their heads. "You know our protocols, Pierce. First we assess the situation, and if we deem it necessary, we inform the Conclave."

"We don't have time for standard operation procedure," I said. "I already called them."

Mr. Proctor visibly bristled. "What? How?"

"Through me," Kale replied.

"As an emissary of the Beast King, Kale has a direct line to the Conclave," I reminded them, and it was one I used after I called everyone else here.

"This is not how we work," echoed the voice of Gerald Wa all around us. A second later the nine robed members of the Conclave appeared in the middle of our library. He pulled back his hood and fixed his angry gray eyes on me. "I'd hoped after what happened last time, you'd have learned a lesson."

"There's only one way to remedy this," said the Warlock Hag who stood at the end of the line of power assembled before us. She still spoke in that strange metallic voice she'd used earlier. "The Blackmoors must be removed from their station."

The rest of the Conclave nodded in agreement.

"Can we get back to that later?" I asked. We didn't have time for their threats. If they were going to replace us with the Edwells, there was nothing I could do about it. That would be a failure in their leadership. It had nothing to do with my family, my place as the future High Priest, or me. The only thing I could be concerned about now was Kale's people. "Ben and Chloe are already on Aeaea."

Gerald regarded me as if I couldn't spell my name. "How is that possible?"

"You tell me," I said. "You're the ones with the secrets."

"Pierce!" my father warned.

"It's true," I said, addressing the other protector covens. "It's not like we didn't already know they had them. They kept us in the dark about Ben, about the blood magic, about so many things that have put all of our lives in jeopardy, and they've done it again with the shifters."

"What are you talking about?" Mrs. Proctor asked. She glanced from me to Gerald and studied the warring emotions that played across his face. "Is it true? Is there more we don't know?"

Gerald scanned the space in front of them as he magically conversed with his colleagues. "Yes," he finally said with a nod.

"Why continue to do this?" Mr. Proctor asked. "We're on the same side."

"We couldn't risk exposing the weakness of the shifters," he responded. "The potential for disaster was too high if that information got out."

"It already has," I said. "Humans have been able to land on Aeaea for years."

"What?" my father asked.

I glanced at Kale, who nodded. "It's true. It first happened many generations ago, but recently more humans have arrived on our shores."

"What?" Gerald asked. He took several steps forward. "We didn't know this."

"How could you not?" Kale asked. "It's *your* spell."

Gerald glanced over his shoulder and studied the robed and hooded figures behind him. What was he looking for? When he turned around, he was an entirely different wizard. All color had drained from his face, and his hands trembled. "We had no knowledge of this," he said. "We find this news… disturbing."

"Okay, so then who are these humans?" Drake asked.

Even I didn't need to be told the answer to that one. "Witch hunters," I replied. They'd hunted us ever since our species first evolved, but a few years ago, their attacks suddenly stopped. Now we knew why. They were planning an inside job all along.

Gerald reluctantly nodded. "That makes the most logical sense."

"What doesn't make sense is why would Ben be working with the witch hunters?" Aiden asked. "He's magical. They'd want to eliminate him as much as they do us."

"That's simple," Thad replied. "Ben, Chloe, and the witch hunters share a common enemy. Us."

Thad was right. Ben believed the Conclave and the protector covens had wronged him, and wanted revenge. My species was responsible for making sorcerers virtually extinct, and the witch hunters believed we were a blasphemy against their god and nature. If they worked together, they had a better chance of eliminating us before turning on each other.

But something still wasn't adding up.

"Ben couldn't have done all this on his own," I said. "He's powerful, but not that powerful. Someone else is pulling the strings here. Do you know who it is?"

The eight robed figures behind Gerald tensed, and Gerald's eyes once again scanned the floor. "Enough!" he said, turning to the Conclave. "The time for secrets has come to an end."

It was about fucking time!

When Gerald faced us again, he shook his head. "We do not." He glanced at Thad, who smiled and nodded. Had my brother already known? "There's another mysterious force at work here. One that we have been trying to uncover but have not been able to ferret out so far."

Kale gripped my arm, his golden eyes wide in fear. I hadn't wanted him to be right, but he was. We had another enemy we knew nothing about, and whoever he or she was possessed more power than even the Conclave.

"WE DON'T have time for this," Kale mumbled to me as we made our way to the living room. The Conclave had asked us to leave so they could talk in private with our parents. It always pissed me off when they did that.

"I know," I replied, rubbing the small of his back and offering whatever comfort I could. We had to get to Aeaea, but for the first time in my entire life, I was thinking beyond the first step we had to take to the ones that came after.

Before we could go to Aeaea, we needed more answers.

Kale and I joined the others in the library, where silence had gobbled up most of the conversation. Edith and Elliot stood statue still across the room, and even their younger siblings, Kate and Keaton, sat quietly on the couch. They usually chatted nonstop about the stupid teen shows they watched on Nickelodeon, but the information Gerald just shared with us had shocked all the Stonewalls into silence.

Adam huddled with his sisters, Charlotte and Miranda, who were whispering to each other. Instead of paying attention to what they were saying, he kept glancing at me with his eyebrows stitched. That look meant he wanted to talk, but there was someone else I needed to speak with first.

"You knew," I said to Thad, who'd been talking in hushed voices to Aiden.

"We can discuss this later," he said before giving me his back.

It took every ounce of control I had not to zap his ass. I grabbed his shoulder and spun him around. "No. Now." My words came out in a low rumble that reminded me of Dad.

Aiden slapped my hand from Thad's shoulder and stepped between my brother and me, his chest heaving. He'd always had a hair-trigger temper even as a fire fae, but now that he was also a vamp, he went from zero to pissed off in under two seconds flat. He was ready to throw down and protect Thad.

I took a step closer and bumped my chest against his.

"Pierce," Kale said. He stood at my side, his gentle touch and voice soothing the anger that once again stirred within my soul.

At any other point in my life, I would have shrugged out of Kale's touch and went on the offensive. I would have zapped Aiden in the face and then beat my brother until he told me what I wanted to know, but I wasn't angry.

I was terrified.

I'd been living my life screeching at the world like an eagle. It was time to try to be the dove Kale saw in my soul.

"We can't keep having secrets, Thad." My voice was calm and low as I glanced over Aiden's protective shoulder at my brother, who stood behind him.

Thad's icy exterior responded to my soothing tone. He'd clearly been ready to enter a verbal showdown, which would have gotten us nowhere. "You're right." He grabbed Aiden's hand and pulled him to the side. Aiden nodded at Thad's unspoken request, but Aiden kept his eye trained on me in case I lost my temper again. "I have been keeping things from you."

"But why?" Mason asked. He and Drake, along with everyone else in the room, moved closer.

"To protect you," Thad answered.

"Secrets don't protect us." I placed my hands on my brother's shoulders and squeezed them. He might be cold and distant most of the time, but he had a good heart. He loved his family, and he'd do anything to protect us. He'd proven that on more than one occasion over the past few months, but even though his heart was in the right place, it still didn't make it right. "They make us vulnerable. That's what the Conclave has been doing to us. We can't do that to each other."

He nodded and glanced around the room, meeting everyone's gaze. It was his way of apologizing. When he settled his eyes back on me, I nodded in acceptance.

"What don't we know?" I asked.

He cleared his voice and studied the floor. The idea of telling us obviously scared him shitless. He didn't settle down until Aiden rubbed his arms and whispered something in his ear. "A week or so after we returned from Otherworld, Gerald came to see me," he began. "He saw how my trust in the Conclave was shaken after we learned they kept the fact Ebenezer was still alive from us."

"And were the ones who taught him blood magic," Mason added. "Ben almost killed us and the fae with it."

Aiden nodded and snarled in reply. Because of their secrets, he'd been turned into a vampyre and exiled from his kingdom.

"Exactly," Thad replied. "He felt the need to rebuild that trust, and he thought that the only way to do that was for us to share things we both knew that we hadn't yet revealed."

That explained the glances Thad and Gerald had exchanged during Yule. They possessed pieces of the puzzle no one else had. "What did he tell you?" I asked.

"What he just told us. That he believed there was another force out there behind all our troubles. Behind Ben."

So the Conclave knew about this for quite some time? But that didn't explain why Thad was on edge these past few weeks. There was more he'd yet to share. "What else?" I asked.

"Ben didn't escape from his prison," he answered. "He was let out."

A collective gasp spread through the room at Thad's answer, and everyone exchanged worried glances with each other. This was even worse than I'd thought. Either our real enemy was an unknown entity or one of the nine members of the Conclave.

Gerald Wa had left that part out back in the library.

"Are you fucking shitting me?" Mason asked. His faced turned a deep red I'd never seen before. He clenched his fists, and the shadows in the room coiled about him. "They've been busting our asses about keeping secrets, about working against them. They even want to replace us with the Edwells because they think *we're* unstable. *They're* the ones on unsteady ground, not us!"

Mason had a point, and this only confirmed what I already believed. The Conclave distrusted us because of our growing powers, but why?

"This makes no rational sense," Edith said as she stepped forward. She was filtering all the information she'd learned through her logical wizard brain. "The Conclave demands obedience and loyalty, and as a wizard, I see the benefits. Without the structure they provide, our kind would devolve back to our warring tribes. They've given us unity and stability. But these secrets, these hidden agendas, undermine the very foundation upon which our magical community was built. Why continue to behave in a way that fosters distrust while at the same time demanding blind faith?"

Now Edith was thinking like the future High Priest of her coven, and not as one of the mindless soldiers the Conclave preferred us to be.

"They're afraid," Adam answered.

"Of what?" his sister Charlotte asked. She balled her fists and shook her head. She had always been one of the Conclave's staunchest supporters, doing whatever they asked whenever they asked it. It was clearly difficult for her to see them in any other light.

"Of losing control," Adam finally replied.

Thad nodded in agreement. "I think so too. Everything the Conclave has ever done has been about remaining at the top of the magical pyramid. Look at what they did to the fae and the shifters. They removed them from our world when it became obvious they were threats to the Conclave's power."

"That's not fair and you know it," Charlotte said. She wrung her hands as she stared at us. "The witch hunters developed the ability to track magic, which led them to the fae. We were being slaughtered, or did you forget that? *That's* why the fae were sent to Otherworld. And the shifters?" she settled her gaze on Kale before flitting them away. "I'm sorry, but they attacked our kind with the sorcerers."

Kale bristled and stepped forward. If his eyes were talons, Charlotte would be cut to shreds. "We were under Sersie's control."

"I know. But you were a liability, and still are," she said with a firm nod. "The Conclave did what they had to do to protect us, and sent your kind to Aeaea. That was their motive. The way everyone is describing the past is making the Conclave sound like they're our enemy, and I won't stand for it."

"You're right," I said. Charlotte exhaled, clearly relieved. She lost some of her previous bluster. "The Conclave isn't our enemy. They've done a lot for our kind. They've kept us safe, but something has changed. We don't know what it is, but it's our job to find out. We're the protector covens. Our duty above everything else is to the Gate; not even the Conclave comes before that. And this new enemy and the Conclave's secrets could be placing the Gate and all of us at risk."

Everyone nodded in agreement, and as I surveyed the faces around us, I could see the distrust that had started with our family spread across the room. Their faces twisted in anger at the lies we'd continually been told, and even Charlotte, who'd fought the truth to the bitter end, had the first traces of doubt track a path across her delicate features.

Normally I'd be pleased that, for once in their lives, the others had started to question what they'd been told and think on their own, but I couldn't help but recall the words that Warlock Hag had spoken to us after Yule.

The defiance of the Blackmoors spreads like a plague. It must be severed before it reaches the rest.

My gut twisted in a knot, and a second later the lights in the room shut off, plunging us into darkness.

"*LUCEM*."

In response to my spell, six globes of light floated in the air above us, illuminating the living room. I drew closer to Kale and studied the shadows that crouched all around us. This could only mean one thing: Ben was here.

We gathered in a defensive circle, standing shoulder to shoulder and staring out into the darkness around us, waiting for the attack. In the middle of the circle stood Kate and Keaton Stonewall. They had yet to tap into their active powers and needed us to protect them from whatever Ben had planned.

"He's here," Thad said, baring his teeth. Ever since Otherworld, he'd been itching to get his revenge on Ben for trying to seduce him, kill his family, and hurt Aiden.

"I know," I said, shifting my gaze from one fluttering shadow to the next. "Stay close," I whispered to Kale.

"I'm not going anywhere," he answered, gripping my hand tight. "I've got your back."

Even in the middle of danger, he made me smile and tiny wings flap inside my chest.

"We need to get out of here," Edith said from my left. "This room is too small. We have no tactical advantage."

I nodded, but when I glanced over to where the hallway should have been, a black shadowy wall stood in its place. Faint thuds reverberated from the other side. Our parents were clearly trying to break in and get us out. I turned to the windows and found they too had been covered by Ben's shadows. "He's trapped us in here."

"We'll see about that," Adam said. He muttered a spell and waved at the wall blocking the hallway, but nothing happened. I wasn't too surprised. If our parents were having trouble tearing down the barrier, our luck wouldn't be much better.

"Let me try," Mason said. He was a shadow weaver, just like Ben. He laced his fingers together and closed his eyes, concentrating on the shadows around us. Normally they bent to his will and turned into spikes or chains or did whatever he commanded, but against a shadow weaver vampyre that was over three hundred years old, my brother couldn't wrest away control of the shadows. "I can't. He's gotten even stronger."

Great. How the hell did that happen?

A cry of fury exploded to my left. It was Aiden. He abandoned his fae form and turned into the vampyre Ben had created. His jet-black hair grew long and ratted, and his fair skin withered and turned ashen. He snapped his razor-sharp teeth together and slithered his tongue, constantly used to search for blood, out of his mouth.

"Face me, you coward," he screamed into the air. The fire he commanded as a fire fairy blazed within his open palms. Besides a wooden stake through the heart, the fire of the fae could kill a vampyre.

Laughter echoed around us. "If I were that stupid," Ben said. "I wouldn't have gotten to where I am now."

Aiden flew toward the shadow wall and punched it with his flaming fists. The impact of the blows sounded like thunder exploding in the sky. No matter how hard Aiden hit or how much fire he poured into the shadows, the darkness absorbed the flame.

Muscle wasn't going to get us out of this.

"What do you want?" I asked, continually scanning my surroundings.

"I'm surprised you're not the one losing your cool, Pierce," Ben's voice said. "You're usually the dumbass hothead."

Taunting me wasn't going to get him anywhere anymore because I wasn't angry, I was scared, and the only person I needed to keep me centered was Kale. I reached for his hand, and he squeezed it tight. That one gesture filled me with more power than rage ever sparked within me before.

I squared my shoulders and gazed deep into the shadows in front of me as if I were staring right into Ben's cocky grin. "You're here for a reason," I responded. "We all know you don't take a shit unless it suits your needs, so what is it? Why are you here?"

"Why else?" he asked. "We're ready for the avian."

That was a half-truth. If that was all he wanted, he would have snagged Kale while we were alone on the beach. "You're such a fucking liar," I said. "You've got something else planned. Otherwise why let us get together like this?"

Ben snickered. "Because it's more fun taunting you all in a big group," he said. "To show you I'm not scared of you. To let you congregate and see how I can trap you while keeping your parents and the Conclave out. So you can see just how powerful I truly am."

He was still lying. There was some other purpose for this, and he wasn't going to share it.

"Oh, and there was one more thing," he added.

"What's that?" I asked.

"So I could snatch the avian out from under your nose."

Blue arcs of electricity sizzled from my clenched fists as I moved Kale directly behind me. "I'll kill you before you get two feet from him."

Ben's laughter detonated around us like a bomb. "You could always tell a good joke," he said as his amusement trailed off. "You have no idea the forces that are gathered against you, working their way into all that you hold dear. I'm but one cog in a grand machine."

That told me all I needed to know. Bringing us together wasn't a part of Ben's plan. It was the will of whoever he was working for. "We're not as in the dark as you might think we are," I said. "We know you're working with a sorcerer and have witch hunters on Aeaea."

"Such silly children," he said with a chortle. "You only know what I want you to know. Now hand over the avian, and no one will have to die," he said. His voice no longer held an amusing air of superiority. It had turned cold and curt. "Yet."

Kale tried to move around me, but I held him back. "What are you doing?" I asked.

"I can't be the reason you or anyone dies," he said. His big golden eyes pleaded with me to listen. "If I go with him, it might buy you some time to stop him."

"No," I said. "I won't allow it."

"It's not your choice," Kale replied. He regarded me with kind eyes and a set jaw. "It's mine."

Drake grabbed Kale's arm. "Don't do it," he said. Concern and fear thickened his Southern drawl. "It's a trick. He'll just kill you."

"If he doesn't come, I'll kill these two now," a voice said behind us.

We whipped around to find Chloe standing within our circle with Kate and Keaton in her arms. They were unconscious, and she held their necks in a chokehold. Purple energy trailed from her hands, which were pointed directly at the youngest Stonewalls' heads.

We moved into formation, the Stonewalls in the center, and the rest of us on either side. I caught Miranda Proctor's gaze and nodded. Her hands glowed as she activated her warp power and teleported Kate and Keaton out of Chloe's clutches and into the force field Edith had erected around us.

The young Stonewalls lay at our feet, and the rest of us switched on our active powers, ready to defend ourselves or die. "What's your next move?" I asked.

Chloe flipped her hair off her shoulders and shrugged. "Nothing big," she said with a grin. "Just your severed heads on a spike."

Snaking tentacles exploded from the shadows and writhed across the floor toward us. The energy around Chloe's fists pulsed with a vibrant purple as she poured even more power into her hands.

"Stop!" Kale said. He shifted into a dove and flew from my side and out of the protective barrier. Black limbs shot from the corners of the room and wrapped around his small form, dragging him toward the shadows.

"Kale, no!" Without thinking, I lunged out of Edith's force field, and Chloe's energy slammed into me, sending me flying across the room.

Adam unleashed a windstorm that slammed Chloe into the wall while Thad quickly encased her limbs in ice. Darkness pulsed around Mason's hands, and a stream of negative energy flew from his fingertips and exploded in Chloe's face. Aiden, still in his vampyre form, descended upon her. He wrapped his snaking tongue around her neck while he punched her in the stomach with his incredible strength.

I scrambled to my feet and rushed toward Kale as Chloe exploded with purple energy that sent the others tumbling across the room. Although I wanted to help them, I had to get to Kale. He was what they'd come for, which meant he was a vital part of their plan.

A dark hole opened up in the corner of the living room, and the shadowy limbs pulled him toward it. He fluttered against the restraints and pecked at the tentacles, but he might as well have been a mosquito buzzing around a giant.

"Let him go!" I yelled as I fired a lightning blast at the withdrawing limbs. The shadows absorbed my energy without flinching and continued pulling Kale across the room. He was only a few inches from the portal that would take him away from me.

There was no fucking way I was going to let that happen.

I lunged forward, but the wall of shadows to my left turned fluid and crashed over me in a giant black wave.

"You bore me, so you might as well die." Ben's voice echoed around me. "Someone has to go first, right?"

I crawled forward as the darkness climbed up my body like a flash flood. It rushed around my legs and up my back. No matter how hard I kicked, it stuck to me like tar. It surged past my waist and up my back as I clawed across the floor to Kale.

He teetered at the edge of the portal. He'd shifted back to his human form, trying to squirm free of the tentacles that pulled him backward.

"Kale!" I cried out as the darkness washed up my neck and flowed toward my mouth.

He glanced at me. Fear didn't crouch in his golden eyes. Despite what was about to happen, they glowed with unwavering hope. "I'll be waiting."

The shadowed arms pulled him through the portal, and the wave of darkness stole all light from my world.

CHAPTER 9

MUFFLED VOICES whispered all around me, and pain spread across my body like I'd just emerged from a burning building. What the fuck happened to me?

I opened my eyes, but the blinds to my room had been lifted. The sun burst through the window like an excited puppy lapping at my face. I couldn't see a damn thing, and my arms were too heavy to block out the light.

"He's awake," said a man's voice I couldn't recognize.

Had I woken up in a trick's apartment again?

The last thing I remembered was talking with Kale, when—

Fuck. Ben and Chloe had attacked us.

I sat up straight, scrambling off the cushions I'd been lying on. My feet crumbled underneath my weight and I crashed to the floor. My world spun, and the throbbing in my head threatened to go nuclear.

"Where's Kale?" I asked the blurry world around me.

"Ben took him." The low, gravelly voice could only belong to my father. He helped me onto my feet and placed me back on the couch, where I'd awoken.

"We've got to save him," I said, struggling to stand.

"We will," Drake said. He was at my other side, helping my father keep me where I was. Normally I was strong enough to break free of both of them, so why did just thinking about fighting back exhaust me?

"What happened to me?" I asked as my world slowly came into focus. Mason, Thad, and Aiden stood in front of me. Aiden was still in his vampyre form, and it must have been his voice I first heard. He never sounded quite like himself in that form. He parted his withered lips, revealing his full set of razor-sharp teeth. Was that a vampyren version of a smile? Whatever the fuck it was, I'd be good if I never saw it again. It was pretty fucking creepy. Mason gave me a thumbs-up while Thad let out the biggest sigh of relief I'd ever heard in my life.

When no one answered, I asked my question again.

"You almost died, Pierce," Drake replied.

I gaped at him. "Are you fucking around with me?"

"No," my father answered. He kneeled in front of me, his eyes red and swollen. "We almost lost you, and we would have, too, if it hadn't been for Charlotte." He glanced over his shoulder to the far corner, where Charlotte, Adam, and Miranda stood. I hadn't even noticed they were in the room before. "She kept you alive until Ben's power faded and let us in."

Charlotte had dark circles under her eyes and leaned against her brother for support. Her healing powers came from her connection to the element of water, and saving me obviously took everything she had. "Thank you," I said. Because of her I still had a chance to save Kale.

She nodded and smiled in reply.

"What about Kate and Keaton?" I asked, suddenly remembering how Chloe had knocked them out and almost killed them.

Dad nodded to the other room. "They're resting but doing well."

"Thanks to you." I jumped at the sound of Mrs. Stonewall's voice behind me. How many fucking people were in this room I didn't know about? I craned my neck around and saw Edith and her mother standing behind the couch, and I caught a glimpse of something I'd never seen before. Rachel Stonewall was smiling.

"That was quick thinking on your part, having Miranda teleport them to safety," Mrs. Stonewall said. She cupped my face with her hands and kissed my forehead. "I'll never be able to repay you for that."

"No need," I said with a shake of my head. "I was just doing the job we all agreed to do."

She nodded in understanding and then took a deep breath. She wiped the tears from her face and attempted to gain control of the emotions wizards didn't enjoy expressing.

"So what happened after I passed out?" I asked.

"You mean after Chloe handed us our asses?" Mason asked.

Yeah, we were definitely going to have to do something about that.

"Chloe vanished shortly after Kale disappeared in the portal," Thad replied. "About fifteen minutes later, the shadow walls fell and our parents came through."

"So you weren't able to break through on your own?" I asked my father.

He shook his head. "And neither could the Conclave."

I buried my face in my hands. Things were getting worse. Ben's magic had somehow surpassed the most powerful of us all. To make matters worse, the butt wipe had Kale. "We have to get to Aeaea," I said, surveying the room. "We've lost too much time already."

"We agree."

The Conclave blinked into the living room and stood before the couch where I sat. Gerald Wa pulled back his hood and stepped out of the line. "I'm pleased you're doing better."

"You and me both," I said, rising to my feet. The world spun briefly around me, but I clutched on to my dad's shoulder for support. "Now tell us how the hell Ben was able to keep you out, or is that a secret you're guarding for our protection?"

Gerald's gray eyes turned to slits, but before he could respond, the Warlock Hag stepped forward.

I winced, waiting for her to reach out with her power and finish what Ben had started. I was surprised when instead she spoke in her strange altered voice. "We can continue fighting each other, or we can cease this needless hostility and do what needs to be done."

I stared deep into the shadows of her hood. I didn't recognize her voice, but the anger and disappointment mixed in her tone seemed familiar, something I'd heard for most of my life. But I had to be imagining it. There was no way that woman was—

"She's right," Gerald said. "We have a plan."

It was about damn time.

AFTER THE Conclave shared their plan with us, I pulled my brothers as well as Edith, Elliot, and Adam into a corner where we could have a private conversation.

"Their plan sucks balls," I said.

Edith sighed and slowly nodded her head. "I wouldn't put it in those words, but I agree. Splitting up our forces isn't the wisest move, especially considering our lack of knowledge of the terrain and the enemies that await us." For only being eighteen, Edith talked more like a grown-up than I did. I must sound like a doofus to her.

"So what do we do, then?" Mason asked. "Tell them to shove their plan up their robed butts and come up with something else?" On the other hand, next to Mason I came off like a genius.

"That's not the most helpful solution," Adam said with an arch of his eyebrow.

Mason flipped him off with a smile.

"Can we focus, please?" Thad asked. He was right. We didn't have time for a circle jerk. I had to get to Kale before Ben hurt him.

Mason made a show of standing at attention while Edith let loose a sigh of frustration. I felt her pain, but she didn't have to live with him. I did.

So what's the plan, then? Elliot asked in our heads. It made everyone but Edith wince. She was used to speaking to her brother telepathically. I wasn't, and I sure as hell wasn't looking forward to the migraine I'd get later. *Sorry,* he said before switching his gaze between Thad and Edith. They were the brainiacs, so it made sense that he turned to them. The only problem with that was he didn't need to.

"I already have one," I whispered.

They couldn't have been any more shocked if I had fired a thousand volts of electricity into them.

"Are you feeling okay?" Mason asked. "I don't think you've recovered yet from your near-death experience."

I uttered a warning growl that shut my little brother's mouth. "Listen, the Conclave thinks their cloaking spell is going to hide our presence on Aeaea. We know that's not going to work."

Thad and Edith nodded. Ben had already proven he could block the Conclave's power. If he could erect a blind spot around Havenbridge like he'd done during Mabon and keep them from breaking down his walls when he'd had us trapped in the living room, he'd have no trouble detecting a cloaking spell.

"I think we all know what's going to happen when we show up, right?" I asked.

"Yes, we do," Adam replied.

"So what do we do about it?" Mason asked.

"After we learned Chloe was a sorcerer, I did some research on them." I grabbed Thad's lower jaw and shut it. "And here's what I think we should do."

I explained my idea. When I was done, they stared at me in silence.

Well, shit. I'd come up with a perfect strategy for dealing with that sorcerer bitch, or so I thought. Maybe I was just the dumbass jock everyone thought I was. "What's wrong with it?" I asked.

"Absolutely nothing," Thad replied with a pat to my back. "It's pretty genius, actually."

"Really?" I asked, surveying the group.

Though their wide eyes communicated their shock, they nodded their heads.

"You're getting good at this," Edith said.

"Yes, he is," Thad replied. He grabbed my shoulders and locked eyes with me. "I was wrong, Pierce. You're going to be a great High Priest."

Those words were like a sledgehammer to the wall of fear I'd been living behind. "Thanks, bro."

"You two can make out later," Mason said, flinching at our sudden outpouring of emotion. "So you have a plan for Chloe, but what about Ben?"

A wicked grin sliced across my lips. "For Ben, I have something even juicier."

FINALLY WE were ready to leave for Aeaea, where I'd be one step closer to holding Kale in my arms again.

"So how are we going to do this?" Mason asked. Even though he wasn't thrilled Drake was joining us on another mission, he understood his boyfriend's magical immunity might be as helpful to us on shifter island as it had been in Otherworld.

"We will open the portal to Aeaea and cast a cloaking spell that will hide your presence," Gerald replied as he and the Conclave stood before us.

Why did they continue to underestimate Ben or overestimate themselves?

"Once you arrive, Oliver will assess the situation. You will then proceed with the plan as we have already outlined," Gerald said as he studied each of our gazes.

Everyone nodded, but when his gray eyes landed on me, he hesitated. A slight grin hitched up the left corner of his mouth. Why did I get the feeling he knew exactly what we were up to, and approved?

"As you know," Gerald continued. "We cannot send the entirety of the protector covens to Aeaea. Some must stay behind to protect the Gate. We have also placed the Edwells on standby. Just in case."

I didn't like it, but I understood it. The Gate was our first priority. While Adam, Edith, Elliot, my family, and I were going to Aeaea, the Gate needed to be protected, even if it was by the Edwells. It was a good thing the rest of the Stonewalls and Proctors were staying back. They would be able to keep an eye on those sneaky bastards.

The plan wasn't ideal, but it was certainly a better show of force than when only my brothers and I were sent to Otherworld with Drake and Aiden. I wasn't sure what made this mission different, but something had changed in our leaders. I couldn't tell if it was fear of the unknown, anger at the havoc Ben was causing across the magical community, or the need to set right the wrongs they had helped set into motion.

Whatever it was, it made me feel better that perhaps our enemy wasn't one of them. Only time would tell if I was right.

"We should make haste," Gerald said.

I couldn't agree more, but before we left, blessings had to be bestowed for a safe return. The Proctors and the Stonewalls gathered around their children while my father took his family aside. "I'm not going to blow smoke up your asses," he said. "This is going to be a bitch of a fight. We have no idea what we're going to find in Aeaea, and we all know Ben's got something up his sleeve. We've got to save Kale and the shifters and put that bastard down."

"Damn straight," Mason said with a nod.

Aiden, who'd thankfully resumed his fae form, nodded his head. He was ready for some payback. "It would be my honor to rip open his throat."

Thad caressed the back of his neck. "I'll hold him down for you," he said.

Drake swallowed hard and nodded. He was nervous, and I couldn't blame him. While he might be immune to magic, he was vulnerable to the claws and teeth of the shifters. He held tightly on to the straps of the backpack around his shoulders. Inside it were some athames that might help him with the shifters, and wooden stakes for any vampyren we might stumble across. Even though none had shown their ugly pasty asses so far, that didn't mean they wouldn't. If they did, how would Drake react to facing his Aunt Millie again?

"Don't worry," I said, draping my arm across his shoulders. "We're family. We've got each other's backs."

Drake smiled, hauling his arm around me and then Mason.

"That's right," Mason said, mimicking the gesture. "We're all family now."

Before long we stood in a circle with our arms around each other, and I surveyed the faces of my growing family. Fear crawled up my spine, and it took several deep breaths to squelch the rising anger. I couldn't lose any of them. We weren't perfect, and we weren't all related by blood, but I loved them all the same.

It had been too long since I admitted that to myself or said it out loud, especially since Mom died. My life had been about power and competition, about proving who was the strongest of us all. About being angry because I was so fucking scared.

But none of that mattered. Together we were more formidable.

There was power in the bond that united us, and it was an emotion I had to learn to embrace.

I'd never have realized that if it weren't for the dove who filled my soul most of all.

"I love you guys. I just want you to know that."

Mason studied me as if I were a stranger. "Who is this warlock, and what have you done with my brother?"

A devilish smirk curled Thad's upper lip. "The next thing you know, he's going to be anointing himself with patchouli and dancing naked in the woods with the Proctors."

Drake and Aiden snorted in response while my father hid his grin behind the back of his palm.

I should've known better than to say that to these jerks. "I changed my mind. I hate all of you."

"No, you don't. You love us!" Mason sang while batting his eyelashes at me.

"Keep that up, and I'm gonna rip your ear off and stick it up your butt so you can hear me kicking your ass."

Mason beamed. "Now *there's* my big brother. Welcome back, dick breath."

I growled, but there was no anger behind it. This was how my family said they loved me too.

"It's time."

Gerald's words broke up our family huddle, and we returned to where Adam, Elliot, and Edith stood waiting. We grasped each other's hands and nodded to the Conclave.

"Blessed be your journey," Gerald said. He glanced over his shoulder at his colleagues who nodded in unison.

Without a spell or a gesture, a bright light flashed around us. When it faded we no longer stood in the library in my house. We'd finally arrived on Aeaea.

IT WAS midmorning just a second ago, but we arrived under the canopy of an early evening sky. Millions of stars already twinkled overhead, and a faint orange glow backlit the forest to the right of the clearing where we'd landed. It cast an eerie shadow on the mountain that towered behind the trees.

"What's that glow?" Thad asked, surveying our surroundings for a threat.

Mason ventured a guess. "The setting sun?"

"No," Edith replied. "Something's burning."

I clenched my jaw. "That's where Aria must be." It was the town where the shifters who worked for the king lived. Before we left I shared the information Kale gave me on Aeaea. "And that must be Mount Oronos." I nodded toward the mountain. "The Beast King's den is carved into its side, and I bet that's where we'll find Ben." But more importantly, Kale.

"Then that's where we must go. But we're going to do this as planned." Dad locked eyes with me and waited for me to respond.

Although we all nodded in agreement, that wasn't what we were going to do. I just hoped when Dad found out, he wouldn't be too pissed.

"Pierce?" he asked, studying me intently.

"Yeah."

"You have a terrible poker face," he said. "What are you planning?"

"Oh, please. Do tell," a woman's voice said from behind us. Chloe was right on time.

We spun around to find her standing behind us in the clearing. She'd traded in her barfly outfit for one made of black leather. She reminded me of Catwoman. All she was missing was her whip. She sneered at us as purple energy pulsed around her clenched fists. "I hate it when I'm not included."

A *chunk* preceded my father turning his body to stone, and Aiden shifted into his vampyre form. Seeing him that way freaked the crap out of me, but I was glad to have Aiden on our side. Everyone else clicked on their active powers. I gestured for them to stop.

She had the ability to cancel out our abilities. We had to wait until the right moment to strike.

We're linked, Elliot's voice said inside my head. During Samhain, Elliot was able to connect our minds together with his telepathy. This gave us a secure channel to communicate.

Although everyone winced, only Dad was startled by Elliot's voice. Mason and Thad had already let their boyfriends in on the plan. Dad was kept in the dark because he was in constant communication with the Conclave before we left.

What the hell is going on? he asked.

Don't worry, Dad, Mason said. *We've got you covered.*

This isn't the plan, he said.

Quiet, I said. *I need to concentrate.*

I blinked on my aura vision, and the darkness around me exploded with color. Various human and animal forms waited in the shadows. As we had feared, Chloe had already used her sorcery to gain control over the shifters. Did that go for Kale too?

We're surrounded by shifters and witch hunters, I told the group. *I count at least a few dozen.*

They knew we were coming and where we'd show up? Dad asked. *But how?*

I glanced over at him and offered him a thin smile. He knew the truth. He just couldn't accept it.

The Conclave? he asked. His voice trembled.

Probably not all of them, Mr. Blackmoor, Adam said. *But at least one.*

I had my money on that Warlock Hag.

"Is there a reason you're just standing there with mouths gaping like inbred hillbillies?" she asked. "I didn't know all of you were from Texas."

"Fuck you!" Drake said.

Mason placed a reassuring hand on his shoulder. *She's trying to goad you. Don't fall for it.*

I'm not afraid of her, Drake replied. *She can cancel out your powers, but I reckon I can do the same to her.*

That's what we're hoping for too, I added. *You're our last resort.*

Chloe stepped forward. "What are you up to?" she asked. Purple energy trailed behind her as she amped up her powers.

Do you see it? Thad asked.

I nodded. The same brown energy remained trapped inside the pulsing red aura that made up her outer form. My gut told me that was her weak spot.

"We're just waiting," I replied.

"For what?" she asked, surveying the clearing.

Everyone ready?

Yes, everyone except my father said in unison.

For what? he asked.

Just follow our lead, Thad said.

"For this."

A dark umbra glowed around Mason's hands. He reached out with his shadow powers and the darkness that surrounded us came to life in snaking tentacles. The inky limbs grasped the unsuspecting shifters and witch hunters that lay in wait, and their angry screams echoed around us.

"What?" Chloe asked, glancing around her. A scowl marched across her face as the pulsing energy in her hands began to glow in her eyes. "You knew?"

I shrugged. "Lucky guess."

She's getting ready to fire, Elliot warned. He was not only able to read our thoughts but Chloe's as well.

Edith threw up her force field just as Chloe's purple energy struck the barrier.

"It won't hold for long," Edith said. Her muscles strained as she fought to hold up the dome that kept us momentarily safe from the magic Chloe expended. While she was powerful and tapped into a different and wilder magic than we did, her access to it was limited.

She would need time to recharge.

When the energy dissipated, we advanced. "Do it now!" I yelled as we broke free of Edith's barrier. Just as we had discussed, Edith cut off her larger force field and projected smaller ones around the rest of us as we charged toward Chloe.

She screamed in our heads from the strain it took to maintain multiple force fields. It wouldn't last long, but with her shields and with Mason keeping the rest of the players off the field, it gave us the chance to do what needed to be done.

Chloe fired multiple shots at us that bounced off Edith's barriers.

Thad unleashed a blizzard, sending wind and ice barreling at her. Though it blinded her, the white veil parted for us under Thad's direction. In his stone form, my father thudded to her and punched her hard and high. She flew up about ten feet where Aiden caught her and slammed her with all his might back onto the ground.

It was important we kept her off balance and unable to focus. If she had time to cancel our powers, we were toast.

She struggled to her feet, but Adam whipped up a wind that sent her tumbling backward across the field.

Everyone had done their part. It was my turn.

I focused solely on the brown aura, the one that represented her fear of letting go, and let loose a thunderous barrage of lightning straight at her center. The aura writhed and fought back, and an orange light flickered amid the brown. The new color meant confidence and power.

That was unexpected.

Pierce, Elliot said in our heads. *Something's happening.*

Can you be more specific? I asked as I poured more power into her. I had to put her down fast, or I'd never make it to Kale.

The ground underneath Chloe froze courtesy of Thad, who began to encase her in ice.

I hear two minds, Elliot replied.

That explained why I saw two auras. Chloe wasn't just one person. She was two. But who was the second one inside her?

The outer red aura that surrounded Chloe completely devoured the brown energy within. Purple-and-orange magic exploded from her body, knocking all of us off our feet.

She laughed as she levitated off the ground and rose into the night sky. "Thank you for that, Pierce," she said, a genuine smile plastered across her face. "I'd been uncertain how I would finally devour Chloe's soul, but the amount of power you poured into me—well, her—weakened her. It allowed me to do what I've been failing to do all these centuries, truly return to the land that should rightfully be mine."

"Who the fuck are you?" I asked.

"Silly, warlock. I'm the one who started all this," she said with a wave of her hand. "If that's still too difficult for you to figure out, you can call me Sersie."

Holy shit! We were in for it now.

SERSIE WAS the one who started the Sorcerer War and created the shifters. Why wasn't she dead, and how the hell were we supposed to fight someone whose magic had grown over the last two millennia? She certainly hadn't broken a sweat when she had us trapped in a mass of purple-and-orange energy. Every few seconds a jolt of power traveled through the field that caused us to scream in pain. It made it hard to think, much less summon my magic, and the telepathic link Elliot established was severed.

Dozens of shifters circled around us. There were wolves, lions, tigers, alligators, snakes, and a whole slew of other mammalians and reptilians. What I didn't see were any avians or aquatics. While it made sense that the ocean-dwelling shifters wouldn't be able to move around on land in their animal form, why were the avians not here?

Along with the shifters were the human witch hunters. They were dressed in clothing similar to the tunic and homemade pants Kale first wore when I met him, but they had guns trained on us and they watched us carefully. Their fingers clearly itched to pull their triggers.

"Your plan didn't quite work out the way you thought it would, did it?" Sersie asked. She hovered above us and laughed.

"We're not dead yet," I said as another surge of energy pulsed through us. I gritted my teeth, refusing to give her the satisfaction of screaming.

"That's the word of the day," she said with a grin. "Yet."

"Then why not do it already?" Mason asked. He glanced at Drake, who had the same grimace on his face Mason had from the sizzling energy that threatened to fry us. Was he faking it like he'd done in Otherworld, or was he not immune to Sersie's magic?

"Oh, you know," she said with a shrug. "Plans must be followed." With a wave of her hand, Mason, Thad, and I flew out of the energy trap and dangled before her. I tried to activate my powers and so did my brothers, but nothing happened.

"What the fuck?" Mason asked.

"Did you forget I can cancel out your magic?" she asked with a grimace. "Stupid boy."

"Let them go!" my father yelled from below. He strained against the magical field that held them, and with every movement, he set off crackling sparks of energy that shot through the field and almost killed the others.

They all writhed in pain, but Drake's thrashing seemed more rehearsed than anyone else's. In fact, he slowly inched his way toward the end of Sersie's magical barrier. He *was* immune to her magic. I caught Mason and Thad's eyes, and they nodded. They'd noticed it too.

"Dad, stop!" I said.

He gritted his teeth and locked eyes with Sersie. "I'll kill you if you hurt them."

Sersie laughed and the shifters around her howled, roared, and hissed. The witch hunters remained quiet, observing. "You boys are putting on quite a show."

"How are you even here?" Thad asked. "The first Conclave killed you."

If I could kiss him right now, I would. Keeping Sersie focused on us would give Drake the time he needed to get free. The faster we kicked her ass, the sooner I could get to Kale.

"It's really quite an interesting story," she said. Her eyes brightened with delight. Like most psychopaths, Sersie enjoyed talking about herself. "Before the Conclave destroyed my body, I cast the ultimate transmutation spell. You know, like the one I uttered that created my shifter army." She clasped her hands together and cast her wide-eyed gaze down at the shifters who stared up at her. "Except I cast it upon my soul and turned myself into a wraith."

We had experience with wraiths. A few years ago, one of those spirits terrorized Havenbridge by possessing the souls of others. It was responsible for a series of murders the local police force could do nothing to stop. It was difficult to catch a killer who hopped from body to body. Thankfully the protector covens had been able to send it into the Gate.

"So you've been possessing the bodies of sorcerers like Chloe all these years?" I asked.

"Of course," she said with a midair twirl. "Their bodies don't last long, which is a pity, so I'm always on the lookout for a new body to take over. It's a real bitch too. They don't like being trapped inside themselves. They fight and complain, but what can they do?" she asked with a shrug. "But now I don't have to worry about that anymore, do I? This body is now one hundred percent mine. Thanks to you, Pierce."

"You're not welcome," I replied.

She grinned and took a deep breath. "You don't know how wonderful it is to actually smell the Earth again with my own lungs. It's the small things you miss in life, like the pollen on the air, a crisp summer breeze, or the blood of your enemies spilled upon the ground before you."

"Is that a threat?" Thad asked.

She clicked her tongue. "No. A promise."

"You're such a fucking liar," I said.

She zipped over to me, purple-and-orange energy glowing from her eyes. "You don't think I'll kill you?" she asked. "Because I *so* will."

I shook my head. "You can't. You need us, or else why trap us or pull my brothers and me out here with you? We're part of the plan, and I'm guessing you need us alive for that."

She shook off her anger as if it were a bad dream and grinned broadly at me. This bitch was crazy. "You're right," she said. She then gazed down at my father and the others still held in her power. She jutted out her lower lip in pretend sadness. "But that's not true for them."

"How about for me?" Drake asked, stepping out of the energy field. The shifters who'd been focusing their adoration on Sersie slowly closed in on him while the witch hunters lowered their weapons and glanced around at each other in shock.

"No," she said. "How is this possible?" She unleashed a stream of purple-and-orange energy at Drake, who closed his eyes and stood his ground.

He was either the smartest or stupidest guy I knew.

"Drake, move!" Mason yelled, but Sersie's power passed straight through Drake and struck the energy field she'd been using to keep the others trapped. The magical prison shimmered before disappearing entirely.

Sersie had canceled out her own spell.

"GET THEM, goddammit!" Sersie screeched.

The shifters lunged, but Edith threw up her force field. They bounced off the energy in pained mewls and growls. My father turned to stone and charged in. Their claws and teeth held no power over his rock armor. He kicked and punched them away, preventing as many as possible from reaching Drake.

He stood beyond Edith's protective barrier as if daring Sersie to attack him again. She dove toward him, but Aiden crashed into her. His talons sliced through her skin and he squeezed his tongue around her neck.

My brothers and I were still held in whatever invisible energy Sersie snagged us with. No matter how much we struggled, we couldn't break free.

As I glanced around at the battlefield, I noticed for the first time the witch hunters hadn't joined the battle, nor were they watching it. Their eyes were trained on Drake.

"Elliot!" I screamed.

What? he asked. *I'm a little busy relaying everyone's thoughts to the people who are actually fighting.*

The witch hunters, I said. *They're just standing there staring at Drake. Why?*

Elliot went silent. A few minutes later, he spoke in my head again. *I can't read their thoughts.*

What? Why?

How the hell would I know?

This wasn't good.

"Drake, watch out!" Mason screamed from my right.

A wolf had circled around the battle, where my father, Adam, and Edith fought off the advancing shifters. Drake readied his drawn athame for the attack, but the shifter was too fast. It pounced on him, sending the weapon out of his hands. It snarled before opening its mouth and preparing to go for the jugular.

A shot rang out, and the wolf whimpered before falling over dead.

One of the witch hunters, a man with sandy-blond hair, had saved Drake.

"It's because he's human," I mumbled. "They'll protect him." We could use that to our advantage.

Adam, I said, using the telepathic link Elliot struggled to keep going. *Drop Drake away from the battle.*

What? Adam asked.

Are you fucking crazy? Mason screamed. *They'll kill him.*

No, they won't, Thad replied. *It's genius.*

I'm ready, Drake replied as he rose from the ground.

Drake, no! Mason pleaded.

We don't have time to debate, I screamed through the link. *Do it!*

With a slight gesture, Adam created an updraft around Drake. He lifted off the ground and floated thirty yards away from where my dad, Adam, and Edith fought. Sensing easier prey, the majority of the shifters ran after Drake.

"Come and get me," Drake said before he took off in a sprint, using the speed and agility he'd gained from years of free running to put distance between him and his pursuers.

"Fire!" shouted the blond witch hunter, and gunfire exploded all around us. One by one the shifters fell over until there were no more remaining.

"What the hell are you doing?" Sersie asked as she reentered the battlefield, surveying the dead bodies of her shifter army. She had Aiden's long tongue wrapped around her fist and dragged his unconscious body behind her.

"Aiden!" Thad yelled, struggling against the power that still contained my brothers and me.

My father thudded over to Sersie with Adam, Elliot, and Edith trailing behind him.

"Oh for crying out loud," she muttered. She flicked her wrist and a wave of purple-and-orange magic crashed into them. They flew off their feet, where they landed in a lifeless heap.

Sersie turned back to the witch hunters who gathered before her. "Hopkins, would you mind explaining just *why* you killed my babies?"

The sandy-haired man squeezed the grip of his pistol and nodded toward where Drake had escaped. "That one was human," he answered in a gruff voice. His narrowed blue eyes told me he didn't like Sersie, and if they weren't working together, he'd shoot her point-blank. "Your 'babies' were going to kill him. We won't allow innocent humans to be caught in the crossfire."

She sighed and let go of Aiden's tongue, causing his limp body to fall to the ground. "Innocent?" she asked, jerking her head up to where we floated. "He's sleeping with the enemy."

Hopkins cringed. "It doesn't matter. He's human. End of discussion."

"Well, all right then," she said. She spun on her heels and walked away a few feet before stopping and turning around. "Just one more thing."

"What's that?" Hopkins asked.

"No one hurts my babies." Purple-and-orange energy exploded from her body, striking the ground where the witch hunters stood. The earth erupted around them, sending them flying twenty feet in the air. When they landed in the huge crater her magic created, none of the witch hunters moved.

Sersie wiped her hands and grinned at the devastation.

"You're sick," I told her.

She barked in laughter before suddenly cutting it off and firing her magic at us. The last thing I heard before I fell unconscious was Sersie's snickering.

CHAPTER 10

MY HEAD hurt like a bitch, and my wrists screamed in pain. What the hell had Sersie done to me now?

When I opened my eyes, I found myself dangling a few hundred feet off the ground, bound to the face of Mount Oronos by shadowy chains wrapped around my wrists and ankles. My brothers and father were on my right and the rest of the group hung to my left. They were all still unconscious.

Below us, a fire raged. It consumed the huts of a small village and the forest that surrounded it. That had to be Aria, where Kale lived. In the distance, other pockets of glowing orange illuminated the night sky.

Aeaea was being burned to the ground.

"It's about time," Ben's cocky voice said. "I thought we'd have to get started without you."

Dressed in a tight-fitting black tee and jeans, Ben stood on a rocky shelf carpeted by shadows that jutted about twenty feet from the side of the mountain. If I could somehow get free, I'd fall right on top of his smug face. "Well, I'm awake," I said, tugging on my restraints. "How about you let me loose so we can get this party started?"

Ben snorted, his brown eyes wide with amusement. "You still have a sense of humor. I respect that."

"I find it annoying."

Sersie levitated in front of me. Her dark hair whipped around her from the steady breeze that blew off the ocean. Several birds of prey hovered behind her and squawked at me. Their steady golden eyes told me they were ready to rip my face to shreds if Sersie would only give the command.

I'd hoped the avians had somehow escaped her control since none of them were with her when we first arrived. I was clearly wrong.

If Sersie had cast her whammy on them, what had she done to Kale?

"Not as annoying as you are, you hag."

I glanced to my right to find Mason glaring at Sersie. My brothers and father had woken up, and so had everyone else. They all struggled to get free.

Ben waved his hand and our shadowy restraints grew taut, pressing us flat against the rock face. I couldn't move my head, much less my hands, and even if I could, the purplish glow around Sersie's fists told me she was still using her magic to nullify ours.

It was time to switch tactics. "Is this your plan?" I asked Ben while nodding at Sersie. "To let Sersie get her claws back into the shifters so you can control her and her army?"

She zipped over to me and slapped my face. "No one controls me," she railed, raining spit onto my face. She balled her fist into my shirt and purple-and-orange energy crackled in her palm. The avians around her screeched and moved in closer.

The shadows that draped across the side of the mountain came to life and turned to hands. They caressed Sersie's face and forced her to turn to where Ben stood below us. "Don't lose your temper, my love," he said.

He had to be fucking kidding. Ben and Sersie were lovers?

Sersie sighed and nodded at Ben before turning her steely gaze to us. "You're lucky we're not done with you yet," she said with a snarl that turned into a big grin. Her mood swings made me dizzy. "We've got a surprise or two in store for you."

"You mean there's something more surprising than the fact that Ben's slipping it to you?" I asked.

She cocked a suggestive eyebrow at me. "Jealous?"

"Hardly," I said with a snort. "I may not have many standards, but I draw the line at psychopathic murderers."

My brothers laughed, which only fueled Sersie's fire. Another sting bit into my cheek as she slapped me.

"Don't let him get to you," Ben said with a dismissive wave at me. "Pierce Blackmoor has never understood matters of the heart."

Who the fuck was he kidding? Whatever he had going on with Sersie had nothing to do with the heart. It was about hate and revenge. That was about as far away from the heart as someone could get. His interest in her was all about furthering his plans, but judging from the smile on her face when she looked at Ben, the only one who didn't know that was Sersie.

"Really?" Thad asked. "You're going to tell us you two are in love?"

"So what if we are?" he asked. He crossed his arms and grinned up at us. "You had your chance. Are you regretting your choice now?"

"I'll rip open your throat," Aiden cried out as he morphed into his vampyre form and thrashed against his restraints. His vampyren abilities should have been enough to break free, but Ben's growing magic held him fast.

A haughty grin sliced across Ben's expression. "Good luck with that."

"You know he doesn't love you, right?" Mason asked Sersie.

She floated down to Ben and stood at his side. "I know I'm here because of him. He found me, stuck in the body of a dying sorcerer. Thanks to you and your damned Conclave who'd practically made us extinct, I couldn't find another body to inhabit." She gazed at Ben. Her lips parted as she reached out to touch his face. "He promised me a new host and took me to Chloe. He made me strong, and he brought me here," she said with a gesture out to Aeaea. "He's the reason I've got my shifters back. He's given me everything he promised. If that's not love, I don't know what is."

"You're right," I said with a nod. "You have no idea what it is."

Ben laughed so hard he doubled over. "And you do?" he asked in between fits. "The man whose cock has seen more action than a hustler trolling the docks for sailors on shore leave?"

He was right. I had no more idea of what love was than he did. How could I? I'd fucked my way through life and never gave anyone a chance to get to know me beyond how I looked naked and how hard I could make them come. That had been all that was important to me.

At least until I met Kale.

I could have had my way with him when we first met in the woods, or in the two days he spent at my house, or when we were in my dad's car. Hell, the old me would have made sure it happened. I would've hit it and quit it, but those innocent golden eyes and that big dimpled smile made what my body wanted not as important as what my soul longed for.

While I might not know what love really was, I knew what it was not.

"You know, throwing red herrings never works," I said. I wasn't quite sure what that meant, but Thad had said that to me often enough that I think I used it right. My brother's smile told me I had. "We're not talking about me. We're talking about you."

The chains that held me to the mountain grew slack and lengthened, lowering me until I was eye level with Ben. He flashed me his crooked Zachary Quinto smile as I dangled only a few feet from the shelf where he stood.

"Don't piss me off," Ben warned.

"Or what?" I asked. "You're not going to kill me. Or us."

His bushy eyebrows arched across his forehead as spikes sprouted from my chains, inching closer to my head. "Are you sure about that?"

I glanced at the approaching pointed edges and then locked gazes with Ben. "One hundred percent," I said with a firm nod.

Sersie stood behind Ben and nuzzled into his neck. "While I'd love to see you skewer this asshole, remember what you were told by Ica—"

"Shut your fucking mouth!" Ben wheeled around in her embrace and grabbed her by the throat. His ruggedly handsome face grew ashen, and razor-sharp teeth filled his mouth as he morphed into his vampyre form. He stood seven feet tall, with long black hair and withered skin, and he dug his talons into Sersie's flesh, lifting her off the ground.

The avians that had perched on the rocks around us flapped into the air and dove at him. Loud hisses exploded all around me as the three vampyren who attacked us in Otherworld leaped from the shadows and descended upon Sersie's feathered saviors.

Their talons easily ripped through the shifters in an explosion of feathers and blood.

She gasped for air, and her wide eyes drew into slits.

"You know my one rule," Ben snarled at her. His tongue rattled like a pissed-off snake. "Don't say the name."

Ica or whatever the hell this person's name was had to be the one calling the shots, and Ben protected his or her identity with a savagery I'd never seen from him before.

When Sersie nodded, Ben released his hold on her, and she fell to the ground.

She rubbed her throat while wheezing and coughing. When she surveyed the shifters that had been torn apart by Ben's vampyren buddies, anger smoldered deep in the pools of her violet eyes.

I glanced up at the others, and they nodded in agreement. This was just what we needed.

WHILE BEN and Sersie kissed and made up, I surveyed the rocky area where they stood. It appeared to be more of a platform than a shelf. It certainly wasn't natural. It had been carved away into the side of the mountain.

Intricate designs I couldn't make out were etched onto the lip, and the walls and the floor were smoothed into a slick, glossy surface. I turned my head as far as I could to determine what the area behind me looked like, but the shifting shadows caused by the raging inferno below made it difficult to see.

The only thing I could make out was a chair sculpted from stone and what looked like a furry rug sprawled out before it.

This had to be the entrance to the Den of the Beast King. If that was true, where was he, and where the hell was Kale?

"Is this what you're looking for?"

I snapped around. Ben and Sersie stood before an altar made entirely from shadows, and their vampyren bodyguards flanked them. On top of the altar rested Kale. He was naked and trembling, but when he saw me, his quivering lips broadened into a smile. "Pierce."

My soul sighed when I glimpsed his dimpled cheeks. "Kale!" I lunged forward, but Ben's shadows held me back.

Fear and relief reflected in Kale's golden eyes while he struggled to get free, but the shadows that made up the altar stuck to him like glue. It kept him from doing little more than thrashing.

"I told you," Sersie said with a grin. She sauntered over to me and ran her index finger down my chest. When she reached the waistband of my jeans, she bit her lip and grinned before grabbing my crotch. "The warlock's got a thing for my dove."

"He's not your dove," I spat.

"And he's not yours either," Ben added. He moved behind the altar. A wicked grin cut a diagonal path across his features as he ran his hands over Kale's naked flesh. Kale whimpered, and he shuddered away from Ben's touch as he fluttered his fingertips across Kale's chest before sliding down his smooth stomach.

"Don't touch me, you perverted freak!"

Kale's protests only urged Ben on. He traveled farther south, moaning in ecstasy and licking his lips as he danced his fingers around the light brushing of dark hair that nested around Kale's groin.

Of all the terrible things Ben had done so far, he'd just fallen to a new low. "Stop that," I said through gritted teeth. Tendrils of electricity sparked off me.

"You stop that," Sersie said. She gestured toward me and my powers shut off. Except this time the magic didn't completely snuff out within me. It flickered.

"He's using you," I said to Sersie. "When he's done with you, he'll kill you."

"You're confusing me with you," she said with a titter.

"Am I?" I asked. "You've seen how he treats your shifters, the beings you helped create. They're your children. Look at what he's doing. See him for what he is." Sersie's gaze drifted over to Ben, who arched an eyebrow at us as he continued to rub his hands up and down Kale's bare flesh. He was putting on a show for me, but the cocky grin told me he was testing Sersie too, seeing how deep her loyalty to him ran. "He doesn't give a flying fuck about them. He wants to find the Gate and hurt the Conclave. *That's* all he wants."

"And you don't think I don't want to hurt the Conclave? Or you?" She got in my face, hatred burning in her violet eyes. "Your kind has killed mine for generations."

"Maybe, but that's because of what you've done. You might be guilty, but your shifters are not. They're innocent, and we're not hurting them." I glanced over at Kale. Every part of me tingled and came to life at once. "We've protected them the best we knew how."

"So it *is* true," Ben said. "You've developed a soft spot for this one." He withdrew his hands from Kale's body and grinned like a wolf about to devour his prey. "This will make what comes next truly delightful."

"What are you going to do to him?" I asked. A familiar burn spread across my fingertips and sizzled up my arms.

"Would you really like to know?" he asked.

Instead of responding, I focused on Kale. Energy surged forward and spread a burning path down my chest and to my legs.

"Tell him," Sersie said. "I want to see his face when he finds out."

Ben nodded. His wide grin told me how much he was enjoying this. "There's so much you don't know about shifters. So much the Conclave has kept hidden from you. You know how much they love their secrets, right?"

I did, and it was those secrets that had brought us here.

"While it's true that Sersie's transmutation spell originally created the shifters by altering their bodies, her spell affected more than just their physical forms." Ben placed his hands on Kale's squirming body. "They were changed on a level far deeper than the flesh. One that travels all the way to their souls."

He had to be talking about the morphogenic field Kale told me about, but I wasn't going to admit I already knew. Playing dumb would buy me a few more minutes. "What the hell are you talking about?" I asked, willing the roiling magic to the rest of my body and urging it to do what it had done for the first time only a few days ago.

"Unlike our kind and the fae, their magic isn't in their bodies," Ben continued. "It's in their souls. Souls that have been linked to the beasts, the most basic, most primitive creatures on this planet, and it's because of Sersie's spell that her shifters have been able to tap into the morphogenic field."

Thad gasped. Of course the brainiac knew what Ben was getting at.

"Will you fucking talk in English?" I asked, still feigning ignorance. Sometimes being underestimated had its advantages. I was almost where I needed to be. My insides felt as if they had been converted to sparks of energy.

"Think of it as a collective consciousness," Ben answered. "One that only animals can access. It connects all living creatures to each other." He paused and smiled. "And to the Gate."

Now his plans made sense. Ben was going to use the shifters and their link to the Gate to find the source of all magic.

Ben clapped and smiled at me. "I'm amazed," he said. "You figured the rest of it out by yourself."

"What do you want with the Gate?" I asked. My aura vision clicked on without me even thinking about it. The world suddenly thrummed around me in a swirl of energy.

Sersie's red aura snorted. "Like we'd tell you that."

"All you need to know is that the dove is the only shifter who still has a mind of his own," Ben said. His energy signature was as black as the shadows he commanded. It told me Ben's spirit was unforgiving and unwilling to let go of the negativity that wrapped around him. Not even the vampyren at his side radiated as much negative energy. Tiny slivers of gray threaded through their mostly ebony auras. "And once he's ours, we'll have a road map to the Gate."

Sersie strolled over to Kale, her magic pulsing from her fists. She was getting ready to cast her spell that would bring Kale under her control. Once she did that, Ben would have everything he needed to hurt everyone I loved.

The churning fear that powered me for years dissolved. In its place burned something far more powerful. There was no fucking way I was going to let that happen. I'd save my family, Kale, and the Gate, even if it cost me my life.

"Think again." In an explosion of brilliant blue, I unleashed the power building within me.

WHEN THE flash of light faded, I'd converted my body into the magical energy it created. Electrical currents spiked off me but didn't streak off in uncontrollable arcs. It calmly pulsed and thrummed, seeking release but waiting for me to tell it what to do.

"What the fuck?" Ben asked.

I pointed my arm at him and let loose a torrent of power that slammed into his chest and sent him flying off the mountain and down to the ground below.

Damn. This power was fucking badass!

A rage-filled scream echoed off the cave walls. Sersie lunged, firing bolts of purple and orange at me, but in this form, her power didn't seem as menacing as it had earlier. They were only colorful bands of energy. I held up my hands to catch them. Upon contact, my body absorbed her magic. It burned, and if I still had teeth, I'd be grinding them in pain, but her power couldn't hurt me like it had before. It was energy, and right now all energy was at my command.

I rerouted Sersie's magic out of my fingertips and straight toward her. The impact sent her slamming into the wall.

The vampyren hissed and leaped toward me. Those fuckers always scared the shit out of me with their fangs and gross prehensile tongues, but instead of turning my fear into anger, I embraced it.

Arcs of electricity fanned out of my body, snagging them in the electrical current. As they sizzled on the ground like bacon, I gazed up at my family and the friends who'd come with me. Spindles of lightning zipped from my body, severing the shadowy chains that kept them restrained.

As they fell, my father extended his arms, using his magic to slow everyone's descent and landing them safely on the rocky shelf.

"That was fucking awesome!" Mason said, as he looked me up and down.

"We'll pat Pierce on the back later." My father stood before us in his stone armor. "We've got company!"

The sky overhead grew dark with avians as they descended upon us.

Edith threw up her force field as a barrier.

"Where's Drake?" Mason asked. Dark energy hummed around his fists as he prepared to shoot the advancing birds of prey out of the sky.

Gunfire exploded below, and some of the shifters fell from the sky. After glancing toward the base of the mountain, I spotted a familiar white energy signature among scores of other regular human auras. It was Drake. The purity of his soul was impossible to miss. "He's down there." I pointed, and though my voice came out in static, Mason understood me. "He found the other witch hunters and he's brought them with him."

"What?" Thad asked, scanning the area below us. "Why?"

I told them there's more humans up there, Drake's voice suddenly said in our heads.

I glanced over at Elliot. His closed eyes and clenched jaw told me he was having difficulty with the link over the distance.

You're fucking brilliant, Mason said.

I know, right? Drake replied.

I can't keep this up much longer! Elliot shouted. Sweat dripped down his face.

Tell them to stop shooting. The shifters are being controlled. This isn't their fault, I said into the link.

Um, I don't know if they'll listen, he replied.

Tell them there are humans in the line off fire. Just get them to stop shooting.

The gunfire immediately stopped, and Elliot collapsed onto the ground, severing the link.

"The vampyren!" Kale yelled behind us.

My father, Thad, and Aiden headed for the vamps. "Leave them to us. You get Kale."

I nodded and rushed toward Kale as the cave shook from the force of the magic being tossed around me.

"I told you I'd be waiting," Kale said. Even though he was still stuck like a fly on flypaper, he grinned up at me as if he no longer had a care in the world.

"Yes, you did," I replied. "I didn't expect to find you naked on an altar, though. That's pretty kinky."

"You know what would be even better than finding me naked on an altar?" he asked, a grin snaking across his soft lips.

"What?"

"If you actually got me off this thing," he replied with an eye roll.

If I were still flesh and blood, I'd be blushing. "Yeah, of course." I sent a rush of electrical current to my right hand. It crackled and hummed with bright-blue energy. "You ready?"

When Kale nodded, I punched the altar. Upon contact with my charged fist, the shadows that had formed the altar dissipated and Kale dropped onto the hard stone.

"Ow!" he said, rubbing his bare butt. "You could have caught me, you know?"

"And I would've electrocuted you," I said as I shut off my lightning form and kneeled beside him. "But I give excellent massages." I rubbed my fingers across his smooth cheek, and his flesh trembled at my touch. "You okay?"

"Much better," he said, leaning into my palm. "Now."

I hooked his chin and pressed his lips to mine. A surge of energy crashed through my body and soul, filling me with more power than I'd felt when I turned to lightning. Whatever had awakened within me quadrupled in response to Kale's flesh against mine.

"It's so sweet, it's pathetic."

Sersie leaned against the far cave wall. She'd regained consciousness, and her fists burned with purple-and-orange magic. I stood in front of Kale, and a second later a familiar burn spread across my body as I reverted to my energy form.

"It's over, Sersie," I said gesturing around us.

Edith's force field still blocked the entrance. Mason and Adam kept the shifters from getting too close and overwhelming Edith with their numbers while my father, Thad, and Aiden battled the vampyren farther within the cave.

"You'd think so," she said. A grin crept its way across her thin lips. What the hell was she so happy about?

She suddenly disappeared.

"But you'd be wrong."

I spun around to find her standing behind me. She held Kale in a chokehold just like she'd done back at the Pig's Eye, except this time she'd surrounded them in a bubble of purple-and-orange magic.

If I were close enough, I could probably absorb the energy, but there was no way Sersie would let me get within a few feet. She'd just teleport somewhere else, and as long as we were in the same room together, I still had a chance to think of something. Firing at the magical field wasn't a possibility. I packed too much power now. I wasn't sure what would happen to Kale, and I couldn't chance hurting him. The bitch knew that.

"When Ben returns, he'll kill you," she said, darting her eyes to the shadows.

"You think he's going to sacrifice himself for you?" I asked with a chuckle. "You're even dumber than you look."

Gunfire rattled again, this time closer to the mouth of the cave. Drake and the witch hunters were getting closer.

"My shifters!" she screamed.

"They're dying because of you," Kale spat.

She tightened her grip around his neck. "I'd never hurt them. I'm their queen," she said with a sneer. "I'm *your* queen."

"You're not my queen," he replied with a grimace. "And when King Alexander gets here, he'll tear your face off."

Sersie cackled. "The first thing we did when we got here was kill your king. His sway over his people was the only thing keeping my spell that you thought was a virus from fully taking hold."

Kale's body tensed. "Liar!" he screeched. I'd never heard him make such an ear-piercing sound before. His tone was always softer, even when he was angry, but the cries that came from him now were much harsher than I'd ever heard.

"See for yourself." She gestured toward the stone chair in the room, and the fur rug that had been placed before it floated toward where we stood. It was a lion, its golden fur covered in dried blood and a huge hole in its regal chest.

A golden crown, which had been placed on its massive head, slid to one side before falling to the stone floor with a clang.

"You bitch!" Kale screamed, and instead of shifting his entire body, his mouth morphed into a hooked beak. It belonged to an eagle, not a dove. With one strike he pecked out her eye. Blood poured down Sersie's face as she screamed and released her hold on him.

The energy field around them wavered.

I sprinted forward, placing my hands on the magical bubble. It crackled and hissed as I siphoned the magic out of the barrier. All I needed was a few minutes, and I could get inside.

But it didn't look like Kale would give me the chance.

He screeched as his razor-sharp beak tore into her cheek, neck, and shoulder. She covered her face, trying to defend against the attacks, but Kale was too swift and too angry. Ribbons of blood trickled down her face and arms.

"Stop!" she screamed, releasing a burst of magic that knocked Kale onto his back.

His feet partially shifted into claws. He gripped her ankles, his talons burying into her Achilles' tendons before ripping the tender muscle to shreds.

Sersie squealed in pain and crumpled to the stony ground. "No," she pleaded. She covered her empty socket, blood gushing from between her fingers. "I'm the one who made you." She held out her other hand toward Kale, hoping for mercy.

Kale had other plans.

His entire body shimmered, and a second later a beautiful bald eagle, not a dove, filled the prison before me. His large brown-feathered body landed on top of Sersie before he sank his golden beak into her throat four times.

Sersie's barrier fell a second later, and when her body stopped convulsing, Kale spread his massive wings and let out a cry that echoed all around me.

Even though Kale believed she was dead, my aura vision saw the truth.

Sersie was a wraith, and her red energy rose from her dead body.

I unleashed her magic that I'd absorbed a few minutes earlier, along with my lightning, into the floating mass of scarlet that attempted to escape. The room exploded with power as sparks of electricity sizzled through the cave, ripping huge holes in the wall and ground. The ricochet of energy spit into the battles surrounding me, sending everyone ducking for cover while the vampyren used the diversion to retreat deeper into the cave.

"Pierce!" Thad screamed. "You're losing control again."

No, I wasn't. This time I was in complete control. More and more power flowed out of me and into the wraith, and arcs of lightning tore holes in Edith's force field.

"Shut it down!" my father yelled as the attacking shifters advanced, attempting to break the rest of the way through.

If I didn't stop, they would converge on us. If I did stop, Sersie could find another sorcerer to possess and return. Ben had already escaped us too many times. I wasn't going to let the same thing happen with Sersie.

I poured more power into the swirling energy until all that remained was a floating crimson particle. With one final surge, the speck of magic that had once been the most powerful sorcerer to ever exist was no more.

WHEN MY power fizzled out, I collapsed to my knees and Kale, who'd reverted back to his human form, darted to my side. He pulled me into his naked embrace and wrapped his arms around me as I struggled to catch my breath.

"Are you okay?" he asked. He nuzzled his cheek against my forehead and sighed.

I gripped his arms and glanced up at him. I'd expended a lot of energy and needed a nap. "I'm better. Now."

"What the hell were you doing?" Mason asked from where he and Adam had taken cover behind an outcropping of rock. "You could've killed us."

"I was in complete control."

Edith snorted. "Didn't look that way to me."

I sighed. Why did everyone refuse to believe I could be more than just an overpowered meathead? "Sersie was a wraith, remember?"

"Oh yeah," Mason replied.

Thad studied the empty air around us. "And you were able to dissipate her spiritual energy?"

I nodded, too tired from my exertion to speak.

"So she's dead?" Aiden asked.

"Even more than you," I replied with a grin.

Several low growls drew our attention to the opening of the cave, where other shifters slowly started to fill the room. Most of them were in their animal forms, their fangs bared and ready to rip us to shreds, but some of them had either not shifted or only partially shifted. Those that had partly transformed approached us on human legs, with claws for hands or beaks instead of mouths.

Though they were ready to fight, their eyes no longer burned with rabid hatred. They appeared to be more confused than anything else. I certainly knew how that felt.

"Stop!" Kale commanded. He rose from where he'd been holding me and stepped between his people and mine. "They aren't your enemies."

"I can smell magic on them," said a blond man at the front, who flicked his tongue out of his mouth like a snake. His cold blue eyes and set square jaw clearly revealed he didn't trust us. "They must die. It is the will of King Alexander."

The shifters behind him nodded in agreement.

Kale sighed and slumped his shoulders. "King Alexander is dead."

The blond shifter lunged forward, changing into a cobra in midair as he headed straight for me. He clearly thought I was to blame, and I was too weak to defend myself magically. I held up my arm, ready for the sting of fang and burn of poison. A majestic eagle suddenly descended on the reptile, catching the cobra in his talons and squeezing it tight before landing with a regal flap of his wings.

Kale had saved me.

The shifters behind him gasped and took several steps back. Kale screeched at them and then down at the snake that coiled about his talons. He snapped his yellow beak once in warning before the cobra released its hold and went slack.

Kale fluttered off him, reverting to the man who made my soul sing. When the cobra returned to his true form, his wide eyes communicated his surprise. "How is this possible?" he asked. "You're a dove."

"I'm not sure how, Caspian," Kale replied. I remembered that name. He had been King Alexander's chief advisor and someone Kale didn't trust. "But I'm not a dove anymore," he said, offering his hand to the cobra he'd corralled.

Caspian hesitantly took the assistance, and Kale helped him to his feet. "Nothing like this has happened before," Caspian said, glancing at the others and me. "What did they do to you?"

"This wasn't them," Kale answered. His tone was firm. He squared his shoulders and stood tall. "This was me."

"You've *always* been a dove," Caspian insisted. He crossed his arms. "Sorcery must somehow be involved."

The gathering crowd at the mouth of the cave muttered in agreement. The shifters' distrust of magic ran deep, and I certainly understood why. They'd been used by our half-breed cousins and banished by the Conclave, but there was one thing they were forgetting—their own history.

"What about King Jerrick?" I asked from where I still sat on the floor. I wasn't as weak as I was after defeating Sersie, but I wasn't ready to go another ten rounds with anyone. Right now a kitten could kick my ass.

"What do you know of our most beloved liege?" Caspian asked. His chin held high.

"I know he shifted into an owl even though he'd always been a bear." My answer surprised everyone in the room, especially my family. If my brothers' mouths gaped any wider, more than one avian could fly down their throats. I rose from where I'd been resting and crossed on unsteady legs to stand next to Kale. "I know he turned into a reptilian and an aquatic. I know he saved your kind's collective asses."

Caspian snorted. "What's your point?"

"My point is Jerrick tapped into the morphogenic field, energy Ben was after, and used it to choose the forms he needed, not just the one that chose him. By doing that, he saved your people from the humans that tried to enslave you. Just like Kale." I put my hand on Kale's shoulder, which earned me a big dimpled smile.

"Save us?" Caspian asked, glancing around the room. "From whom?"

They didn't remember. Was that a side effect of Sersie's spell?

"From Sersie," Kale answered.

A murmur filled the room like a tidal wave.

"Sersie?" someone asked. "She's here?"

"I remember," another muttered, her voice low and faraway. "She appeared above Aeaea in an explosion of purple right before the humans attacked."

"She ensorcelled us. Again," Caspian added. He wrinkled his brow as he regarded Kale. "But not you?"

Kale shook his head just as Drake ran into the cave. The shifters snarled, but one nod from Kale quieted them down.

"Drake!" Mason shouted, but before he could draw Drake into an embrace, the army of witch hunters, scrambling into the cave behind him, raised their guns. Though only a handful stood at the cave's entrance, hundreds of them gathered on the mountain's slope.

"Stay right there!" commanded a blond haired man. It was Hopkins, the one who had saved Drake from the shifters shortly after we arrived. Sersie didn't kill them after all, but why? "Where are the other humans?" he asked, glancing around the cave.

"There aren't any." Drake grinned and stepped inside the magical barrier Edith once again had raised. "I needed your help to save my friends."

Hopkins sneered. A second later the muzzles of their guns sprouted fire as they fired at the force field.

"That's enough!" my father railed. With a flick of his wrist, their weapons flew out of their hands and tumbled down the side of the mountain.

"I couldn't agree more."

Ben appeared behind them, floating on a black cloud. "Your usefulness has come to an end."

The darkness around the witch hunters rose in a giant black wave that crashed down upon them. When the shadows parted, every single human was gone.

CHAPTER 11

EVERYONE RUSHED to the edge of the cave in disbelief. All the witch hunters, including those who were climbing the mountain, had been swept away by Ben's shadows.

"You killed them?" I asked.

"Of course," Ben said with a shrug. "They were only a means to an end and were going to die eventually. Just like Sersie." He nodded toward Kale and grinned. "Thanks for taking care of her for me. One less loose end for me to tie up."

That told me everything I needed to know. All this had been a ruse. "You never gave a shit about Sersie or building a shifter army, did you?"

Ben laughed as the vampyren hovered in the sky behind him. Those damned things were like cockroaches. Just when you thought they were gone, they scrambled back out of the shadows. "Pierce, no matter how hard you try, you always fall a few feet short, don't you? Of course I cared about Sersie's plan, no matter how foolish it might have been. Helping her regain control of her shifters would have led me to the Gate."

"But that's not what you were really after," Thad said. "Just like in Otherworld, you're here for something, aren't you?"

"Are you just now figuring that out?" he asked. "Damn, you guys are slow!"

"Whatever it is, you won't get it," Kale screeched. The shifters added their voices to Kale's.

Ben rolled his eyes as if idiots constantly surrounded him. "I already have it," he said. Suddenly, a golden object appeared in his hand, and he twirled it around his index finger.

"The king's crown!" Kale yelled.

The avians behind us cried out and shifted, launching their bodies into the air. Kale was about to join them when I wrapped my arms around him and pulled him tight. He struggled against me, but when the vampyren sliced through them with their talons, he stopped fighting, even though his body remained tense.

Ben was too powerful alone. With the vampyren, he was unstoppable. That didn't matter to my family or my friends. They were ready to fight, but I wasn't ready to let them.

"There's nothing you can do to stop me," Ben taunted. "I've won, and I'll always win."

"Not this time." I charged forward, changing into energy, and leaped off the edge. Instead of falling, I cut through the sky on a collision course with Ben.

"You can fly?" Ben asked, shifting into his vampyre form.

It was news to me too. I was still learning what this energy form could do, but I wasn't going to tell him that. "You have no fucking clue what I can do," I said, channeling a buttload of lightning into my fists.

We collided in an explosion of energy that sent me flying backward into the side of the mountain while Ben soared in the opposite direction.

"Pierce!" Kale yelled from the entrance of the cave. The shifters with him morphed into animals, and my family clicked on their powers. "We're coming."

I couldn't let them out here with Ben. If he could stop the Conclave without breaking a sweat, I couldn't imagine what he'd do to them. In response to my thoughts, spindles of energy spooled from my fingertips, forming a giant electric net across the opening of the cave.

"What the fuck?" Thad asked, stepping away from the lightning field.

My father growled. "What do you think you're doing?"

"Stay there," I said. "Where you'll be safe."

"Pierce!" Kale cried out. "Don't do this. Not by yourself."

"I have to. I love you," I said, sweeping my gaze over my loved ones before lingering upon Kale's big golden eyes. "All of you."

"Watch out!" Drake screamed.

I whipped around as the vampyren who were stunned by the force of the impact dove toward me, claws extended.

Kicking off the side of Mount Oronos, I launched myself at them, forming a ball of compressed lightning in my hand. I hurled it at them like a fastball, and they reacted as I suspected. They veered to the right to let the projectile pass, but grenades didn't have to touch their targets. They just needed to get close.

The ball lightning exploded in a blinding flash. Snaking tendrils of energy ensnared the vampyren. Their bodies convulsed for a few moments before going limp and falling from the sky.

"Three down. One to go."

A dark cloud formed around me, and shadowy arms grasped at my waist, neck, and limbs. But instead of ripping me apart, they passed harmlessly through me. "Nice try," I said, releasing a wave of energy that tore the cloud to shreds. "But you can't touch this."

"Impressive," Ben said. He floated a few feet from me, studying me with his cold, dead eyes. He most likely had no idea what to do. How was he supposed to fight an opponent he couldn't touch? "I've never encountered this ability before."

"That's because I'm one of a kind." One glance at his aura revealed his energy had changed. It wasn't just pure black as it had been earlier. While patches of umbra swirled around him, muddied reds, dark pinks, and cloudy blues made up the majority of his signature. His emotions were changing. "Feeling a little insecure?"

"Because of you?" he asked with a chuckle. "Never."

I was far from convinced. His laughter had lost some of its edge. "You can't lie to me. I can see it. Your aura is practically a rainbow."

"What you see is confusion and surprise," he said. "I know you're the oldest and supposed to be the most powerful, but I never really gave you a second thought. Sure, a tank can be devastating, but you can hear that motherfucker coming. It's always been your brothers I've been worried about. They're sneaky, and you never know what they're going to do. But you? You may have power, but you're too predictable to be truly a threat."

If Ben thought I was falling for that, he was even stupider than he thought I was. But as long as he underestimated me, I had an advantage, so I did as he expected.

"Fuck you!" I amped up my powers, sending snaking trails of energy slicing through the sky. I even bared my teeth and shook my fists. Although he tried to hide it, the corners of his lips slightly hitched. "I'm not predictable, you asswipe."

"No," he said with a shake of his head. "Not at all."

I fired a lightning bolt and dove at him. Ben laughed as he easily dodged my choreographed moves.

"I'm tired of everyone not taking me seriously." I unleashed lightning bolt after lightning bolt that bounced off the shadowy rampart he'd erected in front of him. "My family thinks I'm a failure, and the Conclave doesn't respect me worth shit. I won't take crap from you too." My last blast exploded in rumbling thunder, and I hovered before him, panting.

"Poor Pierce. Unappreciated and misunderstood."

"Just like you," I said. "You didn't ask for any of this. I know that. You were the one burned at the stake and whose father turned you into this."

Ben tensed, gnashing his razor-sharp teeth. "Don't speak of my father."

As I suspected, Bartram Kane remained an open wound. If I picked at it long enough, I could get it to bleed. "He was a stupid, self-centered man, wasn't he?"

"I warn you." The darkness around Ben pulsed.

"Come on, you can admit it," I said, slowly gliding my way closer. "He was a member of the fucking Conclave. He had the power to save you from the witch hunters, to pull you down from the stake before they set you on fire, but he didn't, did he?"

"No," Ben said through gritted teeth. "He didn't."

"And why not? Because the Conclave didn't want him to. It's always about them, isn't it? Always what the Conclave wants. They don't give two shits about anyone else. I mean, look at how they've treated the fae and the shifters. They crapped all over them. I'd bet they'd screw over their own mothers if it worked in their favor."

"Maybe not their mothers," Ben replied. He balled up his fists, which spiked with building negative energy. "But their children? Most definitely."

I closed the distance between us to about twenty feet. Ben didn't notice. His eyes had grown glassy and faraway as he gazed into a past filled with death, imprisonment, and torture. If he weren't such a psychopath, I'd feel sorry for the guy because, even though he'd done terrible things in the name of revenge, it was the Conclave and his father that had started him on this path.

"You're right," I said with a nod. "Your father screwed you over big time, turning you into a vampyre. And why did he do it? Why did he cast the *immortalitas* spell? Because he felt guilty for not doing what he should have done in the first place—standing up to the Conclave and protecting his own son."

Anger stormed across his eyes. "My father was a self-righteous asshole. He expected more from me than he was capable of giving." The shadow wall separating us fell, and Ben didn't seem to notice. Instead of staring at me, he gazed at his withered skin and talons. "He turned me into a monster."

I drifted closer. In a few more feet, I could do what needed to be done.

"He's the one who should've been imprisoned and experimented on. He's the one who started all this." Ben gazed up at me, desperation etched into the lines across his forehead. "Right?" he asked.

"He's the bad guy," I said with a nod, hovering directly in front of him. All I had to do was reach out and I could end this with one touch.

"Not me?"

"No," I said. "Not you."

I placed my arm on his shoulder, ready to absorb his energy and his magic and redirect it into him as I had done with Sersie. What I wasn't prepared for was the searing pain that sliced through my body like a hundred scalpels.

"Nice try," Ben said. A mocking grin cut diagonally across his lips. "But you're not the only one here who can act."

Ben's energy flooded my body like a tidal wave rushing onto the shore. It was too much power, too much energy for me to absorb. If I didn't release it, I'd explode, but Ben's power blocked my outlets.

"I must admit that I underestimated you." He locked eyes with me as he clutched my shoulders. He transferred even more power into me until dark energy muddied my lightning form, turning my brilliant blue into gray murk. "I won't make that mistake again."

Every part of me throbbed and ached as black lightning streaked from me and across the sky. I had only a few seconds before I exploded, so I gazed down at where I'd trapped the others for their safety. I was too far to hear their words, but their energy signatures swirled in a tempest of yellow and orange that told me they were afraid. Not for themselves, but for me.

The only aura that was different was Kale's. Those colors that pulsed through everyone else were just specks and threads within him.

He was made almost entirely of the same vibrant pink I first saw in the sky over Havenbridge. The warm flutters that spread through my chest told me it was the love and hope he had in the world and in me.

Even though he was afraid, he had faith I would overcome Ben.

I wrapped my big hand around Ben's neck, and the laughter in his eyes died as he struggled against my grip. "Underestimating me was your first and last mistake." I reversed the flow of energy that poured into my body and sent it back to Ben. I cried out in pain as the currents of power collided like dueling tsunamis.

"What are you doing?" Ben muttered. The muscles in his neck fanned from the strain. He was fighting me with everything he had, trying to block the channel he'd opened up between us, the one he was going to use to kill me. The one I was now using to kill him.

"I'm ending this once and for all." Lightning sliced through the sky, and the darkness around us came to life. Our powers, our energy, our magic clashed in streaks of blue and rumbles of darkness.

"You can't defeat me," Ben said. "I have more power than you can imagine."

He was right. Ben's magic was stronger than mine, but I had something he didn't. The love and faith of a man who filled my soul with energy that couldn't be measured or contained.

I dug my fingers deeper into Ben's flesh, noticing how the bright-blue energy I was made of suddenly developed threads of pink. They wove together, creating specks that grew into floating islands of pink.

"What the hell?" Ben asked, watching as the new hue slowly spread throughout my form.

"That's a power you could never understand." I shoved every ounce of energy in my body into Ben in one final explosion of radiant pink that reminded me of the first blush of dawn.

Ben's mouth opened in a silent scream. His flesh bubbled and ignited in a fire that quickly consumed his body. A second later I held nothing but ash and the crown Ben had stolen.

After all these months, it was finally over. Ben and his threat were gone.

KALE FLEW into my arms when I dispersed the energy net and landed at the mouth of the cave.

"You did it!" he said, pressing his lips to mine and grasping at my neck. "I knew you would."

"I know you did." I nuzzled my face into his, grateful to have him in my arms again. I'd been afraid that it wouldn't happen, that Ben would defeat me, but Kale's faith and love in me gave me the power I needed to make it back to him. "Thank you for that."

"For what? I didn't do anything."

"Yes, you did," I replied, rubbing my thumb across his lips. "More than you know."

His knitted eyebrows told me he had no clue what I was talking about, and though I wanted to explain, we had too many other things to deal with right now. That conversation would have to wait for when we were alone. "How is everyone?" I asked, turning my attention to my family. Proud smiles stretched across my brothers' faces while my father grimaced.

"That was stupid," he said. "You could've been killed."

"But I wasn't." I strode over to him. I didn't need my aura vision to tell me he was more afraid than he was angry. I was his son, after all. "I couldn't take the chance of Ben hurting any of you. I knew he wouldn't be able to touch me in my energy form."

"You didn't know that," he said in a growl. "You gambled."

He was right. I had gambled, but it was better to bet on my life than theirs.

"Come on, Dad," Mason said. He rubbed his hand up and down our father's back. "Pierce kicked ass, and you know it."

"It was a foolish move," Thad said, moving to our father's side. "But it was also a wise one."

I couldn't have been more surprised if Thad shifted into a unicorn. Everyone's gaping mouths told me they agreed.

"We would've been a distraction," Thad said. "When Ben realized he couldn't touch Pierce, he would've gone after us. Pierce would've been too busy trying to protect us to take Ben out."

"But is he dead?" Drake asked. "I mean, really dead. Not vampyre dead."

"Yes," I said with a firm nod. "I don't know how I managed it, but the energy I dumped into his body sparked a magical fire just like that of the fae. He's dead."

"And we have the crown," Kale added. He laced his fingers with mine. "But why did he want it?"

Thad chewed on his bottom lip. His hazel eyes turned glassy as they gazed off into the distance. That look confirmed everything I already suspected before Sersie attacked us back in the living room at home.

"You know, don't you?" I asked.

Everyone stared at him, waiting for his response. Finally he sighed and said, "I'm not certain, but I have my suspicions."

"What suspicions?" Dad said. "Why am I just hearing about them now?"

"Because I was afraid what kind of danger knowing would place everyone in," he admitted.

"It doesn't matter now, does it? Just tell us."

"Ben was collecting talismans."

"Like the Hearthstone?" Aiden asked.

"Yes," Thad said. "But I don't think that was his first one."

"What do you mean?" Adam asked.

"When we met during Samhain, Ben wore a green pendant he constantly played with. At first I thought it was some family heirloom, but I have a feeling it was more than that. I think that pendant was what he was after in Havenbridge during Mabon."

"Wait a minute!" Drake grabbed Thad's shoulders. "Describe it."

Thad glanced around before answering, "It's an emerald stone encased in gold."

Drake turned to look at Mason, whose eyes grew into big circles. "Did it have a lily with its petals open carved on the face?"

Thad stitched his eyebrows together. "How did you know?"

"Holy fuck!" Mason said. He turned to our father and clutched at his shirt. "That was Aunt Millie's pendant. Ben had it all this time, but why? And where is it now?"

"I don't know," Thad said. "Everything that's been happening on Aeaea has been about the crown all this time."

"That is correct."

The Conclave suddenly appeared before us.

"You knew?" I asked, scanning their hooded faces for a response, but they stood before us in silence. "Why the hell didn't you just tell us?"

Gerald Wa pulled back his hood and stepped forward. "There are many things the Conclave knows that cannot be made public."

"For our protection?" Mason asked in a snort.

Gerald nodded. "You may not like the answer, but it doesn't make it any less true. When we learned Ben had stolen the Hearthstone, we suspected what he might truly be after."

"And what was he after?" my father asked. "We know working with Sersie was a ruse."

"Not entirely," Gerald replied. "Had Ben and Sersie gained control over all the shifters, they would have had access to the morphogenic field and been able to track the Gate's location."

"But we stopped that," Edith answered with a smug jut of her chin.

"Yes, you did," Gerald said with a smile. "For that we are truly grateful."

"Grateful?" asked the Warlock Hag. She broke the line and regarded us carefully. "They were given a specific plan to follow. Had they done that, lives could have been saved."

"Don't blame them." Kale and a crowd of shifters gathered behind us. Their eyes were trained on the Conclave, and their tense muscles revealed they were ready to pounce. "This is *your* failure, not theirs."

"This is none of your concern," said the Warlock Hag as she waved Kale and the shifters away.

Kale bristled and took several steps forward. "This is *our* island, and the crown belongs to *our* king."

"Both of which the Conclave gave to you," she replied.

I exchanged glances with the others. If anyone had already known that piece of information, it would have been Thad. His O-shaped mouth told me he was learning this for the first time. With as much animosity that existed between the shifters and my kind, it didn't make sense the Conclave were the ones to hand over a ceremonial relic that would be symbolic of the Beast King's rule.

There was something else going on here.

"*You* gave the crown to the shifters?" I asked.

"Yes," Gerald said, trying to lock gazes with the Warlock Hag, who refused to meet his eyes. "It was an offering of peace between our species."

"Like the Hearthstone you gave to the fae?" Aiden asked. "The magical relic upon which the cornerstone of Otherworld had been built."

If the Conclave saw the fae or the shifters as challenges to their authority, they wouldn't be giving them gifts. That wasn't what you did to people who might turn against you. However, if you wanted to hide something from everyone else, the best place to keep it would be with those no one would ever expect.

"You were hiding these talismans Ben was looking for, weren't you?" I asked. Everyone turned their eyes to me as I closed the distance between the Conclave and us. "It makes sense. You weren't offering gifts of friendship. You were using your enemies to hold on to relics you didn't want anyone to find. That's why you gave the fae a power source for their land and the shifters a crown for their king. You knew they'd protect those objects with their lives, and you wouldn't have to."

Aiden tensed, his jaw clenching shut. "You used us?"

"Is this true?" Kale asked as he joined my side.

Gerald attempted a smile, but it died on his face. He locked eyes with me briefly before drawing in a deep breath. "It's true."

His answer riled the shifters, many of who transformed into their beast forms, ready to attack. The Conclave didn't move or even start. They turned toward the advancing beast horde as if they were ready to take them out with a stray thought.

Kale shifted his left hand to a wing and fanned it outward. "No," he commanded. His people immediately stopped as if they'd been obeying him their entire lives. My insecure dove had changed in more ways than the animal he shifted into. He'd turned into a leader. "Why betray us in this manner?"

"It wasn't a betrayal," Gerald answered. "We needed to put the relics in places of great safety, where no one would know what they truly were and where they would be safe."

"So why not just tell the fae and the shifters what they were doing?" Adam asked. "I bet they would have helped you out willingly."

Aiden and Kale nodded in unison.

"Perhaps, but we couldn't chance it." Gerald's usually kind face tensed and grew grim. "Too much was a stake."

"Like what?" I asked. I was getting tired of all this pussyfooting around the issue. It was time for the Conclave to finally tell us what the hell had their panties in a bunch. "What are these talismans you've been keeping secret for so long?"

Gerald scanned the air in front of him while the Conclave spoke to each other in private. This was the moment of truth. They'd either finally trust in us or continue to lie and forever strain our relationship. When they were done, he sighed and said, "They are the Crests of the Five."

Thad, Edith, and my father gasped and glanced around nervously. I had no fucking clue what he was talking about, and it pissed me off. When I got home, I was locking myself in the library and not coming out until I was as much of a brainiac as my brother. "Five what?" I asked.

"The five elements of magic," Dad whispered.

Yeah, that cleared things right up. The five elements were earth, fire, air, water, and spirit. They were the source of our powers. The wizards accessed spirit, the witches tapped directly into whichever of the five elements became their guiding life force, and warlocks combined two elements into a powerful hybrid. Water and air were mine, which was how I could command lightning, but what did these talismans have to do with any of that? "And?"

"And?" Thad asked. His exasperation clearly knew no bounds. "The Crests of the Five are physical manifestations of each element. Their power is directly fed by the Gate, and whoever holds these talismans can access the power that comes with it."

That was how Ben's magic had surpassed the Conclave's. Though they represented the most powerful of us all, they were still bound by the rules of magic as we were. Ben wasn't. He'd found a magical loophole.

Plus he had an ally. "Was Ben collecting these crests for himself or whoever he was working for?"

That got the Conclave's attention. They'd already guessed that Ben had been working with someone of great power, someone who'd let him out of the prison they had kept him in. "What do you know of this individual?" Gerald asked.

"Not much," I answered. "Only that he or she is called Ica or something." I studied the Warlock Hag's body language. My gut told me either she was the one Ben was working with or she knew more than she let on. If she was either of those things, I couldn't tell. Her posture betrayed nothing.

"This name means nothing to us," Gerald said after speaking with the others through their mind link.

"Or us," Thad answered. "I'm not even sure that's the full name. Ben shut Sersie up before she could say anything more."

"So Ben or this Ica person wanted the crests for their power?" I asked.

"It's more than that," Gerald admitted. The eight figures behind him tensed, and they stepped forward all at once.

"You will be silent," said one of the robed figures in white.

The two other figures who wore gray like Gerald nodded in agreement.

Gerald spun around, his cool demeanor vanishing into thin air. "Secrets are all you care about," he railed. "I've pleaded with you time and again to speak the truth, but you insist on keeping those we should be working with in the dark."

"He's lost his objectivity," the Warlock Hag said to the others. "As I have already warned."

"That's ridiculous coming from you," Gerald told her. "And you know why better than I do."

More than anything I wanted to turn on my aura vision and take a look at her energy again. There were secrets there, and my gut told me they involved my family. But I couldn't chance pissing her off any more than she already was.

Whatever secrets she held, she stiffened in response and took a step toward Gerald. I darted in between them before they could come to blows. I didn't even want to imagine the devastation they would cause if they started fighting.

"We don't have time for this shit," I said. "We may have stopped Ben and prevented him from stealing the crown and the crest it contains, but we need to find out who he was working for and take back the two crests he'd already stolen."

"You're mistaken," the Warlock Hag said. "He has one, not two."

"That's where you're wrong," I said. "He's got the Hearthstone and Aunt Millie's emerald pendant."

Gerald stumbled backward. "He has Millicent's pendant? The one I gave her?"

"The one that cost my aunt her life," Drake answered in a thick Southern drawl. A scowl marched across his face as he regarded the wizard who was once in love with his aunt. "You thought it would be safe with her, didn't you?"

He nodded, still unable to speak.

"Yeah, well, she wasn't safe with it. Was she?"

"Why didn't you tell me?" Gerald asked, speaking to no one in particular.

"Because I didn't trust you," Thad answered. "You were keeping too many secrets from us, and I worried that telling you or anyone else might put more people in danger."

"These are the individuals you've been putting your neck on the line for?" the Warlock Hag asked.

"We're the individuals who stopped Ebenezer Kane," I said. "*That's* who we are."

When the stunned expression on Gerald's face disappeared, an arctic chill spread across his features and hardened his gray eyes. "You've known since Samhain, haven't you?" he asked Thad. "When I asked you to trust me, to tell me what you knew."

My brother nodded.

"I see." He folded his arms in his robes and stepped back into line with the rest of the Conclave. I didn't need Thad to tell me what that meant. Whatever support or information we'd gotten from Gerald before this had just come to an end. The other members of the Conclave nodded in approval and turned their gazes upon us. "I offered my assistance. I went beyond the call of duty to give you as much as I could in order to deal with the crisis we all face. You have thrown those good deeds back in my face."

"That's no different than what you've done to us," I said.

"Enough!" Gerald's voice cracked like a whip. "You've placed us and all of magic in great danger. Had we known more than one of the crests had been taken, our actions and discourse would be vastly different, but because of you, what we've feared the most might very well be upon us."

The fear beneath the anger terrified me. "What is it?" I asked. "What have you been afraid of?"

"The Spell Fall," Gerald answered. A second later the Conclave was gone.

AFTER THE Conclave left us stranded in Aeaea, everyone began talking about the Spell Fall. No one, not even Thad, had any clue what Gerald had been talking about. Whatever it was, it sure as fuck didn't sound good.

It soured our victory over Ben and told us whatever we'd believed had ended had only just begun.

So not only was our already-strained relationship with the Conclave in shambles, we'd lost the support of our greatest ally among our leaders, the shifters lost a king, and I was a few moments away from saying good-bye to Kale and heading back to Havenbridge.

"It won't be forever," Kale said. He laced his fingers with mine as we strolled through the part of the forest around Aria that Sersie and Ben hadn't burned. Huge, majestic trees danced to the wind above us, and the sudden rush of air filled my nostrils with the scent of citrus and cedar.

I'd never be able to smell either again without thinking of him.

"I know," I replied. "I just wish you were coming back with me."

"Me too," he said with a nod. "But you've got a lot to figure out back home, and we have to rebuild."

Yeah. Even though we defeated Ben, I didn't expect the Conclave's attitude to change toward us one bit. In fact, I'd be surprised if the Edwells didn't take our place as the black magic protector coven. If that happened, even if we learned what the Spell Fall was, we wouldn't be able to do anything about it.

The Conclave and the Edwells would make sure of that.

The shifters had a difficult task before them as well. Most of their villages had been destroyed, and they had to find a new Beast King.

"You'll be right there leading the way," I said, nudging my shoulder against his.

He snorted. "Not if Caspian has anything to say about it. He has enough supporters from the king's previous council that he thinks he's a shoo-in to be our next leader." Kale grimaced up at me and shuddered.

With the way the shifters had been looking to Kale since he transformed into an eagle, I suspected Caspian had another think coming. "How will it be decided?" I asked.

"It'll be put to a vote among the council," he said with a shrug, as if he didn't care. His pressed lips told me he did. "Chances are good that it'll be Caspian. The king trusted him, and everyone loved the king."

"And what about you?" I asked.

He glanced up at me, his eyebrows stitched. "I loved the king too."

"I'm sure you did, but that's not what I was asking."

"I don't understand."

"What do you think your chances are of being the next king?"

Kale came to a dead stop and looked at me as if I'd just turned off the radio in the middle of a Backstreet Boys song. "Are you crazy? I'd never be chosen as a king. I'm just a—"

I grabbed his hand and pulled him into my arms. "Don't say it," I said. He smiled and looked away. "You're not just a dove. You've *never* been *just* a dove. Kale, you're so much more than you even realize that I sometimes wish you could see what I see."

"You really do see something, don't you?" he asked. He gazed up at me with his big golden eyes and placed his hands on my chest, causing my heart to flutter. "No one has ever looked at me like you do. Not my parents, not the king, not even Brit. Whenever I see that look in your eyes, it's like I have to do whatever I can to be exactly what you see."

I cupped his smooth cheeks in my big hands and brought our faces closer together. His warm breath plumed across my face, setting my flesh on fire. "You don't ever need to be anyone other than who you already are: a man who defended himself and his people, someone who took out one of the most powerful sorcerers who ever lived, and a man of great strength and courage."

"Really?" He locked his gaze on my lips. "That's what you see in me?" He asked the question as if it was the most bizarre concept in the world.

I ran my thumb across his lips and nodded. "But that's not even the best part about you. It's not your strength or the fact that you turn into either an eagle or a dove." I laid my hand flat across his bare chest. "It's your soul. That's where your true strength lies, and that's what hit me like a lightning bolt the first time I saw you."

His eyebrows arched high across his forehead. "Is that really true?"

"Why would I lie about that?"

"I'm not saying you would." He traced my jawline with his fingertips, as if he were memorizing every line and curve before we had to part ways. "It's just, well—" He looked away, his cheeks blushing red.

I hooked his chin and brought his eyes back to mine. "What is it? You can tell me anything. I promise."

He bit his lip, apparently trying to chew the words free from where they refused to move. "It's silly, really, and I don't want you to think it means anything. Because it doesn't have to. Honest. But some people, most of the older ones, really, the younger generation not so much—"

"Kale," I whispered, moving my lips so close to his I was inhaling every breath he exhaled. "Just tell me."

He nodded, resting his hands on my chest and leaning his full weight against me. "I don't know about your kind, but my people believe that when they find their mate, it's like finding a part of your soul."

I smiled. "Like a soul mate?"

"Kinda," he said with a dimpled grin. "Except we call it being soul struck. It's one of the perks of the morphogenic field. It allows us to find the one we're supposed to spend the rest of our lives with, and when we do, it's like this exchange of unseen energy between two who are meant to be one."

Funny enough, I liked the way that sounded. I used to think the idea of two people becoming one was stupid. No, even worse than that, it was pretty fucking ridiculous. We were meant to be individuals and do what the hell we wanted, not live according to someone else's rules.

Since Kale, I learned how wrong I'd been.

Becoming one didn't mean losing yourself. It meant gaining a part of yourself you never knew existed in someone else.

"That's what makes this so hard," he said.

"What do you mean?"

"Well, when you punched me in the nose—"

I groaned and shook my fist at the heavens. "You're never going to let that go, are you?"

Kale flicked the tip of my nose and grunted. "Will you let me finish?"

"Fine," I said with a loud exhale.

"When we first met—"

"Yeah, that's much better," I said with a big smile. "Always start that way, okay?"

He took a step back and placed his hands on his hips. That look told me he was about two seconds away from turning around and walking back. I pulled him into my embrace and made a big show of zipping my lips.

After studying me for a few moments and realizing I was going to keep my trap shut, he continued, "I saw something inside you fighting to get free. You were so sad and lost and angry. I wanted to fly into your arms, tell you it would be okay, and give you the hug you so desperately wanted but didn't know you needed."

I nodded and swallowed hard. Kale was right. I was all of those things, and he was the only one to have ever seen it.

"But you weren't ready," he said with a snicker. "You were too busy hiding beneath all the bullshit you thought was important, like being the baddest warlock in all the land."

I scrunched up my face. "Are you saying I'm not?" I asked. "Because I'll prove it to you right here. Right now."

"How? By turning into pink lightning again?" he asked in complete deadpan.

Yeah, I was going to get shit about that from my brothers for quite some time. "So what if I turned into pink lightning," I said with a mock scowl. "That was because of you."

"Me?" he asked with an arch of his eyebrow.

"That's the color of your aura," I replied. "When I first saw it, you were flying over Havenbridge as a dove. I hadn't even met you yet, but I'd wanted to chase after you and find you."

"So you shot me out of the sky instead?" he asked. "You couldn't just ask me out?"

I shot him a grimace. "Will you stop that? I'm trying to be serious, here."

Kale flashed me a dimpled smile and settled into my arms.

"I turned into pink lightning because of you. Your color, your soul, has called out to me from the start, and instead of questioning it or running from it, I embraced it and you. When I did, it was like my soul caught on fire and burned with more energy than I knew what to do with, and I used it to knock Ben on his ass. The only reason I was able to do that was because of you."

Kale shook his head. "That's not true. You did it because of us. Because when I first laid eyes on you, I knew I'd found my mate."

I liked the way that sounded. It meant I belonged to Kale, and he belonged to me. I'd never wanted a relationship like that before, but now

I couldn't imagine my life without it. I craned down to Kale, hovering over his lips and wanting to taste the sweetness of his kiss again, but the fear I'd learned to control pushed forward again.

This might be the last moment Kale and I shared together.

No matter how much we wanted to see each other again. The decision was up to the Conclave and the next Beast King, not us.

"That's what makes this so hard," Kale repeated. Tears pooled in his eyes as he grasped my shoulders. "Finally finding my mate and having to say good-bye."

"Then let's not say it," I said, sucking back the emotion I refused to let drip down my face. "I'm your mate, so we'll see each other again. Some way. Somehow."

Kale smiled through his sniffles. "That's right. We will."

I pressed my mouth to his, and when our lips met, every part of me surged forward in a tidal wave to meet the better part of me that lived within him. Our kiss cut through our tears and sadness and found the joy that existed deep within, the one that told us this wouldn't be the end. That it could never be good-bye.

Our bodies responded to the unspoken promise. My flesh tingled to life as our tongues writhed together in and out of each other's mouths. His hands squeezed my shoulders before sliding down my sides to my hips.

"I need you, Pierce," Kale muttered. "Please say you need me too."

Was he crazy? There wasn't a part of me that didn't. Every cell in my body was ready to jump ship and swim over to him. "I do," I mumbled between our kisses. "I want to touch every part of you with every part of me."

"Then do it."

I pulled Kale harder against me, grinding his hardness against mine. The friction made my flesh tingle and the hair on my body stand straight up. I slid my hands down his sweat-slick back to the swell of his plump ass. I kissed my way from his lips to his neck as I massaged his butt in my palms. Kale moaned and held my face against his neck, urging me with his labored breathing to nibble harder and faster on his sensitive flesh.

"More," he panted.

That was exactly what I wanted too. I'd denied myself his touch for too long already, too afraid that once we shed our clothes, I might somehow ruin how special Kale had become to me like I'd done so many times before him. But touching him and kissing him only sweetened the bond that had formed between us. I didn't have to worry about the warlock I had been.

I had only to embrace the warlock I became because of him.

I slipped my fingers beneath the waistband of his pants, tickling the swell of his ass. He moaned and clutched at my back, realizing that this time, I wouldn't stop him or pull back. Our lips found each other again, and as we dove our tongues in and out of each other's mouths, my flesh sizzled from the energy we produced.

I slid his pants from his hips and Kale wrapped his arms around my neck, pushing his lips harder against mine. I drew him into me, his hard cock pressed against my erection, which was still confined by my jeans. As he thrust against my groin, I gathered the perspiration that slid down his flesh upon my fingertips before slipping my finger into his crevice. I traced lazy circles around the outer edge of his hole, using the sweat to lubricate his opening.

When I pushed one finger inside him, Kale whimpered. "Yes."

"Does that feel good?" I asked, sliding the digit in and out of his body.

Kale chewed on his lower lip, thrusting backward onto my palm. "God yes," he mumbled. "But I still need more."

With wide, frantic eyes, Kale tugged his tunic over his head and stood before me completely naked. I removed my finger from his body and stepped back. I took in his smooth tanned flesh, the swell of his heaving chest, his flat stomach, and the gorgeous six-inch cock that throbbed before me.

"Fuck, you're beautiful," I said.

I closed the distance I'd put between us, tracing my fingertips down his abs before grabbing my prize.

Kale melted into my arms, brushing his lips against mine as I stroked his prick. He pushed his tongue into my mouth, clawing at my skin as I slowly jacked my hand up and down his throbbing shaft. "Why am I the only one without clothes on?" he asked in short breaths.

That was a good question. I pulled my shirt up and over my head and shimmied out of my denim while Kale stepped out of his pants. When I was about ready to lose my briefs, Kale placed his hand over mine.

"No," he whispered, kneeling before me. "Let me."

I leered down at him and cupped his cheek in my hand. "It's all yours."

He licked his lips and slowly lowered the fabric, revealing the shock of dark hair that rested at the base of my cock. He buried his face in my groin, sniffing and licking crazy trails through my musk. I wound my fingers in his dark locks and groaned when he nibbled on my shaft covered by my briefs, soaking the fabric with his spit.

"Damn, that feels good," I whispered.

Kale flashed me a devilish grin that told me he was only getting started. He tugged my underwear down the rest of my body and oohed when my fat nine-inch cock flopped out of hiding.

"Wow," he muttered before taking the heavy prick in his hand and slowly massaging its length with his fingers. His warm grip ignited the energy we produced and sent sparks of electricity shooting through me, and when he ran his tongue along the sides, I almost short-circuited.

Kale delivered feathery kisses to the swollen head before popping it in his mouth. He sucked on my cock for several minutes, bobbing up and down its length and swirling his tongue around the head, only pausing to slurp up the precum that wept from the slit.

The combination of his mouth, tongue, and hand on my balls brought me close to critical mass. "Stop," I mumbled.

He pulled off my cock and gazed up at me with wide eyes. "Am I doing it wrong?" he asked.

"You've got to be kidding!" I took to my knees in front of him and placed my hands on his cheeks. "It was great. Too great. I almost lost it."

"What's wrong with that?"

"Absolutely nothing," I replied. "But I want more too. I want to hold you in my arms while my body slides inside yours."

"Yeah," he said with a vigorous nod. "Let's do that."

I took his sweet face in my hands and pressed my lips to his. As we kissed, I shivered with the anticipation of joining my body with Kale's, of the two of us finally becoming one. I gently nudged him backward onto the cool grass and hovered over him. I longed for his flesh, but my eyes, my heart, and my soul had to savor every minute, every second of this experience. I traveled my gaze down his body, taking notice of how Kale's nipples pebbled in response to the cool night air and how a small trail of hair began at his belly button before charting a path to the wiry nest that sprouted around his cock.

"What are you doing?" Kale asked, folding his arms around my neck.

"Just looking," I replied. "Memorizing everything about you."

"There's more than one way to make memories," he said, pulling me onto him.

I inhaled sharply the moment we touched. The warmth of his flesh triggered a chain reaction inside me. The energy we'd generated pulsed to life, creating a charge I'd never be able to generate alone. I'd spent my life trying to become the most powerful warlock in my family, but I finally found it in the arms that held me tight and the lips that pressed against my skin.

I hadn't been looking for power. I'd been looking for Kale.

I fell onto his lips, devouring the sweetness of his kisses that served to fuel the building energy. I cradled his face as he scratched down my back to my ass, which he used for leverage to grind our cocks together in the sheen of sweat that coated our bodies.

"I need you," he said.

"I need you too. So bad," I replied before licking a trail down his chin, across his chest, and down his stomach to his cock. I seized his hardness, swabbing my tongue across the engorged head and drinking in the sweetness he produced.

Kale groaned as I slipped my tongue into the slit to coax more precum from the head of his prick. He grabbed my shoulders and thrust upward, sliding his cock between my lips. I inhaled deeply as he invaded my mouth and my throat. The scent of sweat and musk drove me wild, and I fluttered my tongue along the shaft while pursing my lips together to create just the right amount of suction.

"Fuck!" he cried out, clawing at the ground around him. "You're gonna make me come."

I gripped the base and picked up the pace. I bobbed up and down, wrapping my tongue around his head on the upstroke and swallowing him to the hilt on the down. Every time I slid my mouth back up, I worked my hand in a circular motion to bring Kale over the edge from which he dangled.

Kale's cock grew diamond hard before it pulsed, filling my mouth with his seed. I greedily drank down his offering as Kale thrashed his body beneath me before finally falling still.

"Damn," he muttered. "You're good."

I grinned at him as I delivered one final kiss to the head of his prick. "You haven't seen anything yet," I said before throwing his legs over my shoulders and burying my face in his ass.

Kale gasped when I darted my tongue across his hole. I lapped at his salty opening, getting drunk on the heady taste before I pried his cheeks apart and forced my tongue inside. His head fell back against the grass as he gave himself over to the pleasure I willingly offered, and his eyes turned glassy and faraway.

I replaced my tongue with a finger, and Kale arched his back with a groan. He pushed onto my digit, forcing more of me inside him. I drew circles inside his body, opening him up for me, and the thought of finally entering him almost made me jizz in the grass.

After a few more minutes and two more fingers, Kale was ready, and so was I.

I sat back on my haunches and reached into my jeans for my wallet.

"What are you doing?" Kale asked.

I pulled out a condom and waved it at him.

He gaped at the square golden wrapper. "What's that?"

I snickered. I hadn't been asked that question since high school. "It's something two guys need to keep each other safe when they're about to do what we're about to do."

He gestured impatiently at it. "Well hurry up, then."

I tore open the package and slid the wrapping over my cock. Kale grabbed his ankles and pulled his feet to his chest. I'd never seen anything more breathtaking in my life.

"Are you ready?" I asked.

Kale's labored breathing and half-closed eyes told me that was a ridiculous question.

I positioned myself over him and aimed my cock at his center. With a gentle nudge, I pushed past the first ring of muscle. Kale inhaled, wrapping his arms around my neck. He pulled me down on top of him, forcing the remainder of my length inside his body.

When my groin rested against his ass, my body shivered, my blood boiled, and my soul sang. Being in Kale's arms and in Kale's body was like finding the most special place in the world that had been saved just for me, and it was a gift I'd never take for granted.

Kale craned his neck up and pressed his lips to mine. I gave myself over to the kiss, to the magic we created together, and thrust my hips. His eyes went wide and his body shook as I pushed myself in and out of him.

His kisses and hands went wild. He clutched my ass, my shoulders, my back, and I held him tightly against me as I rocked our bodies to the frenzied pace my heart had set.

"Pierce," he called out, licking my neck and nibbling my ear. "You feel so good inside me. Like you were made just for me."

That was exactly how I felt. The curve of his body fit perfectly against my larger frame. We were two pieces of a cosmic puzzle, two souls that had been waiting for an eternity to be reunited.

I molded my lips to his once more, the pressure in my balls growing more intense. The tight grip with which Kale's internal muscles massaged my hard cock brought me to the precipice.

"Fuck," Kale mumbled. He thrust his hand beneath our writhing bodies and furiously jacked his cock. "You're gonna make me shoot again."

I pistoned inside him harder and faster, trying to send both of us over the edge in one creamy explosion.

Kale's head slammed back against the grass as he cried out, coating our stomachs with his spunk. His orgasm sent me flying. I slammed inside him, and with a loud grunt, my cock pulsed, filling the condom with my seed.

I collapsed on top of him, sweat dripping off my face and sliding down my back. Kale wrapped his arms and legs around me, doing his best to keep my withdrawing cock inside him for as long as he could.

When I finally slipped free, I slid off him and landed on my back on the cold, wet grass. "Damn, that was good."

Kale's body still trembled from the aftershock of his orgasm. "Yeah, it was." He snuggled into my chest and draped his leg around my waist. "It was like flying."

"Well, we can go flying together anytime," I said, kissing the top of his head.

"I'd like that," he replied with a big devilish grin, but it retreated as quickly as it had appeared. "I just hope we get the chance."

The worry and fear we'd hoped to send away with our lovemaking was back with a vengeance. It crouched at the edges of his eyes and within the giant hole that gaped in my chest. It was as if what we had shared fed the beast, making it stronger and more powerful than it ever was.

Kale needed reassurance we'd see each other again. Hell, so did I. I didn't even want to contemplate any other alternative. There had to be something I could say, some magical spell I could utter that would cast some light onto our uncertain future.

My brain couldn't find the words, so I listened to the song Kale's touch had started in my soul.

"It's not a matter of hope." I pulled him on top of me and gazed deep into his golden eyes. "It's a matter of time."

His big dimpled grin returned as if it had never left. "Really?"

"Really," I said with a firm nod.

He sat up and wiggled his bare butt against my cock. The previous gloom had been banished by the light of my words. "So what are we going to do when we see each other again?" he asked with a wiggle of his eyebrows.

"Well, besides this," I said grinding my slowly hardening dick against him. "I figured I'd take you on another date."

"Oh, a second date!" Kale giddily bounced up and down, and the movement brought me back to full mast. "You promise?"

That was the easiest promise to make. "Of course."

"And of course there'll be more whiskey."

I scrunched up my lips. "Maybe."

"Don't forget the Backstreet Boys," he said, pointing his finger at me.

I rolled over and pinned him underneath me. "Now you're just pushing your luck."

"Maybe," he said with a shrug. He wrapped his arms around my neck and brushed his lips against mine. "But I'm adorable, so I can."

I groaned and laid my forehead against his. I knew when I accidentally called him adorable at the Pig's Eye, I'd live to regret it. "You're going to use that against me from now till the end of time, aren't you?"

"If you're lucky."

I gazed deep into his golden eyes and smiled. Right now I considered myself the luckiest warlock in the world, and that was a power more potent than any other magic in existence.

It would get us through whatever distance would separate us.

That was a fact I knew from the deepest depths of my soul.

THE FIRST week after leaving Kale in Aeaea was painful. The week after that was torture. By the third week, I wanted to die, and my brothers would have been glad to help me. I turned into quite a moody bastard who growled at anything anyone said, and my hair-trigger temper grew shorter.

Even Drake, who was always so positive about every damn thing, turned and went in the other direction when he saw me coming.

My brothers tried to help. They told me it would get better in time and other bullshit, but what the hell did they know? They had their boyfriends living with them. The fuckers!

This was my first relationship where I'd just happened to find my soul mate, and of course it had to be long distance. If it was just miles keeping us apart, it wouldn't be so bad. The magic that separated us was the real bitch.

I couldn't just hop on a plane or cast some spell that would take me to him. Aeaea was safely hidden by power I could never hope to break.

It was so damned frustrating I wanted to punch something so hard until it felt as badly as I did.

"There's Mr. Grump," Mason said. He and Drake entered the kitchen where I'd been drinking my early morning protein shake before the gym. Of course they were holding hands and cast sideways glances at each other that told me they'd spent most of the night fucking their brains out. Maybe if I kicked the crap out of Mason, I'd feel better. It sure wouldn't hurt.

"I'm not in the mood," I growled.

Drake came up behind where I sat at the bar and gave me a tentative hug. At least he still tried to make me feel better instead of being an asswipe like Mason. "I'm sorry you're hurtin' so much," he said. His Southern drawl was as comforting as his embrace. "I wish there was somethin' we could do."

"Me too," Mason said as he plodded to the refrigerator. "I'm tired of the Debbie Downer routine."

"Keep it up and you'll be wearing your orange juice," I warned.

"Are you threatening physical violence again?" Thad asked. He sauntered into the kitchen, wearing a button-down and jeans instead of just pajama bottoms. Ever since Aiden, he'd gone to bed early and slept late. Not that I blamed him. If Kale were here, I'd spend every opportunity I could naked in bed with him. When Aiden followed closely behind dressed in jeans and a T-shirt, my gut told me something was up.

"Cut him some slack," Aiden said after stifling a yawn. "He misses Kale."

Missing Kale didn't even come close. It was like I'd lost a part of myself and had no idea how to put the broken pieces back together again.

"I miss him too," Drake said, taking the glass of OJ Mason handed him. "He's a nice guy and always had a smile on his face. Even when Thad was so mean to him."

That was the truth. Thad had been ready to string Kale up as one of Ben's accomplices. Maybe my younger brother wasn't such a brainiac after all. The dumbass.

Thad harrumphed in reply. "I was just being cautious."

"You were a dick," I said, chugging down the rest of my drink.

Thad's arched eyebrow told me he wasn't in the mood either. The two of us had spent most of our time since we'd been back in the library with our noses in just about every book we had. We were on a mission to find out everything we could about this Spell Fall Gerald had mentioned, but while I researched along with him, I went to bed hours before he did last night.

"Learn anything new?" I asked.

He shook his head and leaned against Aiden for support. "Nothing more than we already know about the crests. They're talismans that are directly tied to the five elements."

Yeah, and two were still missing, most likely in the hands of this Ica person. What would happen when he or she had all five?

I rose from where I sat and tossed my plastic cup into the trashcan. It was time to hit the gym and blow off steam. There was no way I was going to stay here with these rays of sunshine. If I did, they'd all be bloodstains in a few seconds flat.

"Where are you goin'?" Drake asked. He scrambled off his barstool and stood in front of me.

I arched an eyebrow at him. "Where I go every morning. To the gym."

"You should really stay for breakfast." He hooked his hand around my arm and led me back to the others. "Like my daddy always said, it's the most important meal of the day."

I pulled my arm from his grasp and shook my head. "You go ahead. I've got to get going."

"Sit down."

I turned around at the sound of my father's stern voice. He blocked the exit with his massive frame and pointed back to the bar. Since we'd returned from Aeaea, he and I had been silently battling for the title of Grump of the Year. Right now he was in the lead.

I couldn't blame him, though. We hadn't heard from the Conclave since they left us in Aeaea, and none of the other protector covens had either. Although I didn't want it to happen, I suspected when they ended their silence, they'd be announcing the Edwells were taking our place. How would Dad, or any of us, take that? The Blackmoors had held this station in our community for the past four generations.

"What's up?" I asked, taking my previous place at the bar.

Dad stood before us and sighed. "I know these past few weeks have been hard. We've been under a lot of stress and had to deal with a shit-ton of crap."

That was a mild understatement.

"Well, that comes to an end right now."

"What does that mean?" Drake asked.

"Ever since Mabon we've been looking over our shoulder, waiting for the next attack or the next secret to be revealed," Dad answered. "I'm done living that way. Sure, we don't know what's going to happen with the Conclave, but I've given up worrying about it. It's out of my hands, and it's time for us to have some fun."

Mason hooted as if he were watching a football game while Thad nodded in agreement. Even Drake and Aiden had smiles plastered across their faces.

I couldn't argue with Dad. We could use some rest and relaxation, but I wasn't ready to celebrate anything yet. It was hard to be happy when it was weeks since I'd seen the dimpled smile that made my soul soar.

"Pierce," Dad said. He suddenly stood by my side, his hand on my shoulder. "I know you're in pain, son. Missing the person you love is the worst kind of hurt imaginable." He paused, doing his best to get his emotions under control.

I was an ass. My misery didn't compare with what he'd gone through since Mom died. Sure, I didn't have Kale with me right now, but he was still alive. I knew we'd see each other again someday. Dad didn't have that luxury.

"I'm sorry, Dad." I gripped his shoulder as he held mine. It was the way he and I hugged. "I know you hurt too."

He nodded and swallowed hard. "But it's time for the both of us to move on. It's not going to be easy, but we have to take the first steps. Otherwise we'll never get out of the fog of pain that drifts around us."

He was right. I had to warlock up. "So what are we going to do?"

"First, you're going back to your room to change," he said with a nod at my gym clothes. "And then we'll meet in the car."

I DASHED into my room, tearing my muscle shirt from my body, and headed for the closet. The familiar scent of citrus and cedar clung to the air in my room.

Fuck. I missed Kale so much I could actually smell him. There was no doubt about it. I needed to get out of the house and do something other than go to the gym or mope.

I threw open my closet door and studied my wardrobe. What should I wear? Were we going somewhere casual or more formal? To me, fun meant casual. For Dad that was another story altogether. Well, shit.

I darted back to the hallway, ready to scream down the stairs, when the familiar purr of the Jag's engine started outside. I sprinted back to my room and over to the window. Before I had a chance to open it and ask what I should wear, the Jag pulled out of the driveway and drove away.

Why the fuck were they leaving without me?

I snagged my phone from the dresser and dialed my dad's cell. When it went to voice mail, I tried each of my brothers' numbers before Drake's. No one answered.

"Did I just get ditched?" I asked my bedroom.

"Looks that way to me."

Instead of turning to the sweet voice that spoke behind me, I froze. If I spun around and he wasn't really there, I didn't know if I'd be able to handle the disappointment. "Kale?"

"You'll have to turn around and find out," he said.

I glanced over my shoulder, and when I caught a glimpse of tanned skin, I whirled the rest of the way around.

Kale leaned against the open bathroom door, a huge grin dimpling his cheeks. "Surprise!"

A second later I held him in my arms, pressing his body tightly against mine and inhaling the intoxicating aroma that followed wherever he went. "You're here?" I asked, cupping his cheeks in my hands and then brushing my lips against his. "How?"

"Is that really what you want to do?" He parted his lips in a devilish grin. "Talk?"

He was right. We'd have time for that later. Right now I needed his body against mine more than I needed answers to questions that could wait until after we were done.

In a blur of motion, I peeled off my clothes before Kale shucked off his tunic. "Someone's excited?" he asked, glancing down at my boner.

"You have no idea," I said, gripping the waistband of his pants and ripping them free of his body. It had been so long since I'd seen him naked that my breath caught in my throat. Judging from the hard cock that stood at attention, it was easy to see I wasn't the only one who was excited. "I see you've missed me too."

Kale stepped into my arms, pressing the full weight of his warm body against my trembling flesh. "More than you know," he whispered. Although joy reflected in the golden pools of his eyes, the pain that hid in their depths was easy to spot.

Since we'd been apart, I'd seen it every morning whenever I looked at myself in the mirror.

But that torment had come to an end. Kale was here and in my arms, but he was still much too far away. I leaned forward, reducing the distance between us to zero, and pressed my lips to Kale's.

Upon contact all the misery of these past few weeks vanished, obliterated by the power of his kiss. My wounded soul took flight as I twirled my tongue around his, coaxing it gently into my mouth. Our time apart made him even sweeter and more precious to me, and I had to have more.

I swept Kale up in my arms and carried him to my bed, where I gently laid him down on the mattress. He wiggled his way up to the headboard while I stood there, mesmerized by the flexing of his muscles as he moved and the hard cock that made my mouth water.

He flipped onto his stomach, peering at me with pretend innocence. "See something you like?"

Oh fuck. Did I ever. My cock grew so hard it hurt. I licked my lips and nodded.

He beckoned to me with his finger. "Then come here."

I climbed onto the bed and crawled behind him. I slid my hands up his lean thighs and along his sides to his smooth, toned back. Tracing a path with my finger, I followed every curve of muscle and dip of flesh until I arrived at his perky butt. When I bent over his body and nibbled at his back, Kale responded by inhaling sharply.

"Stop teasing me and do me instead."

I grabbed his cheeks with both hands and spread them wide. Kale moaned when I teased my tongue across his exposed hole.

"Shit, Pierce," he panted. "Take me. Please. I've been thinking about doing this again for the last three weeks, and I can't wait anymore."

Yeah, neither could I, but we were going to enjoy this, not rush it.

I shoved my tongue into his ass, flattening and wiggling it inside him. Kale balled up the sheets in his fists and groaned into the mattress. He was ready to crawl out of his skin. I withdrew my tongue, tracing lazy circles around his shuddering hole and inhaling his heady scent that made my cock throb.

I wasn't just teasing Kale. I was torturing myself.

My dick longed to replace my tongue and experience the warm, sweet grip of Kale's body again, but I wasn't finished exploring the rest of him.

I grabbed his legs and spread them farther apart, giving me the access I needed. After withdrawing my tongue from his butt, I swabbed it across his balls and along his taint. Kale sucked in his breath as I sucked one testicle into my mouth and tickled it with my tongue. I did the same with the other, and by the time I was done, Kale had turned into a writhing, moaning mass.

"Please, Pierce. Fuck me now."

"Almost." I shoved my hand between his body and the mattress, pulling his hard cock backward between his legs. I fluttered my tongue along the head, slurping up the juices my teasing had enticed. Leaning forward, I swallowed him all at once.

"Holy shit!" Kale cried out. He gripped the headboard, his knuckles turning white as I slid back and forth along the shaft. He lifted his ass in the air, allowing me to work his dick with my hands and my mouth. I flickered my swirling tongue across the head while I stroked his cock or fondled his balls with my hand. Kale was soon on his knees, thrusting backward into my mouth. His labored breathing and light mewls told me he was almost there.

I braced myself with one arm and increased my speed. Kale cursed and bucked his hips even harder, trying to match the rhythm with which I sucked and tugged. He threw back his head and screamed as his cock went rigid in my mouth before spraying my throat with his hot cum.

Kale collapsed on the mattress, breathless and exhausted. Sweat dripped down his face. He clearly was unable to move, which meant it was time.

I crawled between his legs and opened the bedside drawer.

"Are you gonna fuck me now?" he asked, his voice dreamy.

"Oh yeah," I said after rolling the rubber down my cock.

"It's about damn time."

I couldn't agree more. I nestled the head of my dick against his hole and pushed. His entrance parted and I slowly slid myself inside, wanting to savor every inch I traveled. Kale rose up on all fours and bucked hard against me, impaling himself on my cock.

The surprise move stole my breath from my lungs as Kale's warm grip completely enveloped my hardness. "Fuck!" I growled. I had to grip his waist and force the cum back down into my balls.

"That's what you get for teasing me," he said with a dimpled smile.

"Are we going to play that game?" I grabbed both of his shoulders and rammed myself into him, hard and fast.

Kale leaned forward, resting his forehead against the headboard for support. "Yeah," he said. "Do that again."

I didn't need another invitation.

With my hands on his waist, I thrust myself in and out of Kale. I started slow and steady, easing my way all the way out before slowly inching myself all the way back in. Each leisurely movement elicited moans that urged me to increase my speed. Before long my measured pace became frenzied.

When my hips developed a mind of their own, I pushed Kale into the mattress with his butt high in the air and leaned over him. I pressed my forehead to his back and delivered gentle kisses to his flesh as I continued to work my cock in and out of his warm tightness.

I lapped up the sweat that had collected between his shoulder blades and took a deep whiff. Damn, this must be what heaven smelled like—cedar and citrus mixed with musk, sweat, and cum.

Kale bucked back against me, meeting my hard thrusts with his own. "Yes, Pierce. Don't stop," he begged.

"I couldn't if I tried," I panted, feeling the impending release as my sac gathered closer to my body. "Fuck, I'm coming!" With one final thrust, I grunted and every part of my body grew rigid and relaxed at the same time as I pumped out six jets of cum into the condom.

I fell on top of Kale, panting. Sweat dripped off my brow and landed in his matted hair.

"Now that's what I'm talking about," he said.

I chuckled. "No fucking kidding." I slipped from Kale's body and dropped to my side. After carefully removing the used condom, I deposited it into the bedside trashcan.

Kale immediately turned around in my arms and nuzzled into the crook of my neck. "You smell yummy," he said.

"Not as yummy as you feel," I replied, running my hands up and down his smooth, sweaty body. I could lie here with him for another day and it wouldn't be enough. A week wouldn't be enough. Hell, would any amount of time be enough?

"I could stay like this forever," Kale said, his eyes lingering on mine.

"How'd you know what I was thinking?"

He placed his hand on my chest. "Soul mates, remember?"

As if I could ever forget. Ever since we made love in Aeaea, our bond had only grown. It was like a part of him lived in me, just like a part of me lived in him. All I had to do was close my eyes and I could sense the happiness that swirled within him. I could hear the heart that beat faster when I traveled my hands across his skin, and

I could feel something else, a childlike excitement he could barely keep contained.

"What is it?" I asked, propping my head up on my right hand and gazing down at him. "You've got news, and I'd say it's pretty damn good news too."

Kale's lips grew into the dimpled smile that made me weak. "It's *great* news," he said.

I sat up. "You're the new Beast King, aren't you?"

He laughed. "No, silly. That's Caspian."

I frowned. I thought for sure Kale would be made king. "How the hell did that happen?"

"He got the votes from the council as I thought he would, but he wasn't as big of a shoo-in as he thought he'd be."

"Let me guess," I said with a grin. "You came in a close second."

Kale beamed up at me and nodded. "Can you believe that?"

Of course I could. Kale was the one who kept everyone in line during the chaos. Because of him, more of his people didn't die at the hands of Sersie and Ben. But if Kale wasn't his people's new leader, what was he so excited about telling me? "So what's your news, then?"

"Guess who's the new chief advisor to the king?"

"If you tell me it's not you, I'm going to be upset."

He grinned. "I guess it's a good thing it's me, then."

I pushed him on his back and pounced on top of him. "I'm so proud of you."

"Then why are you trying to kill me?" he asked through strained breaths. "You weigh like a ton!"

"Are you calling me fat?" I asked, grimacing at him.

"Can't. Breathe," he said, pretending as if he were just moments from death.

After grabbing his legs, I wrapped them around my waist and redistributed my weight so it no longer pressed on his chest. I did make sure my cock rested against his sweaty butt, though. "Better?"

He wiggled his ass against my lengthening hardness. "Much."

"So that's why you're here, then? Because Caspian let you come?"

He nodded. "I convinced him it's a good idea to keep up friendly relations with the rest of the magical community."

"How friendly?" I asked, nudging myself against his hole.

"*Very* friendly," he replied as he wrapped his arms around my neck and brought our foreheads together. "We've got a lot of work ahead of us. Do you think you're up for it?"

Was he kidding? As long as I was with him, I was ready for anything.

We had a slew of problems to deal with. Improving relationships between our species was just one among many. Ben might be gone, but whatever threat he started, whatever this Spell Fall was the Conclave feared, my gut told me it was going to take the entire magical community working together to weather the storm.

But for the first time in my life, I wasn't afraid. The fear that had driven me since I was a child had vanished. What powered me now was my faith in my growing family and in the magic being soul struck created.

It made us more powerful than a vampyre shadow weaver and a millennia-old sorcerer. Whatever new threats loomed in the darkness had better watch out.

The Warlock Brothers of Havenbridge were ready to kick their asses.

For bonus content from

The Warlock
Brothers of
Havenbridge

check out

www.havenbridge.me

The Warlock Brothers of Havenbridge: Book One

Mason Blackmoor just can't compete with his brothers, much less his father. They represent the epitome of black magic, strong, dark, and wicked, and though Mason tries to live up to his respected lineage, most of the spells he casts go awry. To make matters worse, his active power has yet to kick in. While his brothers wield lightning and harness the cold, Mason sits on the sidelines, waiting for the moment when he can finally enter the magical game.

When a dead body is discovered on the football field of his high school, Mason meets Drake Carpenter, the new kid in town. Drake's confident demeanor and quick wit rub Mason the wrong way. Drake is far too self-assured for someone without an ounce of magical blood in his body, and Mason aims to teach him a lesson—like turn him into a roach. And if he's lucky, maybe this time Mason won't be the one turned into an insect.

Not surprisingly, the dislike is mutual, and Drake does nothing to dispel Mason's suspicion that the sexy boy with a southern drawl is somehow connected to the murder.

If only Mason didn't find himself inexplicably spell bound whenever they are together, they might actually find out what danger hides in the shadows.

www.dreamspinnerpress.com

JACOB Z. FLORES

BLOOD TIED

THE WARLOCK BROTHERS OF HAVENBRIDGE, BOOK TWO

The Warlock Brothers of Havenbridge: Book Two

Thad Blackmoor's heart is as cold as his icy magical abilities. He considers emotions a waste of his time and prefers to study the arcane, using the sacred books of his coven to grow in his craft. He aspires to supersede his father and elder brother Pierce in power, and now that his younger brother, Mason, has tapped into the rare warlock power of darkness, he needs to work harder than ever.

But Thad's ambitions are halted when he saves Aiden Teine, a fire fairy, from a banshee. Thad's immediate attraction to Aiden catches him off guard and thaws his cold heart for the first time. As Thad, Aiden, and his brothers investigate the connection between the banshee attack and the vampyre and shadow weaver who almost killed them, Thad tries to dodge Ben, a sexy warlock who won't let him be after a one-night stand.

Their search for answers leads them to the Otherworld, where something even more insidious is at work—something Thad will need more than logic to stand against.

www.dreamspinnerpress.com

JACOB Z. FLORES lives a double life. During the day, he is a respected college English professor and midlevel administrator. At night and during his summer vacation, he loosens the tie and tosses aside the trendy sports coat to write man on man fiction, where the hardass assessor of freshmen-level composition turns his attention to the firm posteriors and other rigid appendages of the characters in his fictional world.

Summers in Provincetown, Massachusetts, provide Jacob with inspiration for his fiction. The abundance of barely clothed man flesh and daily debauchery stimulates his personal muse. When he isn't stroking the keyboard, Jacob spends time with his daughter. They both represent a bright blue blip in an otherwise predominantly red swath in south Texas.

Blog: jacobzflores.com
Facebook: www.facebook.com/jacob.flores2
Twitter: @JacobZFlores
Pinterest: www.pinterest.com/jacobflores2
Goodreads: www.goodreads.com/author/show/5142501.Jacob_Z_Flores
Google Plus: plus.google.com/u/0/+JacobFlores9595/posts

JACOB Z. FLORES

Justin Jimenez has loved his partner, Spencer Harrison, for ten years. He'll do anything for him—including bury his feelings for a man he met while he and Spencer were separated last year. Justin never planned to fall in love, and he certainly never planned to tell Spencer about it—but when a phone call wakes them in the middle of the night to inform Justin that his former lover, Dutch Keller, has been in an accident, he doesn't have a choice.

Justin's revelation shatters the fragile relationship he and Spencer were trying to rebuild. The weight of his guilt—both for hurting Spencer and for leaving a heartbroken Dutch to find solace in a bottle—crushes him. But what Justin doesn't know is that Spencer and Dutch guard an explosive secret of their own. All three men are tangled in a communal web of lies, and unless they find the events in their lives that ultimately led them to friendship, passion, and betrayal, they won't see the love at the heart of the pain.

www.dreamspinnerpress.com

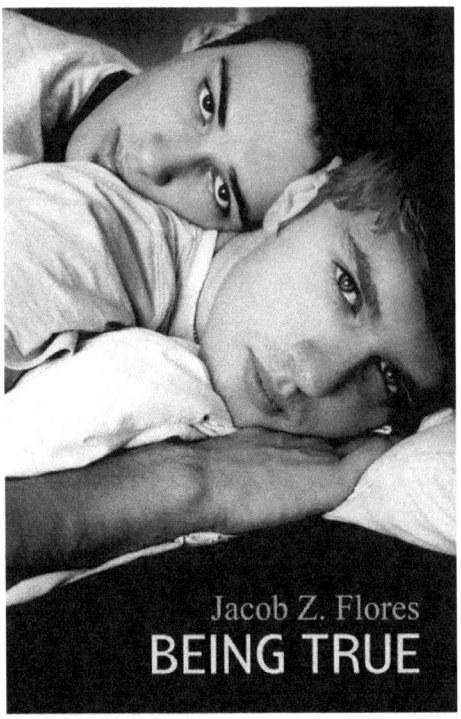

Jacob Z. Flores
BEING TRUE

Truman L. Cobbler has not had an easy life. It's bad enough people say he looks like Donkey from Shrek, but he's also suffered the death of his policeman father and his mother's remarriage to a professional swindler, who cost them everything. Now dirt poor, they live in the barrio of San Antonio, Texas. When Tru transfers to an inner-city high school halfway through his senior year, he meets Javi Castillo, a popular and hot high school jock. Javi takes an immediate liking to Tru, and the two become friends. The odd pairing, however, rocks the school and sets the cliquish social circles askew. No one knows how to act or what to think when Mr. Popular takes a stand for Mr. Donkey. Will the cliques rise up to maintain status quo and lead Tru and Javi to heartbreak and disaster or will being true to who they are rule the day?

www.dreamspinnerpress.com

As his birthday approaches, Matthew Westlake fears more than just growing a year older. He fears never seeing another year at all. Each birthday brings a close call with death, leaving holes in his memory, recurring nightmares, and one more glimpse of his guardian angel. This birthday Matt must stand against ancient evils that have hounded him since birth, because he is a Gifted One—a seventh son of a seventh son.

Within Matt rests the unlocked potential of a force for good, but it also makes him a target. Being the Gifted One and dodging demonic attacks aren't Matt's only problems, though. He's fallen in love with his protector, the Archangel Gabriel, and Heaven will condemn that love to save Matt's soul. But Heaven doesn't count on Gabriel loving Matt in return, defying divine law and placing them in danger from demons and angels alike.

www.dreamspinnerpress.com

JACOB Z. FLORES

Please
REMEMBER
Me

Successful lawyer Santi Herrera couldn't be happier with the direction his life is taking. Not only is he on track to becoming a partner in his law firm, but he's planning his wedding to Hank Burton, a south Texas contractor who has made a name for himself despite his humble beginnings. The introverted lone wolf Santi and the friendly, outgoing Hank complement each other perfectly. From the moment they laid eyes on each other, they were hooked, and as far as Santi and Hank are concerned, a happily ever after is their destiny.

But fate deals them a devastating new hand.

A construction accident leaves Hank with severe head trauma and brings him precariously close to death. When he finally awakens, Hank doesn't remember Santi or the love they shared for the past three years. Santi faces the greatest challenge of his life. Can he respark a flame his lover can't recall? And can he stop the diverging paths that fickle fate charts between them?

Santi has faith in the love he and Hank shared and in the words his father once spoke to him: "It's never too late to fall in love. All over again."

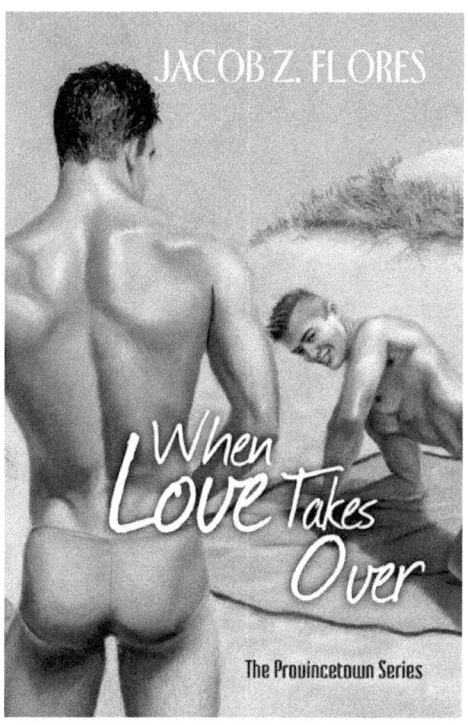

Provincetown: Book One

Zach Kelly's life is a shambles. His boyfriend of three years dumped him, and his writing career is going nowhere. On a whim, he heads to Provincetown, Massachusetts, to nurse his broken heart and figure out his next step. He's expecting to find rest and relaxation on the sandy beaches of Cape Cod. Instead, Zach meets a hunky porn star during a chance encounter at a leather shop he mistakes as a place to buy a belt that is definitely *not* for whipping.

Van Pierce is smitten when shy and inexperienced Zach crashes through a shelf of fetish gear. Though Van's got an insatiable appetite for men on and off the set, his porn persona, Hart Throb, hides a broken heart. He's struggling to find the reality the porno set doesn't offer, and Zach is fighting to find the fantasy that will set his writing on fire. The odd goofball and the suave beefcake may either find love amid Provincetown's colorful pageantry where summer never seems to end—or more heartbreak than either can imagine.

www.dreamspinnerpress.com

Provincetown: Book Two
A Spin-off of *When Love Takes Over*

As a physician and prominent citizen of Victoria, Texas, Dr. Gil Kelly took a hard fall when his vengeful wife revealed his infidelity with other men. Closing ranks around her, the town's elite ostracized him, and his relationship with his children was nearly destroyed.

After spending his life focused on living for others, he has no idea how to live for himself. He wants to find love but now settles for anonymous sex that only further clouds his world with shame and guilt. Gil believes finding true love is an unobtainable dream, what his father used to call "chasing the sun."

Then he runs into Tom Martinez, his son's childhood best friend, who returned to town a grown man and offers everything Gil needs. But Gil hesitates to fall into Tom's arms, because after his high-profile divorce, the potential scandal of loving a younger man could separate him from his children permanently.

Provincetown: Book Three

As vain as he is beautiful, Nino Santos happily lives life waiting for the next ferry full of fairies to bring him new conquests. As long as they aren't hirsute, he's all in. So he's shocked to wake up after a beach party he cannot remember with a hairy naked man lying next to him.

Teddy Miller doesn't remember the "Bear Week" party either, much less the Abercrombie & Fitch model wannabe next to him. Teddy doesn't give two cents about appearances, but guys like Abercrombie don't return the favor. That's why he prefers men with extra fur and padding over carbon copy clones of perfection—a type of man Teddy is far too familiar with.

When Nino and Teddy glimpse each other the next morning, it's loathing at first sight. Instead of exchanging phone numbers, they exchange insults and vow never to see each other again. In Provincetown, however, escaping a trick best forgotten isn't easy. Mutual friends and chance circumstances keep Nino and Teddy in each other's orbit. But are they fighting each other or the attraction growing between them? The answer lies amid Provincetown's windswept dunes and the night neither of them can recall.

www.dreamspinnerpress.com

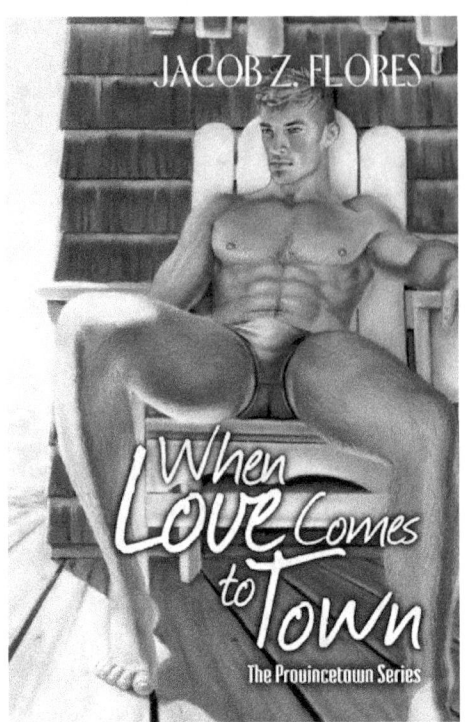

Provincetown: Book Four

Brody O'Shea isn't looking for much, just a hot guy with a decent job, who is sane and doesn't have kids. The son of a former rock star, Brody has lived through the pain of bankruptcy and bad parenting, and he doesn't want to experience it again. As a reformed horndog, he wants the security and stability of a relationship. But almost every guy he meets seems satisfied with Mr. Right Now, and he wants to find Mr. Right—now!

The only men Eric Vasquez chases are criminals. As a deputy and single father, he has no need for a relationship after his last one ended disastrously. He lives for and through Maddie, his nine-year-old daughter. Everything else is a needless distraction, but distraction is what Eric gets when he comes to Provincetown to attend the wedding between his cousin Van and the man of his dreams.

When Brody and Eric meet, what they want and what they find conflict. An ocean of expectations separates them. If they cannot move past their reservations to reach each other's shores, they might miss the boat when love comes to town.

www.dreamspinnerpress.com

STYGIAN

SANTINO HASSELL

FOR
MORE
OF THE
BEST
GAY
ROMANCE

DREAMSPINNER
PRESS
dreamspinnerpress.com